The Goddess Tribe

Publisher's Cataloging-In-Publication Data
(Prepared by The Donohue Group, Inc.)

Names: Satterfield, Radiance.
Title: The Goddess Tribe / Radiance Satterfield.
Description: [Pompano Beach, Florida] : Aqua Creative Marketing, [2018] | Series: The Goddess Tribe ; [1]
Identifiers: ISBN 9781732350717 (hardback) | ISBN 9781732350700 (paperback) | ISBN 9781732350724 (ebook)
Subjects: LCSH: Divorced women--Fiction. | Life change events--Fiction. | Gifts--Fiction. | Christian women--Societies and clubs--Fiction.
Classification: LCC PS3619.A8225 G64 2018 (print) | LCC PS3619.A8225 (ebook) | DDC 813/.6--dc23

Hardcover: ISBN 9781732350717

Paperback: ISBN 9781732350700

E-book ISBN 9781732350724

The Goddess Tribe

RADIANCE SATTERFIELD

Chapter One

I slowly turned the key in the lock. Although I had always wondered what secret lay within the ornate old jewelry box, now that I was at the brink of discovery I felt hesitant. The jewelry box—a large, egg-shaped vessel ornately carved out of ebony—had always held a place of fascination for me. The carvings appeared to be Art Nouveau styled leaves, flowers, and butterflies, rubbed smooth to a shiny, satiny black as if to confirm the passage of time. Attached at the top was a forest green tassel hanging to one side. All my life, this mysterious jewelry box had occupied the corner of my grandmother's dresser. It stood upon a round base and was always locked. As with many of the fine antiques in my grandmother's home, I was never allowed to touch it. As a child, I imagined that it held a pirate's treasure—black pearls, gold coins, and stolen diamonds. Now, as an adult, I was simply curious and honored that my grandmother trusted me with this uniquely shaped old treasure chest.

My grandmother, or "Ma," as we all called her, was a petite lady with a lightning-quick wit and an infectiously joyful laugh.

Ma had grown up as a farm girl in Waco, Georgia, but she'd easily adapted to city life in Atlanta after marrying my grand-father. She was elegant, artistic, and magical in the kitchen. Always dressed immaculately in colors to suit her complexion, she favored ice blue because it set off her bright blue eyes and golden skin. She had silvery white hair, which she had colored and styled each week at the beauty parlor. Chanel No. 5 was her signature cologne; and on her lips and fingernails she always wore the same shade of classic red. Ma meticulously scoured antique shops on the weekends for each unique piece of art and furniture that adorned her home. She took painting and ceramics classes, and often gave her creations to friends and family as cherished gifts. Her time she managed wisely as the owner of her own catering business. Ma's holiday feasts delighted and amazed, and everyone looked forward to being together around her table.

When I think back to all she did, I'm astounded. Not only was she a superwoman, she was incredibly caring and kind, a genuine soul who left happiness in her wake. She and my grandfather were happily married for almost sixty years, raised three children, and even helped to raise their nine grandchildren.

The odd thing was that my grandmother had passed away six years before. My dad, while cleaning out the garage, had only recently found the jewelry box packed away and he real-ized that it had been intended for me. It came to me at a time when my life was a haphazard mess. My marriage of twenty years had ended in divorce; and my children, aged sixteen and nineteen, were not adjusting well. I thought that since they were almost grown up my waiting would make things easier for them, but it had not. It was heart-wrenching to see them both so sad and worried. My youngest was taking it the worst. He had moved to Florida with me and had had a rough time adjusting to his new school. My daughter, a freshman in college, now worried about money and paying her tuition, to the point that her hair had begun to fall out. While my husband and I had been married, the kids felt insulated and safe from worries and stresses like that. They had a safety net, or so it seemed to them. Now, with the divorce, they realized that nothing in life has a guarantee. I tried to help them, but I was ill equipped to deal with their pain. Plus, they took much of their anger out on me. I tried therapy with my son, but after one session he refused to return. Finally, after months of heartache and strife, my son had begged to go back to Georgia to live with his father. Nothing in my life hurt me worse than the knowing that my son did not want to be around me. My whole life had been planned around my children and now I felt as though I had ruined everything.

I was, in fact, starting over; back at square one after having lived a predictable family life, married a man, owned a home, and raised our children. After the decision to divorce, I felt fortunate to have a place to go. I moved into my aunt's old farmhouse in Heritage Springs, Florida. She was my dad's older sister and had passed away the year before. Having no children, she'd left the small farm to Dad. Under different circumstances, it would have been idyllic; ten acres in west Florida near the Crystal River where all the springs are a clear sky blue. It was Old Florida at its best—a quaint downtown, tea houses and open-air cafes that beckoned people to linger, and Spanish moss draping the mammoth oaks that framed the picturesque scene. Swimming with manatees and scalloping were both popular hobbies for the locals, as well as big draws for tourists. In fact, my dad's old cabin cruiser was stored there, abandoned years before under a live oak just beyond the gravel driveway. He had stored the twenty-nine-foot Wellcraft with every intention of fixing her up. I recalled how Dad had just replaced one of the two engines, when the other one blew, dashing his hopes of making her seaworthy again. She also boasted a tiny bathroom, shower, sink, stove, and two beds.

I remembered taking the kids snorkeling with Mom and Dad. The kids and I were adventurers. I was so proud of ten-year-old Ian, swimming around the reef in the open water; and my daughter, Ava, gleefully pointing out brightly colored fish before darting off herself under the gentle waves, her long blonde hair flowing like a cloud behind her. "Just like a mermaid," I reminisced. Jonathan, my husband, was ever-cautious and refused to get in the ocean for fear of sharks. He instead employed himself as the lookout and spent a disgruntled day in the hot sun, scanning the blue ocean for the distant but menacing sharks that never came to eat his family. Now, six years had gone by and the new engine had not been run and the blown engine remained in the same condition as when it took its last breath.

When I was married, I had only had a part-time job, but now I had to work full-time. I decided to try something new that I hoped would be more lucrative. So, I left my comfortable part-time position at an educational software company to try marketing. What I found was that I was way out of practice. I was also bored, overworked, and grossly underpaid. I kept to myself, did my job, and ran out of there at five o'clock on the dot. In short, I hated everything about it.

Every day when I walked into the office I felt the weight of all my mistakes which had led me to that exact point in my misery. Instead of making things better, I had made them much worse. My strategy became working from home three days a week. This, I reasoned, was necessary for my family situation when Ian was living with me. But now that one kid was in college and the other lived with his dad, my family situation boiled down to me spending the day alone, wallowing in self-pity. On these days, I usually just hung around the house in my big gray robe—a good find on clearance in the men's department, and one of the few comforts I had. On those days, I made sure to check my phone and email every hour or so, doing little else. It was on a day like this that things began to change.

I slowly opened the jewelry box, revealing its pristine forest-green velvet lining and there, tucked into the velvet, were twelve brightly sparkling rings. My eyes filled with tears, and my heart with love, as I gazed upon the unique rings with excitement. My grandmother had left me twelve beautiful rings! The rings were all different in style, color, and gemstone, but each one sparkled brightly in the light—pink, royal blue, orange, bright green, smoky topaz, red, olive green, yellow, purple, and light blue. Two rings had no stone—only a gold band with a tiny butterfly pattern engraved on the outside, and a sterling silver spoon ring. I reached out to touch the delicate velvet and realized that my hand was shaking. I chose the purple ring, a large pear-shaped amethyst which was my birthstone. As I slid the sparkling ring onto my finger, I was startled from my reverie by a knock at my front door.

"Ignore, ignore the door," I whispered to myself. Even though it was noon on a Thursday, I was still in my bathrobe. The bothersome knock came again.

"Relentless," I muttered under my breath, thinking that if I hid in the hallway, whomever was knocking would just give up and go away. But, the insistent knock came again, this time louder and more determined.

"Okay, I'm coming!" I chimed in my most fake-nice voice.

As I yanked the door open, I squinted at the harsh, offending sunlight that assaulted my eyes and cast its bright spotlight on me. I threw my hand up to shield my eyes, aware that I looked like a disheveled vampire in my too-large plush gray robe, my hair an unruly mass of auburn tangles, and my green eyes a little bloodshot and shielded from the life-giving sunshine.

"Well hello there, Honey. I was about to give up on you."

As my eyes adjusted to the light, I looked down and saw a little old lady of indeterminate age standing on my front porch. She was pale and fragile as she looked up at me, about four feet tall with a poof of tight white curls upon her little head. She thrust a flyer at me, which I accepted, more to get her to leave than to be polite.

"What a pretty ring," she gasped as she came in for a closer look.

"Thank you. It belonged to my grandmother," I replied, suddenly assaulted by the idea that Ma would never have been caught dead on her front porch in a robe at noon on a Thursday—ring or no ring.

"Do you have any donations today?" she asked. "Our church is accepting clothing, housewares, and toys for the less fortunate."

Given my recent divorce and move into my aunt's small farmhouse, I was aware that I needed to downsize. I kneaded my forehead as I began making a mental inventory. Having noticed that the wheels were starting to turn in my brain, she perked up.

"We're right around the corner. Just off of 13th." She pointed down the driveway as she spoke.

"Yes, as a matter of fact, I do have a lot of old stuff to get rid of, but it's not bagged. Can I bring it by later?" I asked.

"Drop off is Saturday morning between 9:00 a.m. and noon," she said as she began to make her way to the sidewalk. "We close after that, so don't be late."

"Thank you," I said as I closed the door and receded back into my cave. I unfolded the flyer which had become damp and wrinkled in my grasp. "That works out well," I thought. "I have all this stuff." My mind began to replay George Carlin's "Stuff" routine when he says, "Trying to find a place for your stuff is the meaning of life." Now, in trying to find a place to get rid of my stuff I was still pursuing the ultimate goal of finding a place for my stuff.

"And who knew there was a church in this neighborhood?" The little winding road was mostly populated with small farms like mine. Hobby farmers who owned animals like pygmy goats and llamas chose to live out here. All I had was me and some chickens. I scrutinized the flyer again. The words on the yellow page proudly read:

The Church of Radiant Light

856 13th Avenue

Now Accepting Donations for the Homeless Shelter

- *Clothing*

- *Housewares*

- *Toys*

Chapter Two

On Saturday, I set my alarm so I would get up early enough to pack up some of my stuff and get it to the church before noon. I threw on an old t-shirt, a pair of gray shorts, and sneakers. I pulled my hair back into a ponytail to keep it off of my face and started sorting. Old clothes, linens, and stuffed animals were piled into hefty garbage bags. Some of the things I fretted over a little before relinquishing them to the anonymity of the bag. These items, having had a life with me and my family, would now go on to a new life with new people who would have no idea of their special or uneventful past. The idea of getting rid of my children's old things made me a little sad.

I comforted myself by saying things like, "Well, someone can use this now." or "This will be of use to someone." The idea that the item was finally going to be used by someone seemed to matter a lot to me in the lifecycle of my children's stuff. "If it's just lying around, then it's of no use." When I was finished, I had four full garbage bags. I packed them into my car and drove around the corner to find the church.

I pulled into the empty church parking lot at 11:55 a.m. Puzzled, I looked around. Not a car in sight. I was worried that I had missed the drop-off time. I looked at the flyer again. "Yep," I said aloud, "It says it goes until noon." I grabbed a bag and began to walk toward the front door, teetering under the weight. As I approached the door, it flew open, startling me so that I dropped my bag. I bent down to pick up and re-stuff the fallen items back inside the bag.

"Oh, I'm sorry, baby. Let me help you," came a voice from above. An African American woman in a royal blue turban and matching bejeweled kaftan then knelt beside me and started shoving things back into the bag too.

"Thank you so much . . . I'm so sorry, I just . . . I guess it got too heavy," I stammered.

"Oh, don't you worry about it, honey. There, it's all put right now," she said, her bright green eyes smiling at me. "I'm Maymie. I run the clothing drive here."

"Are these for the homeless shelter?" she asked.

"Yes, and I have three more in the car." I pointed.

"That's real nice of you, honey. I'll take this one if you want to bring the others in," she said as she disappeared into the doorway, a cloud of blue chiffon.

I went back to the car for the other bags and piled them inside the doorway of the church. When I finished, I stood for a moment and wiped my brow, noting that I was more exhausted than I should have been. "Jeez, I must be getting old," I thought, feeling more than a little disappointed at the current state of my physical fitness. I had been active before—jogging, yoga, even a gym membership. But since the divorce, I had not exercised at all.

"Well, that's that," I said to myself, and I walked across the hot parking lot to my old red Volvo wagon. I opened the very sturdy door and slid onto the hot leather seat. I turned the key. The engine sputtered and sputtered, but it would not turn over. I tried again. And again. No dice. "Just great! Just what I need! For my car to quit now! I don't have the money to fix it. I don't have any help! Shit. Shit. Shit," I muttered. Then remembering that I had a free tow from AAA, I got out of the hot car and made the call. "At least I can have it towed to the house for now," I thought.

The sun was shining so brightly it hurt my eyes. My very pale skin, which was more accustomed to cave-dwelling, had started to turn pink. It honestly felt like it was about a hundred degrees with 99.9 percent humidity. I began to imagine my skin turning red, sun damage setting in, then wrinkles—like deep crevasses etched into my skin as happens to the elderly beach bums. Knowing that it was closing time, I wondered if I could wait it out in the church narthex. Yearning for some shade, I figured that it was worth a try, so I crossed the parking lot toward the building.

I crept in, trying to be as quiet as possible. I was hoping to wait inside unnoticed. Instead, Maymie came right in from a side door, as if she had supersonic hearing. She was smiling and holding a glass of what looked like lemonade.

"Here, Sugar, you look like you could use this."

I did not really want to stay and drink lemonade with a total stranger. I had become sort of a recluse and loner since my divorce. But something about Maymie, or maybe it was this place, made me feel very safe. Maymie was bright and bold and beautiful. She looked to be about fifty years old. She had mocha skin, green-gold eyes, and fine high cheek bones. She was taller than me, which, owing to the fact that I am only five feet tall, is no great achievement. She was about five feet five and stood very regally in her blue bedazzled kaftan. Although I spent my days alternately in my bathrobe or business casual,

I immediately wanted one just like it. "I'm sorry, but my car won't start. Do you mind if I wait here for the tow truck?" I asked.

Maymie shook her head and clucked her tongue. "Car won't start? Mmm, Mmm! In this heat! Well, come on in here, Sugar. You can wait with us. We're just about to start our ladies meeting." She kept calling me "Sugar." A term of endearment I had not heard since I was a little girl growing up in Georgia. Now, at age forty, the term carried me back to my childhood. My great-aunts used to call me "Sugar" and I liked it. It felt familiar and it made me smile.

I carried my lemonade and followed Maymie into the next room. As Maymie opened the door, the smell of rose water washed over me in a cool, air-conditioned breeze. The room was decorated in a way that reminded me of a parlor in an old Southern home. The wallpaper was yellow with tiny pink roses and white stripes. Victorian parlor chairs lined the walls to form a circle. The Queen Ann table in the back of the room was stacked with a few used dessert plates and what appeared to be the remains of a blueberry cobbler. As we entered, I became so uncomfortable that I almost turned and ran into the roasting badlands of the parking lot. I was not, in fact, a sweaty kid, being called in for lunch by my Southern aunts. I was a sweaty adult, dressed for manual labor, who really had not planned on being social—not even for a couple of minutes.

Sitting in the chairs were ten women, all chattering vibrantly. The room fell silent as they ceased their conversations abruptly, all eyes on me as Maymie and I entered the room. "Ladies, this is—I'm sorry, Sugar, tell me your name," Maymie said, turning to me.

"Diana Williams . . . er Davis. Diana Davis," I caught myself, having made the choice to return to my maiden name.

Suddenly I regretted my decision to ever change it in the first place. "What foolishness," I thought, "Now I've got to pay $160 for a new passport. Not to mention the pain in the butt of all the paperwork and online accounts I need to change—credit cards, driver's license, Netflix, even my email address."

"Diana dropped off a donation for the homeless shelter and decided to stay for the meeting," Maymie announced.

Not wanting to correct her and feeling a little bit of pressure due to the smiling faces and nodding heads in the group, I took a seat and began to sip my lemonade and check my phone compulsively. AAA had left a message. "They estimate two hours! Oh goody! Joy! Great! I get to wait here for two hours," I thought to myself sarcastically. "At least it's comfortable in here," I reasoned, sadly realizing that I had absolutely nothing else going on that day, or any other. I sat up in my chair to tune into the meeting, silently hoping that the air conditioning would dry the vast armpit circles on my t-shirt.

"Ladies, this month's meeting of the Goddess Tribe will come to order," Maymie announced from the front of the room.

"The Goddess Tribe?" I pondered. "That's a cute name for these church ladies." I smiled as I mulled it around in my mind, imagining them flying through the air with sparkling crowns and fairy wings to the next bake sale or bingo night.

"Our topic this month is Faith and will be presented by Isabel," Maymie proclaimed, sounding very official. Maymie then gestured toward a dark-haired woman seated directly in front of her.

Isabel looked to be about thirty-five years old and was very pretty. She was slender and petite, and she wore her long black hair in a braid down her back. Her skin was flawless and slightly olive toned, which contrasted nicely with the white cotton sundress she was wearing, and the very chic brown leather sandals that were laced up to her ankles. Around her neck she wore the most beautiful blue necklace I had ever seen. I could hardly take my eyes off it. It appeared to be a Native American design—a squash blossom in silver and turquoise. "She has fashion simplicity down to an art, that's for sure," I thought, feeling a tinge of both admiration and sadness at the same time. Admiration because I wanted to be her, and sadness because I recognized a part of myself that used to care about things like fashion.

"Hello everyone!" She said cheerfully in a lovely Spanish accent, and then smiled joyfully and waved at the room. "I'm happy to talk to you today about the Goddess Power, Faith," she began.

"When you have Faith in your ability to shape substance, you have the foundation to create an abundant life. Substance refers to the universal stuff in which we all live. We, as creators, have the ability to shape this substance, and our own lives. Therefore, the power of Faith is the foundation of prosperity."

"The Goddess for today's lesson is Lakshmi," Isabel continued, lifting a poster board with a glued-on picture of a beautiful Goddess. "Lakshmi is the Hindu Goddess of wealth, good fortune, luxury, beauty, and fertility. She was born out of the ocean and she is often depicted standing on a lotus flower. The lotus flower represents purity of body, mind, and spirit," she explained, sweeping a stray hair from her face.

"The Goddess Lakshmi embodies the power of Faith because she represents the idea of abundant life in every way—financial abundance, good fortune, and happiness." She paused for a moment as if to gather her thoughts. Then she set the poster down, carefully leaning it against the nearby easel.

"How have you used the Goddess Power of Faith to bring greater abundance into your lives?" she asked, gesturing to the group. To my surprise, several hands flew up. "Lil, how about it?" she prompted, smiling at a tall, dark haired woman in a blue dress. I suddenly noticed that they were all wearing blue in some way—top, bottom, or accessory.

Lil stood up to better address the group. "I have been feeling very fearful about money lately. So, this week, I really made an effort to affirm every day that I am grateful for the abundance in my life. Yesterday, I received a check in the mail for $1200! This was money that an old landlord owed me from years ago and then out of the blue, it shows up!" Everyone cheered and clapped as Lil giggled, took a bow, and sat back down.

"These church ladies are a wild group," I thought to myself.

Hands flew up again.

"Virginia," Isabel called to a petite woman with light brown hair.

Virginia, too, stood up to speak. "I have been thinking about starting my own business, but I was really scared to actually do it. However, since I've been coming to this group, I've realized that these nagging ideas won't go away, and they must have a greater purpose. So as of this week, I have incorporated my brand new wedding cake business! I have the Goddess Power of Faith and I know that I will be successful!" Once again, the group cheered, and Virginia did her best beauty pageant wave, then sat down.

One by one, the ladies shared stories of good fortune that they had received through Faith. One had gotten a great new job. Another had been asked out on a date by someone special. And each story closed to raucous applause from the group.

As I listened, I began to feel a tightness in my stomach and shoulders. My jaw clenched. What was happening to me? I was getting really pissed off at these nice ladies. First of all, they were too nice. And secondly, they were too freakin' perfect. My mind began to race from one life event to another, picking all the worst ones. "Remember the time I got pregnant in college and had to get married instead of graduating? Remember the time I had to give up all of my stock options to stay home with baby number two? Remember the time I bought all those art supplies so that I could really focus on my painting, then never had the time? Remember how we used to fight about money constantly? How was I supposed to save any money when we were living on such a tight budget? Remember how Jonathan used to discourage me at every turn, and I believed him? Remember how I thought divorce was the answer and now my life sucks even worse? And now my car has broken down and I'm too broke to fix it and these ladies are here just cheering about how great everything is!"

I must have been really fidgeting in my chair, because just then, Isabel called on me. "Diana, what would you like to share with the group about your Goddess Power?"

She did not ask if I would like to share. She asked *what* I would like to share.

"I," I stammered, "I don't know, I mean—You can't always be positive when . . . ." In my frustration, I knew what I was thinking, but I couldn't find the words to convey the gravity of my situation.

"Okay," I said, "I'm recently divorced. I'm broke and my kids hate me. Also, I am only here because my only form of transportation, a '94 Volvo wagon, is dead in the parking lot. I'm waiting for AAA. That's all I've got." Then I bowed and sat down. No one clapped.

"Diana, I hear you. I hear what you are saying." Isabel said quietly. "I hear that you are hurting and you are frustrated," she continued, "Would it be okay if we pray with you?"

Isabel's calm demeanor made me feel not only like I had behaved like a grouch, but also that I had been a hysterical grouch—a crazy grouch—and that was their first impression of me. I felt small and I wanted to match that feeling by disappearing, but all eyes were on me. So, I said, "Sure."

Isabel closed her eyes and began.

"We are the presence of Pure Being,

The Sisters of the Goddess Tribe.

We affirm that Goddess Power lives within us,

Flows through each of us,

Connects us all to each other, to our world, to our universe.

Thoughts such as lack, fear, hatred, and poverty have no power over us

For they are just thoughts.

We live in joy, abundance, and prosperity.

Every day it is ours to claim

And we are grateful in this knowledge.

And so it is

Amen."

I had never heard a prayer like this. Something about the words being spoken this way hit me hard. I was overcome with all of my loss, sadness, and fear. I began to sob uncontrollably. A few of the ladies gathered around my chair. I felt hands on my back, attempting to console me.

After a several-minute-long catharsis, I wiped my eyes and stood up. The women of the Goddess Tribe were saying their goodbyes to each other. A few came over to invite me to the next meeting. One gave me the homemade class booklet—a thin stack of papers stapled together with a title page that read "The Goddess Tribe—A Meeting Guide". I smiled and made vague responses about having to check my schedule. I honestly had no intention of ever seeing these women again. I had humiliated myself in front of a group of total strangers. I just wanted to go home.

"Home! How am I getting home?" I suddenly remembered my car situation which had brought me to the meeting in the first place. Just then, the tow truck driver from AAA called to tell me that he was pulling into the parking lot and needed me to meet him. As I started to walk out, Maymie stopped me.

"Diana, thank you so much for coming today. We all really enjoyed having you here," she said, smiling brightly.

"Thanks, but I . . . ," I tried to reply, but she was on a roll.

"And we would just love for you to join the group. Now, we meet on the first Saturday of every month at noon—rain or shine," she said, placing the flyer into my hand and closing my fingers over it with her hands.

"Thanks, but I . . . ," I tried to cut in again, but to no avail.

"And don't you think that you're alone, Honey, because you're not. We've all been through some tough times. The difference is that we've had each other. We've been there to support one another and that's what you're missing, Diana. You are missing a tribe. You just moved here, isn't that right?" She nodded at me as if trying to get me to nod along with her in agreement.

I obliged and began to nod yes. "Yes, I just moved here, but I . . . ."

"And you don't know many people?" She nodded at me again, and I nodded back as if mesmerized.

"So, you'll come to next month's meeting," she stated matter-of-factly, still nodding at me. So, of course, I nodded back.

"Sure, sure I'll come," I responded reluctantly.

"Now, just one thing, Diana. You will need to bring the dessert," she added. "Next month is Strength and key lime pie," she continued. "The recipe is in the booklet, Sugar," she said, patting my hand that held the rolled-up booklet. I hadn't noticed, but she had walked me to the door and was then opening it for me and guiding me out. "There's your tow truck! I'll see you at the next meeting, Diana!" she said, waving as she closed the large white door.

Next thing I knew, I was in the blinding sun again and had just agreed to make a pie for next month's Goddess Tribe meeting—a meeting that I had no intention of attending. But now I had to go, because I was expected to bring the dessert!

I meandered over to the tow truck driver. "Let's just see if it'll start," he said, holding out his hand for the keys. I dropped my key ring into his hand and stood nearby. My jaw dropped open as the car fired right up, purring to life as if it were brand new.

Chapter Three

The next day was Sunday and I awoke with an unusual curiosity about the Goddess Tribe. This was unusual because I had not been genuinely curious about much of anything lately. In my loneliness and depression, I had lost my sense of wonder, forgotten any desire to dig deeper or make discoveries. I sat up in bed and reached for the little hand-made booklet that had made its way to my nightstand. "Meeting One: The Power of Faith," I read. "Hmm?" I puzzled. "Meeting One? How were they already prepared for the discussion? They must have read the booklet ahead of time. Show-offs," I mumbled aloud to the empty house. In my solitude, I continued to read about the Goddess Power of Faith.

I began to read about how in our connectedness—our universal consciousness—Faith is the power that brings ideas into being. Faith is the foundation of a prosperity consciousness, in which one believes that prosperity is readily available to all—if we claim it. Faith is the power that brings our hopes and dreams into reality. Faith is ultimately the force that shapes our world. In discussing how the power of Faith has shown up in their lives, the ladies of the Goddess Tribe were thinking, feeling, and then experiencing how their thoughts literally shape their world.

The ladies at the meeting had related happy events such as a dinner invitation, an unexpected check in the mail, and new job. "So," I questioned "if my thoughts are shaping my life right now, then what kind of life am I creating for myself?" I adjusted in the bed, fluffing my pillows so as to sit up more comfortably. I began to roll the tape back on the weeks and months since my divorce. In so doing, it became clear to me that my thoughts were, if not creating my unhappiness, certainly reinforcing it. I had read religious doctrine many times, only to feel that as a woman and as someone whose behavior would be labeled as 'sinner', it was not for me. However, something in this idea resonated deeply within me. I felt no urge to disagree. I did not feel excluded from this principle. Rather, what I felt at that moment was a deep knowing—a sense that this was a truth that I could feel deep into my being—into my cells, into my memory, into my soul.

That week at work, I vowed to put the power of Faith into practice. My goal was to think about what I want—not about what I do not want, and certainly not what makes me miserable. In setting that goal, I realized that I had not spent much time in thinking about what I want. My days had always been so full of complaining, that I had not stopped to imagine what peace and happiness might look like.

It took quite a bit of effort, thought, and creativity to come up with some things that I wanted in my life. I started by listing the things that I do not want and then their direct opposites. I sat down and made a list with the goal in mind to read and reread the list several times each day.

What I Do Not Want	**What I Want**
Debt and Financial Worries	*Financial Freedom*
Loneliness and Depression	*Supportive, handsome, encouraging, romantic life-partner, and a community of friends.*
Strife, blame, anger from my children and ex-husband	*Peace in my relationship with my children and my ex-husband*
Tiredness, laziness, weight-gain	*Energy, excitement, desire to exercise and reclaim my healthy body*
Dreading going to work—job I hate	*Happiness, creativity, & respect at work*

Since loneliness and depression were on my "What I Do Not Want" list, I reluctantly decided that I should go into the office each day rather than pretending to work from home. What I had been doing was wallowing in sadness and self-pity—reliving my mistakes and polluting my thoughts with negativity. If I really wanted to feel better, I had to get my thoughts under control. If I was in the office every day, I posited, my mind would be occupied with work, not my personal failings. This meant setting an early alarm, showering, putting on make-up, and wearing nice clothes every day. I figured that meeting these requirements would be good for me given the state that I had gotten myself into.

Next, I decided to take a trip to the health food store to pick up some vitamins. I found that St. John's Wart was good for depression. I also got a multivitamin and a few other supplements to help me with my energy level. With the goal in mind of getting my health back, I shopped for healthy greens and some snack bars to take to work. When I returned home, I packed my vitamins by days of the week and stocked my cabinets with New Vegan protein bars. I was not exactly sure how a vegan protein bar contained protein, but I took their word for it, in my new-found determination to get healthy.

On Monday morning, I begrudgingly heeded the chime of my alarm clock, staggered out of bed, and found my way to the kitchen, directed by the welcoming smell of fresh coffee. I had been kind to myself the night before by setting the timer on the electric percolator and now I was greeted by hot coffee as my much-needed reward. I had also chosen my outfit for the day—an oversized off-white silk blouse, a wide brown leather belt, and a pair of old Levi's. This was an ensemble that I would have chosen in 1990 and it made me smile to know that fashion had come back around, as it always does.

In the '80s, we were recapturing the '60s with big hair and mini-skirts. As I put on my makeup, I plugged my phone into the speakers and put it on '90s music. I sang along as I applied contour to conceal the force of gravity under my chin. I twisted my auburn hair up on my head and drove to work. When I arrived, I let out a reluctant sigh, untwisted my hair and let it drop into a mass of waves. I said a mantra as I nervously strolled across the parking lot. "Today will be a good day. Today will be a good day . . . ." As I reached for the door, it was usurped by a very big hand. Startled, I turned my head to see a very tall, very handsome man smiling down at me with the bluest eyes I'd ever seen. "Let me get that for you," he offered in a deep voice. "Thank you," I smiled back, very aware of the butterflies in my stomach. As I walked into the office, I realized that he worked there too. With his laptop bag casually swung over one shoulder, he sauntered down the hallway and entered the IT department. "Wow," I thought, "I'm going to say this mantra every day!"

In making a considerable effort to keep my thoughts on the "What I Want" list, my first full week at work went well.

I had a few minor road blocks, but all in all, I can describe it as painless. I focused on the work rather than on my troubles, and the days went by quickly if not particularly enjoyably. My boss, a man named Jacob, was friendly and as easy to get along with as he had been while I was working from home. I met a few new coworkers and in all, my first full week in the office had gone well.

As the week came to an end, the thought of returning to an empty house for the weekend filled me with both fear and sadness. Fear, because I had done so well this week in focusing on my list. I was worried that I would go back to that negative place that I was trying so hard to climb out of. And sadness because I envisioned being lonely all weekend and the thoughts that loneliness would bring up—missing my children, my old life. I shut down my computer, put my legal pad in my top drawer, and placed my pen in the holder. Then as I was slinging my purse over my shoulder and striding toward the door, I heard someone calling my name. "Diana, Diana!"

I turned to see Shyla, a graphic designer whom I didn't know very well walking in my direction, also with her purse slung over her shoulder. From what I did know of her, she had a bubbly personality and kind face. She was a pretty young woman, a little bit shorter than me, with a mass of waist-length curly hair that she had dyed a lavender-gray color. She had olive skin and brown eyes, and I remembered she had told me her parents were from Puerto Rico and that she had been a military brat growing up. She had recently moved from New York City.

"Diana, we're going to happy hour at Jake's. We do it every payday. You want to come with?" she asked, curtailing her sentence expectantly. I was all set to say no. However, remembering my list item "a community of friends" and "respect at work," I dusted off the words, "Yes, that sounds like fun," which had been long packed away inside the very recesses of my brain, and forced myself to speak them.

We walked across the street to Jake's, a casual restaurant that served burgers about thirty different ways. As we made our way to the bar area, I saw our group from work. Monique, a content writer, was an attractive African American woman of about thirty. She mentioned that she had gone to University of Maryland and had moved to Florida last year. Paul, in affiliate marketing, was a very thin man of about forty-five, with strawberry-blond hair. He was witty, hilarious, and, at six feet seven, by far the tallest of the group. He had invited his partner, Marco, who worked as a florist in the shop down the street. Mike, a graphic designer, looked to be about my age and, quite handsome and funny. He was married, and smiled and laughed easily. A happy man, secure in the knowledge that his family was intact and would be waiting for him at home. My assessment of Mike made me think of the man who had held the door for me on Monday morning. I couldn't help but scan the restaurant hopefully. I dreamily recalled his deep voice and blue eyes. I also noticed that Jacob was not there. I wondered if that was because no one had invited him to come along. I made a mental note to invite him next time.

As we approached the group, I felt fearful and nervous. Socially, I was way out of practice. Other than school events or occasions revolving around my kids, I hadn't had much of a social life. I had not been out with friends in years and was unsure of what we would talk about. What I discovered was that my fears were unfounded. Happy Hour conversation turned out to be a piece of cake. We talked about work and the various places we'd come from (it seemed that none of us were actually from Florida). I finished my glass of white wine and said my goodbyes, not wanting to over-stay the conversation. As I headed home, I did so with a smile on my face. "I'm finally making a life for myself here," I thought.

Chapter Four

The first Friday night in July, I was up late baking the promised key lime pie to take to the Goddess Tribe meeting the next day. Since the recipe noted a cooling time of eight hours, procrastination was not an option. I remembered last month's meeting, and how it seemed that I had changed so much in only four weeks. I was no longer a recluse. I actually had some people at work that I might venture to call friends. My relationship with my kids was still strained, but I was determined to try my best to repair it. They were coming for a visit in a few weeks and I was so ready to see them. I missed them like one would miss a lost arm or leg. I could feel their presence from time to time, and I longed for their return to me.

But all in all, I was feeling better emotionally and was even looking forward to seeing the women at the church, especially Maymie, who had been so kind to me. I also wondered what everyone would wear. The mystery of the color blue last time was easily solved by reading the booklet. Faith was to be represented by royal blue and Strength by emerald green, hence the key lime pie dessert. Although key limes are not technically green, I saw that the intention was there. "Anyway, who wants a green Jell-O pie these days? If you're going for green, what else is there?" I asked aloud, to the house. After refrigerating the pie, I went to scour my closet for something to wear.

I searched my closet for something, anything, emerald green. Pushing through hanger after hanger of size six dresses and tops, which were now way too small for me, I managed to come across a green summer dress which I had recently bought on clearance. I thought it would be too big judging by the label, but it fit perfectly. "That's lucky," I joked to my reflection. It may have been aging or just my sedentary life-style, but I had managed to pack on a good fifteen pounds since the divorce. "Divorce," I mumbled, "the gift that keeps on giving." Satisfied that I was well prepared for the Goddess Tribe and determined to make a better impression than I had last month, I hung the dress back on its hanger and got ready for bed.

I climbed into bed and fell asleep only to be visited by my grandmother as soon as my head hit the pillow. We were in her old house and I was telling her about my sunflowers. I had five Mammoth Sunflowers as big as dinner plates growing in the garden. She looked at me quizzically and said, "You only have two." Knowing that she was mistaken, I said, "No, I have five as big as dinner plates. Did you ever see such beautiful sunflowers?" I pointed to my flowers and sure enough, I only had two. A large monarch butterfly was perched atop one of the flowers. Suddenly, it flew toward me and as it did, the other three sunflowers appeared from behind. I did indeed, have five bright yellow sunflowers, now swaying in the summer breeze. When I awoke, I was sure that Ma had been there visiting me—or I had been somewhere else visiting her. Everything about it was so vivid. "What could it mean?" I wondered. At the same time, I was filled with love and gratitude that Ma would come for a visit, even if the conversation made no sense to me.

I walked over to my dresser and opened Ma's jewelry box. I felt wealthy having this box of jewels. Each one was a lovely example of vintage jewelry. Then I noticed something—a sparkling green emerald! "Perfect!" I thought, slipping it on my finger, "I can wear it in honor of Ma today."

I arrived at the church a little early, noting that I was in charge of the food. Once again, despite my timing, the parking lot was empty. "I guess there's a back parking lot," I thought as I carried my pie toward the door, more concerned with my dessert offering than the parking situation. As I was fumbling with my purse, pie, and booklet, the door swung open and there stood Maymie, with her welcoming smile.

"Well hello there, Sugar," she beamed. "Look at you in your green dress. Don't you look pretty!" She was looking very regal again, just like a queen, this time in a green and white kaftan. The fabric was chiffon, adorned with green fern and palm leaves all over the white background. The neckline was embroidered with silver thread and beads. She wore a matching turban on her head, silver bangle bracelets, and matching silver sandals. "Where does she shop?" I puzzled, "Not Ross Dress for Less, that's for sure."

We walked from the narthex into the meeting room where the ladies were standing, casually chatting and holding their cups of coffee or tea. "The pie's here!" Maymie declared with great authority as I walked toward the table carrying the dessert. The ladies of the Goddess Tribe began to meander in my direction, still holding their conversations. They were soon serving themselves and finding seats. I hoped that my first effort at key lime pie was edible. "It looks like the recipe picture anyway," I reasoned. After everyone was served, I got a slice for myself along with a cup of coffee, sampling the pie as I made my way to the only empty seat. The creamy dessert hit my tongue with tartness and then the comforting flavor of evaporated milk. I thought of Ma and wished that she could be there to try it. Still savoring the bite of pie, I sat down next to the woman I remembered from last month as Lil. She looked to be in her mid-fifties, but her dark hair was done up in a bubble hair-do from the 1960s. She was tall and slender, and her lime green pantsuit and accessories were perfectly put together. "Diana, hello!" she chimed, her green eyes sparkling "I'm so glad you could make it." I was shocked that she had remembered my name, but then again, I guessed that my visit had been pretty memorable. I nodded at Lil, swallowing my bite of pie, and was just about to say hello, when I noticed Maymie making her way to the front of the room. She boldly called us all to order and all the chattering subsided as Maymie introduced this month's topic and speaker.

"Good morning, ladies and Happy Saturday," Maymie said. "What a blessing to join together as the Goddess Tribe once again. Today, our power is Strength which will be presented by our sister, Margie."

Maymie smiled brightly, welcoming us with bold hand gestures as if she would like to hug us with her words.

"Let's start the meeting in prayer for Strength. Join hands, my sisters," she said, closing her eyes and stretching her arms out before her. "Today we invoke the two most powerful words in the Universe. I Am. Thousands of years ago, the ancient Hebrews' name for God was Yahweh, which translates to 'I Am,' meaning that God dwells within. Jesus knew this as he proudly claimed the words, 'I Am,' striking jealousy and fear in the hearts of the Pharisees. And we too, Ladies of The Goddess Tribe, shall call forth the Power of affirming 'I Am', as The Goddess dwells within." Maymie continued.

I am the Power of Strength which dwells within my soul.

I release false beliefs in my heart which separate me from Oneness.

I embrace The Goddess Power of Strength which holds me steadfast, strong, and sure.

I am The Goddess who stands firm in my Strength.

I am The Strength which guides my destiny and claims my voice.

I am The Mother who proudly protects all children.

I am The Goddess who shields the meek.

I Boldly walk the path of peace.

And for this I am so grateful, and I say Thank You.

Amen.

Once again, I was moved to tears by the prayer. Maymie spoke with such assurance—such power. She truly embodied The Goddess, if there was such a thing. I could suddenly feel the intense energy in the room and it was electrifying. "I am the Mother. I am The Goddess. I am the Protector," I thought. These bold words gave me strength. Instantly, I felt an inner power that was completely new to me.

A young woman named Margie moved to the podium carrying her Goddess on a poster board, just as Isabel had the month before. "This month's Goddess Power is the Power of Strength and our Goddess is Kali," she began.

As she leaned the board against the easel, I regarded the blue-skinned Goddess, Kali. She was very beautiful, with long wild black curls and a necklace made of men's heads! She seemed to be waving her four arms in a dance of sorts.

"Kali is a Hindu Goddess known as Mother of the Universe, divine protector, and liberator. The necklace of heads represents a liberation from the ego. When we are caught up in our ego, we are not truly free. Kali frees us from earthly trappings. She affirms our oneness. She joins us together as the Goddess Mother. She is Mother and Protector to all children. With these qualities, Kali embodies the Power of Strength. The strength to advocate for those who are powerless is a gift that mothers all share. Strength to persevere in difficult situations can lead to us liberation. Think about it. If you work hard and persevere toward a goal, the end result is indeed freedom," Margie added tentatively.

"When we combine our Goddess Powers of Faith and Strength, we have a recipe for success," she continued, now shifting her weight from one foot to the other. "We have Faith in our ability to create our own reality, but this must be combined with the strength to persevere in achieving our goals. When we stand firm in our principles, beliefs, and goals, we create our destiny. Ultimately, we reach our spiritual goals."

I thought about the changes I had made in only one month. I have displayed the Power of Faith in my new job, in making friends, and in stepping out of my comfort zone. Now, I thought about using my own Goddess-given strength to persevere in tough times—that is a gift that I have not used in a very long time. I have always been one to give up too easily when the going gets tough. "Maybe," I thought, "that's why my marriage ended—because I did not use my strength to persevere." I thought about my spiritual goals, for which I had created a list after the last meeting. "So," I thought, "applying my inner gift of Strength, is the perfect complement to expressing Faith that I will achieve all the goals on my list."

Margie, finishing her presentation, cleared her throat. "It often takes a strong commitment to strength and perseverance when it feels like nothing that you do is working," her large eyes looking out at the group expectantly. Margie was a very pretty young woman. She looked to be about thirty-two years old. She was about five feet six, with a slender build; her brown hair cut in a very stylish bob. She was wearing a sage green suit. The perfectly tailored jacket had three-quarter length sleeves and a pencil skirt. She wore cream-colored pumps to complete the ensemble. As I regarded her, I thought, "All of the ladies in the group are really pretty. And perfectly put together. Do they ever do stuff like yardwork?"

I was startled out of my musing as Margie addressed the group.

"Does anyone have an example of how you are using your Goddess Power of Strength? Or how you are combining Faith with Strength to achieve your goals?" she asked.

Again, enthusiastic hands flew into the air as if on a timer.

"Yes, Lil," Margie directed.

"I have used the power of Strength to persevere every day since my husband left," Lil recounted primly.

"He was an alcoholic and after Patsy was born, I knew that I had to be strong for her. One day, he just up and left. I never heard from him again. Raising a daughter all by myself has been the most difficult and the most rewarding job of my life." Lil said, her voice cracking just a little. "I have been a school teacher for thirty years now. All alone, I managed to raise my child on a teacher's salary due to Faith, Strength, and Perseverance."

Just then a woman, who looked to be Lil's twin, patted her on the shoulder. It was then that I realized that this woman must be Lil's daughter, Patsy; although they looked to be about the same age! These ladies were full of surprises. It had not occurred to me that any of the Goddess Tribe ladies had endured heartache or strife. They all seemed so happy and so perfect.

After the meeting, I approached Lil. "Thank you for sharing your story," I said as I placed my hand on her arm. "I've been feeling totally alone since my divorce. I've lost friends. My kids are mad at me," I continued looking down at my feet. "It . . . it just really helps to hear that you made it and that you're okay.

And that your daughter is okay." Lil beamed at me as Patsy came up beside her. "She's beautiful, as a matter of fact," I smiled. Then, turning to Patsy, I said, "Your mother looks so young! I thought you two were sisters. What is her secret?" I questioned.

"She lies about her age." Patsy laughed, her red lipstick illuminating her white teeth. "She even lied about it on her driver's license. She's lied about it for so long that she believes it!" Patsy laughed as Lil pretended to elbow her in the ribs, both ladies laughing and giggling up a storm.

"Laughter is the best medicine," said Lil. "Who has time for sadness and misery? Those thoughts and feelings won't serve you. You've just got to pick yourself up and do what is yours to do. Don't spend time and energy on trying to do what is not yours to do. You can't fix anybody but yourself." She said, nodding at me as she spoke. "Smile, laugh, and be happy, Diana. That's the only plan that God has for you, Sugar. Embrace happiness." She then gently took hold of both my hands and smiling brightly at me repeated, "Embrace it!"

I drove home from the meeting thinking about what Lil had said. "If I am to embrace happiness and do only what is mine to do, where do I start," I thought blankly. I continued to ponder the question as my car bumped up the gravel driveway to toward the house. I parked, gathered my purse and pie plate, fumbling with the car keys and door. As I made my way up the front porch steps, I noticed a letter sticking out of the mailbox. I smiled excitedly, thinking that it was from my daughter, Ava. She still preferred letters to email, a quirk that I shared with her. We both loved writing funny letters and embellishing the margins with silly illustrations of cats, flowers, superheroes—anything goofy that might also help to illustrate the story. But as I drew closer, my stomach tensed as I saw the handwriting and read the name. It was from my ex-husband, Jonathan Williams. "I will come back for it," I thought, leaving the letter in the box as I proceeded into the house with my hands and my mind already too full.

Dear Diana,

I am writing to let you know that Ian and I are doing well. Ian is very sad and depressed without you, but he is adjusting okay, and I try my best to be understanding. But he is a moody teenager and it's not always easy. You were always better at this stuff than me. Ava drove up from Savannah last week and said that she misses you too.

I also wanted to let you know that I have been seeing a therapist. Her name is Kelly and she is very down to earth. Not like that judgmental marriage counselor that we saw a couple of years ago. Kelly is great and has given me a lot of insight into your emotional problems and why you chose to leave us now, instead of waiting for Ian to grow up. You know how hard this is on him and yet you remain totally selfish. Thinking only of yourself once again.

Kelly says that I am doing great and will make someone a wonderful husband one day. She says that I should start dating because I am such a catch. But I don't think I will ever get married again. I can't endure having my heart stomped on again.

The kids told me that you are working all the time now and that when they visit, you can barely spend any time with them. Let me remind you that when you lived here in our home, you did not have to work at all. Your only job was to be a mom. You worked part-time for pocket money and to get out of the house. You had your money to spend at the mall or at the makeup store or whatever. While I worked to pay the bills, and put food on the table, etc. And I never got a word of thanks. I sacrificed plenty. Now, I can't believe you don't miss that. What are you doing? What's the point of this?

I hadn't really planned on getting all sappy, but I want to say that I miss you too. I know that in your mind, we are divorced and it's

*over. But for me and the kids, it's not over at all. Please come home.
I love you and miss you.*

Your devoted husband,

Jonathan

I sat and stared at the paper for a long time, feeling guilty and indignant at the same time. I was speechless. I just stared with my mouth open, holding the letter in my hand.

"He's going to a therapist to analyze *my* problems?" I finally yelled. "I never thanked him and I should what? Be grateful and come back to him because he loves me *now*?" I said aloud to the empty farmhouse. After these past few months, I imagined that the house was getting pretty accustomed to me talking to it.

"The nerve!" I breathed, dropping the letter on the table. "The kids are coming for a visit in a few weeks! I'm only six hours away!" I blurted. "He makes it sound like I never see them!"

"That right there!" I pointed at the letter, "That is exactly why I can't live with him!" I fumed. "Condescending, guilt-tripping, smothering—I mean, REALLY? Unbelievable!"

I thought about how he made light of my part-time job. He made it sound like we didn't need the money, but we did. He made it sound like I did not contribute, but I did. I paid for the kids' activities, the Easter Bunny baskets, and the Christmas extravaganzas of wrapping paper flurries strewn all over the living room. I paid for the birthday parties, the July Fourth fireworks, and the beach vacations. I bought the Halloween costumes, pumpkins, and candy. I funded and cooked the Thanksgiving feasts. I signed them up for riding lessons, paid for football uniforms. My part-time job made it possible for the kids to have extras—to have all the things that I wanted for them. I wanted them to have experiences and to have happy childhoods. And now my full-time job was paying Ava's college tuition. He was asking me to come home in the most insulting, most asshole-ish way possible. Even if I was sad and lonely here, even though I missed the kids desperately, I could not and would not go home to *him.*

"I will persevere, and I will make this work." I announced to the house, vaguely recognizing that this, too, was part of my spiritual journey. I had listed my relationship with Jonathan and the kids as something to work on, "I'm now presented with a rich opportunity," I thought sarcastically. I imagined what Maymie might say, "Well, Sugar, don't let that trouble you right now. How about a cold glass of lemonade?" Or what Lil would say, "God's only plan for you is that you should be happy." Or even Margie, whom I had just met, "It takes a strong commitment to strength when it feels like nothing that you do is working."

Later that day, I took myself to my favorite little makeup store in downtown Heritage Springs and paid twenty-five dollars for the perfect shade of red lipstick. The irony was not lost on me in remembering Jonathan's smarty-pants comment in his letter. Since I was making my own money and did not have Jonathan to answer to, why shouldn't I indulge myself now and then. As I happily took the little yellow and white striped bag from the cashier, I noticed the sorry state of my nails. "These don't really go with the whole red lipstick theme," I lamented, regarding my closely clipped unpolished fingernails. They were more suited to clicking computer keys than anything else. I made an abrupt detour into a nearby salon where I proceeded to get "The Works"—mani, pedi, hair-color, and blow out.

When the stylist was finished, she handed me a mirror. The woman looking back at me looked familiar. She was someone like the old me. Gone were the weary under-eye circles. The dull, gray roots were covered with shiny chestnut, copper, and gold strands gently framing her face thanks to the rounded brush that the stylist had used. On her lips, fingers, and toes, she wore the perfect shade of red. And she was smiling.

Since I hadn't bothered to change clothes after the Goddess Tribe meeting, I was clicking down the sidewalk in my green dress and high heels. Proudly sporting my freshly applied red lipstick along with my matching fingers and toes. I felt defiant and rebellious. I felt as if I was showing Jonathan that his veiled insults and attempts at guilt-tripping me only made me stronger. "Why does he do this?" I wondered, "When we lived together, he barely acknowledged my presence and now that I'm gone, papers filed, divorce granted, he wants me back," I thought. "Why didn't he want to work it out a year ago? Why, if he didn't like our marriage counselor, didn't he say something at the time?" I considered. "Or maybe he just wants to vent his anger at someone and I get to be *it* this time."

I walked along the cobblestone sidewalk deep in thought, still carrying the yellow and white striped bag from the makeup store. It was now evening and the street lanterns were alight in the purple and gold dusk—sunset on Florida's West Coast. Groups of tourists were cheerfully setting out to enjoy cocktails. Couples walked hand in hand toward their dinner reservations. As I passed my reflection in a shop window, I was brought back to reality. I thought, "I look like one of the Goddess Tribe ladies," and I chuckled to myself at the idea.

The evening was so idyllic that, in a very uncharacteristic move, I decided to eat dinner out—all by myself. Up ahead I heard the far away sounds of someone playing Spanish guitar. As I approached, I saw a quaint open-air restaurant. The old building was made of stone and looked to be about a hundred years old. The sign that hung above read "The Rusty Hook Restaurant & Tavern—Live Music Tonight." Outside, was a welcoming patio area with wrought iron tables and chairs. Oak trees draped with Spanish moss encircled the courtyard. The branches were decorated with white lights and glass orbs which contained gently flickering candles. Each table was lit with a small golden lantern. The occasional firefly illuminating beyond the oaks. A gentle breeze blew, rustling the leaves, and blowing my hair away from my face. I suddenly felt electrified. I walked up to the gate, intending to request to see a menu, but instead was startled by someone calling my name "Diana, hey!" I scanned the patio crowd to find Shyla and Monique sitting at a table and waving enthusiastically in my direction. I waved back and weaved my way through the groups of diners toward them. I happily arrived at their table, relieved that I did not actually have to do this alone. After further consideration, and seeing the families, groups of friends, and tourists hanging out together, I felt my heart begin to yearn for company, familiarity, and friends. As I looked around the table, I noticed that one more person had joined them. There, smiling back at me, were the bluest eyes I've ever seen.

Butterflies! If ever the expression, 'I got butterflies in my stomach' applied, now was the time. Mr. Blue-Eyed I.T. Guy From Work was there smiling at me, saying his real name, and extending his hand to shake mine. I introduced myself as well, and smiling, shook his hand, then sat down. No idea what he said. Didn't catch his name either.

Shyla and Monique soon noticed my new hair color and began to chatter on and on about how nice I looked and what salon did I go to and who did my nails. Although I appreciated the compliments, I was nervous and uncomfortable discussing my makeup and hair color with Mr. Blue-Eyes right there. I know it's silly, but I wanted him to think that I roll out of bed every morning looking like this. Fortunately, the server came by to take drink orders. I ordered a glass of white wine, attempted to relax, and hoped that they would tire of the subject of my hair. The server brought out our drinks—white wine for me, a Prickly Pear Margarita for Shyla, Cabernet for Monique, and an Old Fashioned for Mr. Blue-Eyes. By listening to the chatter, rather than contributing, I gleaned that his name was Matthew West, he was an application developer, and that the three of them volunteered together at a local foster children's assistance agency.

We all decided that it would be fun to order appetizers and a bottle of wine to share, rather than ordering dinner. When the food was served, our table was overflowing with abundance. Toasted brussel sprouts, escargot, garlic herb chicken wings, basil polenta, barbequed shrimp, grilled octopus, and a char-cuterie platter featuring various meats, cheeses, and olives. It was so much fun chatting and sampling the different dishes that I forgot to be self-conscious around Matthew. "What's your favorite so far?" I asked him. "I think I like the chicken wings best," he smiled.

"Have you tried the grilled octopus?" I asked.

"I don't know about that," he shook his head squeamishly.

"It's the best. I promise!" I declared enthusiastically. "But you have to try it with wine.

He hesitated for a moment, then smiled, "Okay, if you promise." I poured him a glass of wine and passed him a piece of grilled octopus. He slowly stabbed it with his fork, then reluctantly put it in his mouth.

"Now have a sip of wine. You have to put them together," I encouraged. "Isn't that great?" I smiled.

Surprisingly, he smiled back. "That is actually . . . really good," he said in disbelief, setting down his wine glass with a smile. As he smiled, he got little crinkles around his eyes. Crow's feet, they call them. But on him, they were little crinkles. I laughed at his tone, thinking how impossibly cute he was—a grown man in his forties, yet so adorable. His hair was shiny, honey-brown, kind of shaggy, and sun-streaked. He seemed to me to be the kind of person who would forget to have his hair cut, only to be reminded by someone at work.

But in my opinion, his hair matched him perfectly. He didn't try too hard. He just seemed to be himself and being in his company was easy. He was tanned but the skin on his nose and cheeks was tight and pink. The fresh sunburn, along with the blue shirt he wore, really set off his eyes making them appear even more brilliantly blue than when I had first seen him.

"We're taking our group paddle-boarding tomorrow," he said turning to me, "If you don't have plans tomorrow, why don't you come along? We can always use extra help. Teenagers can be a handful."

I was stumped by the question for many reasons. First of all, I was elated that Matthew was inviting me anywhere. However, we had just met and now he would see me in a swimsuit right away. I worried that this might be a deal-breaker due to the recent fifteen pounds or so that I had gained. Yet, I knew myself to be highly qualified for this activity in every other way. "I am an excellent swimmer. I have great balance and can absolutely handle a paddle-board. I am adventurous, and great with kids," I silently reasoned, trying to convince myself.

Therein lay my dilemma. Should I let the fact that I think I'm fat keep me from going paddle-boarding with this great guy? When I put the question to myself that way, it seemed simpler. "Because I think that I am fat, I am willing to lose out on life. Yes, I had gotten comfortable in a twenty-year marriage, and now the thought of someone new seeing my body sends me into a panic. Yes, I have flaws. I'm a little chunky. I have cellulite on my thighs and the thought of being judged on my physical appearance is terrifying to me. But what I am basically saying that this would be a great activity and it would be fun. I can be of service, have friends, and engage in a worthwhile organization . . . but I won't do it because I might look fat. That is so ridiculous. Don't be so shallow, Diana," I chastised.

"What would the Goddess Tribe ladies say?" I wondered again, posing a question to which I already knew the answer. "Put your ego aside and just be happy!" I imagined Lil saying. "I am going to have a life here and I will power through, fat or not." All this conflict going on in my mind finally resolved itself and I smiled back at him.

"Thank you for the invitation, Matthew. I would love to," I answered.

"Great, I'll come by and pick you up at 9:00 a.m. What's your address?" he asked. And that was that.

Chapter Five

Sunday morning, I woke up early to the sound of a rooster crowing. It was dawn and the sky was just beginning to lighten to a medium bluish-gray. I went to the kitchen and took my coffee cup outside onto the porch where I sat down on the cool cement of the top step. A slight breeze was blowing and I worried a little that it might rain and cause my plans to be cancelled. A few cold drops landed on the porch, making little dark spots here and there. I remembered being a child and how I loved to play in the rain. The pure joy I always felt at the onslaught of raindrops. Singing "Raindrops Keep Fallin' on My Head," running and giggling as little girls do. Collecting rain-soaked Cedar Apple Rust in tin cans intended for experiments. Coming in the house soaked to the bone and not caring. Hopping into a warm tub that Ma had filled for me and luxuriating in the bubbles. Chattering with excitement as Ma wrapped me in a warm towel. Not giving a thought to how lucky I was or how much I was loved.

Today, I would go chaperone teenagers who had been taken from their homes—kids who, for whatever reason, could not live with their families. In many cases, the teenagers could not be placed in foster homes either because of their age. According to Matthew, it's difficult to place teenagers in foster homes and practically impossible for them to be adopted into families. I tried but could not imagine the fear that a child must feel in being taken from their home, from the only parents they know, only to be placed with strangers. I was stirred from my daydreaming by a sudden cloudburst. The infrequent droplets had instantly become a summer downpour. I sat on the porch with my coffee cup for just a little while longer, watching the rain.

Fortunately, it was just a summer shower and was over in less than ten minutes, leaving behind a clear blue sky and a gentle breeze. I rose and walked into the farmhouse to get ready for my paddleboarding adventure. I dug around in my swimsuit drawer for something not too revealing. I figured that since we were chaperoning teens, it would be best to cover up somewhat. I opted for a white palm-leaf tankini top with a heart-shaped neckline and black spandex skort. The effect was flattering without being too revealing. This was also a good excuse to not wear a bikini on my first planned outing with Matthew. Next, I twisted my hair up and pinned it with a black clip, pulling a few newly highlighted strands to frame my face. I slipped my feet into a pair of matching palm leaf flip-flops and grabbed my beach bag. Just then, I heard a car up the drive. "Perfect timing," I thought. Feeling butterflies in my stomach once again, I walked out onto the porch.

Matthew was driving an old Jeep Wagoneer, atop of which he had secured brightly colored paddleboards. The car rambled up the gravel drive, teetering from side to side as it lazily splashed in the fresh puddles. I smiled and waved as I walked down the steps toward the car, noticing that he had two passengers in the backseat. As I approached, I could see that they were teenage boys. "Good," I thought. I was a bit relieved that we would not be alone. Having the kids there would be a nice buffer and would remove the pressure of keeping the conversation going with just the two of us. They would also very likely talk, play music, and be generally loud. This would help just in case my stomach decided to start making noises during the drive. It seemed to me that my stomach only made odd noises when I was alone with another person, usually a stranger, in an elevator, doctor's office, job interview, and now a date. "This is not really a date," I thought, "It's a work thing. Shyla and Monique are meeting us there, so it's definitely not a date. It's really silly to jump to that conclusion after one dinner with a group of friends."

As my mind was going on and on in all sorts of directions, the car slowly came to a stop, resting just in front of the house. Matthew then got out, walked around, and, smiling his adorable smile, opened the door for me. "My lady, your coach awaits," he said bowing slightly. "Oh, thank you, sir," I chimed, climbing inside. His car smelled nice, like his cologne mixed with coffee and biscuits. "Diana," he said, gesturing to the two boys in the backseat, "this is Noah, and this is Bryan," pointing to each as he spoke. "Hi, guys," I waved, "nice to meet you both." The boys both nodded at me casually, giving me a disinterested "Hey" before receding into their phones. "Quiet after all," I thought.

"I brought breakfast," Matthew said, handing me a small paper bag, "I hope you like coffee and biscuits."

"Matthew, you're mind-reader," I said. "I love coffee and biscuits," I smiled as we rambled down the gravel drive. I looked out at the farm and took a big bite of my biscuit. A few crumbs fell onto my black skort and I looked down at them, flicking them away with targeted precision. When I looked up, Matthew had stopped the car at the end of the driveway and was smiling at me. "What?" I asked, raising my eyebrows.

"Nothing," he smiled, as he turned the wheel to merge onto the road. "How about some music?" he offered, gesturing toward the center compartment. "Pick whatever you like."

I dropped my biscuit into the bag and began flipping through his CD collection. I picked The Eagles, Greatest Hits. It just seemed to fit the mood of the morning. Matthew took a sideways glance at me and smiled again. I absentmindedly began to sing along to "Peaceful Easy Feeling" and we didn't need to talk much after all.

We arrived at Hunter Springs with a plan to paddleboard around Kings Bay, to Three Sisters Springs. Although manatees were sometimes known to be evasive, Matthew mentioned that we might see a few today. Our group was already at the rental shop when we arrived. Shyla and Monique had driven the van, across which read "Teen Harbor" in big blue letters. They had brought a group of ten kids, both girls and boys, ages twelve to seventeen. The company where we all worked, Web Synergy, sponsored Teen Harbor and gave time off to its employees for volunteer hours. I learned that Matthew had been with the organization for five years and was a mentor to Bryan and Noah. Thus, he was allowed by the center to drive them separately if they wanted to go with him. Of course, they jumped at the chance to shun the group home's van and what I imagined to be oppressive rules. Briefly, they could trade in that reality for one in which Matthew was their dad taking them paddleboarding, and all was well with the world.

Upon arrival, Matthew quickly took charge appointing Noah and Bryan to divide the group into teams, help with life jackets, and go over safety. The kids joined their teams—Team Manatee and Team Stingray, with Noah and Bryan as Team Leaders. Shyla and Monique would head the expedition. Team Manatee would follow behind them, followed by Team Stingray, and finally, by Matthew and me. That way the teens were flanked on all sides by either an adult or a Team Leader.

I imagined that ensuring a safe environment for the kids was paramount to the center and our group was not taking any chances.

After several minutes of both teens and adults falling off the boards at random intervals, we pretty much had our sea legs and were on our way. This part of Florida is called Crystal River for a good reason. The water in the rivers and springs is like blue glass. As we paddled lazily, we could clearly see the bottom. Tiny fish darted back and forth as aquatic plants swayed silently. The intense blue color of the water was magical.

"Hey, you're pretty good at this," Matthew smiled. "Is this your first time?"

"It sure is," I beamed. "I guess you do this all the time?" I asked.

"I take the boys out a lot," Matthew answered, paddling closer to me. "When I started volunteering for Teen Harbor, Noah and Bryan were twelve years old. They had both been in and out of foster care their whole lives," he said furrowing his brow. "They didn't know how to swim, ride a bike, skateboard, play football, much less cook or clean. They had no life skills. They didn't do their homework, fold their laundry, or even brush their teeth regularly. They didn't have a constant parent figure to teach them those things, or to ask more of them. So, they just didn't do them. I try to teach them what I can, and to help them to just be . . . regular kids, I guess," he said, looking down at the water.

"Wow, that's really kind and caring of you to do so much for them—to make such a huge commitment," I said, nodding at him. I was really wondering why a single guy would want to give up so much time, energy, and money to help troubled teens. I couldn't find words to ask the question without sounding shallow or accusatory.

"I was having a rough time back then myself. I was going through a really painful divorce," he continued, answering my unspoken question for me. "Teen Harbor was an organization that I could throw myself into. And they really needed help. The volunteer background check is exhaustive. Most people won't go to all the trouble just to be approved to mentor teens. I needed to stay busy to get out of my head. It seems like I am helping Noah and Bryan. But the truth is they have helped me so much more."

I had not expected Matthew to open up to me even though I had been wondering. I guess he sensed that. He had answered my question and in so doing, had revealed that we have our pain in common. "I know what you mean," I said. And then we were quiet for a while. Rather than talk, we fixed our attention on the kids ahead of us. They were laughing, showing off, and acting silly. Just like teenagers do—stuck in that place, almost adults, but still mostly children. They just don't know it.

"So, how about you, Diana?" Matthew finally said. "What brought you here?"

"To Crystal River?" I asked. "I wanted to paddleboard today," I laughed, knowing that was not what he meant.

"No, I mean, why did you move here?" he asked again.

"Ah, yes," I began, pretending to scratch my head and think. "Well," I said, "I got divorced and I thought I could make a fresh start here." Now I was the one staring blankly at the water. "I thought my kids would love it here with the rivers, the ocean, the weather. They don't." I said, wiping my brow. "They're teenagers too—sixteen and nineteen, the oldest is in college. I was very naïve. I thought they would just want to pick up and move to a new place with me. I hadn't considered that they felt safe in their home. They have never lived anywhere else. In the end, they chose their lifelong home over me." I frowned. "I guess that place just never really felt like home to me, so I didn't consider . . . well. I just didn't consider their feelings. I was pretty foolish."

He looked at me quizzically, "You don't look old enough to have kids that age. What are you, about thirty, thirty-two?" he asked in disbelief.

Caught off-guard by the comment, I smiled just a little at his mistake, but didn't correct him. Then returning to our conversation. "Well, anyway, I sometimes feel like I've made a mess of things in coming here."

"What about your husband?" he asked. "You said you got divorced. What happened there?"

I was a little surprised at the forwardness of the question, but we seemed to have entered a place where we were both opening up. Matthew's blue eyes were so bright next to the blue water. "Well," I paused and took a breath, "I didn't feel free to . . . ," I trailed off. "I didn't really feel free to do much of anything other than be a mother and a homemaker," I said. "I have ideas. I have dreams—things I want to do. Whenever I brought them up to my husband, he shot them down. I still remember the feeling I would get in my stomach when he did that. I was excited about something and he would give me a million reasons why I couldn't do it," I recounted. "I felt like my wings were clipped. I wanted to try a new career, maybe even start my own business, make my own decisions. I wanted to travel and I wanted adventure. I wanted him to want that, too, but he didn't. He felt like he needed to protect me from everything. He wanted to play it safe all the time. I guess freedom to explore my ideas was more important to me than . . . my family," I said, shaking my head. "Again, I was foolish and naïve."

"That doesn't sound foolish or naïve, Diana," he said. "Your kids can visit you any time, right? I mean, you've got an awesome place here! That farm! Look, you've got chickens! And that big old boat! And, come on, one of your kids is technically an adult, right?" He chortled. "Your adventurous spirit sets a good example for them. I think you're being way too hard on yourself."

I smiled back at him, "Maybe I am looking at this the wrong way."

Maybe?"

Just then I heard someone up ahead yell "Manatee!" Suddenly the group was all abuzz with the excitement of seeing the gentle giant. As Matthew and I approached, we saw a mother manatee with her baby swimming effortlessly along-side us in the crystal blue water.

"You think your son would like to come paddleboarding with us?" Matthew asked.

"I think he would love this," I smiled wistfully.

We had a glorious morning on the water, then headed back to turn in the rented boards and get the kids back to the center. As Matthew was checking in boards and wrangling life jackets, I stood by the car. I saw him walk over to Noah, take out his wallet, and give him several bills. He then said something to him, pointed at Bryan, slapped him on the back and turned to walk toward me. "What was that about?" I asked.

"I asked him to ride back in the van and order pizza for the group," he said, nervously running his fingers through his hair.

"Oh," I said, feeling the distinct fluttering of butterflies again. "You're not going back to the center?"

"My guys are okay, they're growing up. Noah is planning on going to college next year. Bryan wants to join the army after high school. They don't need me as much anymore. They need money and unsolicited advice about girls. But they don't need me hanging around all day today. They're fine. I'll just text them later," he said, opening the car door for me.

"Anyway, I wanted to ask you something without the boys around," he said tentatively. I immediately felt queasy and I could feel my face, ears, and neck turning scarlet red. "Is he going to ask me out on a date date?" I wondered feverishly. "I don't think I'm ready to go out on a date date. It's too soon. What if I screw this up?" Beep Beep, Panic Mode!

"Diana," he continued, "I noticed the old boat on your property and I was wondering . . . ."

"Yes?" I prompted, not really knowing where this was going.

"Feel free to say no if I'm overstepping here," he went on.

"Okay?" I questioned.

"I was wondering if we could make restoring it a project for Teen Harbor."

"Oh," I said, now a little bit disappointed. "Of course, you can. Sure. I'm guessing that you know a lot about boats and would be supervising this project?"

"Yeah, I could bring the group out to work on it on Saturdays when we don't have other activities planned. This would be a great project for them and you will get a shiny new boat out of the deal!" he said, smiling brightly. Suddenly, he looked very cute and childlike.

"Okay," I said "Just as long you're in charge. I don't really know a whole lot about boats. I know how to ride in a boat, drink champagne on a boat, and jump off of a boat if needed. But that's about the extent of my boating knowledge," I confessed.

"But you said you were an adventurer and that you wanted to try new things," Matthew teased.

"Yes, I guess I did say that, didn't I?" I laughed.

"Great, so we can plan on Saturdays?" he asked.

"Well, I have a meet . . . I have a thing the first Saturday of the month," I said, not really wanting to explain the Goddess Tribe to Matthew just yet, if ever. "But you can work on it if I'm not home. I'll leave the gate unlocked for you."

"Sounds great!" He beamed as we were turning onto my gravel driveway. He pulled up close to the house again and he got out to open my door. I climbed out and dusted off my skort. "Thanks for today, Matthew. It was really a lot of fun. I think I needed that," I said, nodding.

"Any time," he said, shifting his weight back and forth. "Hey, before I forget, can I get your number? So I can call you about the boat?" he asked, again running his fingers through his hair.

"Sure, of course," I said, taking his phone and punching my number in as a contact. I entered "Diana Davis—Boat" and handed it back to him. "Thanks again. See you Monday." Then I turned and smiled all the way up the porch steps and floated into my farmhouse on butterfly wings.

Chapter Six

The rest of the day was peaceful and uneventful. I spent most of my time thinking about Matthew and reliving our day together. Sunday night, however, I did make sure to touch up my nails. The color was a little bit chipped from paddleboarding. When Monday morning rolled around, I took more care than usual in getting ready for work. I styled my freshly colored hair just as the stylist had shown me. I applied my makeup and spritzed perfume. Suddenly it was important to me to look my absolute best for work. Then I looked in my closet for something to wear.

"I want to look nice without trying too hard to look nice," I thought. "I should definitely wear jeans, so that I look casual," I thought, skimming my closet. I decided on a light blue peasant blouse with eyelet lace and a pair of slightly faded jeans. Checking the mirror, I wondered if Matthew would grab the door for me like he had the first time I saw him. Arriving at work, I looked around and saw that the familiar Wagoneer was already parked in the parking lot. My spirits felt dashed, knowing that I probably would not see Matthew at all today, since we worked in different departments. Crestfallen, I headed toward the door. As I reached out to open it, a big hand caught it before I had the chance. I looked up smiling, prepared to say hi to Matthew. But instead I was looking at my boss, Jacob, smiling back at me. "Oh, good morning," I said, startled. "I wasn't expecting you."

"Who were you expecting?" he chuckled.

"Um, I didn't mean that. You just surprised me, that's all." I replied.

"You look nice today," he said, and continued casually into the building.

"That's sweet," I thought. Although I would have preferred to hear that phrase uttered by Matthew. Still, it was nice to know that my efforts were appreciated in some way.

My workday became busy early on, which was a blessing. I had less free time to think about Matthew. Before I knew it, it was 1:00 p.m. and Monique was standing at my desk asking me if I wanted to go to lunch. "What? It's lunch time already?" I asked in disbelief.

"Yes, and I'm starving. Let's get out of here for a while. I'm sure you could use a break too," Monique replied wearily. It seemed that her morning had been just as busy as mine.

We headed over to the Salad Stop, where, I was informed, we would be meeting Shyla and Paul. They had gone a few minutes earlier in order to grab a table. The Salad Stop was a madhouse at lunch time. We entered and both got in line with the herd of salad eaters and patiently waited our turn to receive the ground breaking invention of salad that was chopped up in a bowl.

"How's your day?" Paul asked as we came to the table to sit down.

"Busy," both Monique and I said in unison.

"Mine too! Crazy day already," Paul replied.

Our conversation continued on work related issues for a while until Paul asked about the weekend. "We took the Teen Harbor kids paddleboarding," Shyla responded. "Where were you and Marco?"

"Oh, we had a busy day at the shop. There was no way I could go. Marco needed my help. Everyone wanted flowers! Who all went? What did we miss?" he enquired.

"Me, Monique, Matthew . . . ," Shyla said, pausing. "And Diana came too. I think she and Matthew really hit it off." she said teasingly. "Where did you guys go, anyway? You left us will all the kids and pizza money! We had to do the movie without you!" she accused.

I could tell that she was teasing, but she also sounded a little bit annoyed. Feeling somewhat exposed, the heat began to rise in my face and I could feel that I was turning bright red, ears and all.

"You're blushing! Diana!" Paul teased. At that point, all three of them joined in poking at me about Matthew. I suddenly felt like I was in middle school.

"Nothing!" I protested. "He just drove me home! That's all!"

"Oh, we're just teasing," assured Monique. "It's nice that Matthew is . . . ," she trailed off. "It's good for him to, well, be interested in you. I heard that he had a really nasty divorce a few years ago and he hasn't dated since. Not that I have seen, anyway. I don't know all of the details," she said, leaning forward "but he was hurt very badly by his ex-wife." She took a sip of her soda thoughtfully. "He just goes to work and volunteers at the center. He does everything for those kids. Noah and Bryan basically treat him like a dad. He even offered to pay for college, if they go," she marveled. "He needs to do something for himself for a change," she said, shaking her head. "It's a good thing. I think you two look cute together."

"No. Wait," I protested. "There is no 'thing' between us. He just drove me home," I said.

"Sure, Diana, keep telling yourself that. Meanwhile, your whole face is as red as your new lipstick," she said, patting my hand.

"No really! I think he's really good-looking and super nice. But he doesn't seem that interested in me. He only drove me home so that he could ask me about bringing the teens to work on my dad's old boat . . . as a project," I insisted.

"So," Shyla began, "how often is Matthew going to bring the teens to your house?"

"They're coming on Saturdays," I replied innocently, "random Saturdays," I stammered. "Well, on the days that they don't have planned activities."

"So," Shyla began, now sounding like the attorney for the prosecution. "He had to get you alone to ask you if he can come over on weekends—and you think he's not interested?" she asked, becoming more intense by the second. "Diana, really, you are way out of practice, girl."

"Maybe I am," I smiled slyly. "I guess I need more practice."

At this, they all laughed loudly, causing the other salad-eaters to look our way curiously.

Just then, my phone began to vibrate. My heart leapt when I saw that the text was from Matthew.

Hi, I had a great time Saturday. Was going to ask you to lunch today, but I can't get away. Too busy. I'll bring lunch this weekend. Your pick :-).

I quickly texted back.

Sounds great :-)

I dropped my phone into my purse. I had endured enough of the third degree. This 'thing' they referred to with Matthew somehow felt very special to me and I wanted it all for myself. I was even the slightest bit jealous that Monique knew so much more about him than I did. I silently smiled as I imagined laughing with him, holding his hand, brushing a stray hair from his face. My daydream consisted of those little familiarities that couples who are very close share. This, I knew, was silliness. But it was fun to imagine anyway.

That evening when I arrived home, I dropped my purse and keys on the table, slid out of my shoes, and put the tea kettle on the stove. When the pot whistled, I poured my tea and took it to bed. I took out my phone and texted Ian and Ava.

How was your day? Miss you both.

No response.

Then I scrolled to Matthew's message and, smiling, read it again. "My pick for lunch," I considered. I had forgotten to return his text earlier because Shyla was being so nosy.

I think I would like chicken salad on rye, iced tea, and Kettle Chips. I texted back, setting my phone on the night stand. My stomach leapt, when it vibrated almost immediately.

My favorite :-), he responded. I smiled, remembering his cute smile and blue eyes.

Next, I took out Ma's jewelry box and opened it to reveal its sparkling treasure. I tried on each ring, one at a time, feeling comforted and close to my grandmother. As I reached for the smoky topaz, I recalled that she used to call it her "root beer ring" because of its smoky brown color. That magical and tasty image had enchanted me as a child, thinking that she had a ring made of actual root beer. I was now enchanted by its beauty, its story, and its connection to Ma. I quietly thanked her for entrusting it to me.

I was startled again by the buzzing noise of my phone.

Good, how 'bout you? Miss you too! was the text from Ava. I instantly felt a tinge of guilt, wishing for a split second that it had been Matthew.

Busy at work, but doing well! I have some friends and I'm volunteering. Can't wait to see you! I texted.

I'm glad you're better, Mom. Love you! See you soon.

I was not surprised that I never got a response from Ian. He was, understandably, still angry with me. Being a teenager is tough. Going through your parents' divorce is no picnic either. I hoped that during his visit, he would meet some of the kids from Teen Harbor and maybe gain a fresh perspective.

Chapter Seven

My week flew by because work was so busy. Before I knew it, it was Saturday morning and I was popping out of my skin with excitement. The night before, my mind had been alive with ideas of how the day would go. I imagined Matthew driving up in his Jeep—his hair blowing in the wind, his bright smile, his blue eyes. I got out of bed early and eagerly put the coffee pot on the stove. Since it was the weekend, I preferred to use the old stovetop percolator that had belonged to my aunt. It took longer to make, but the result was heavenly. With the first delicious sip, I could feel it waking me up with the high-octane potency that only comes from a percolator. I looked forward to that first cup every Saturday morning.

I carefully dressed, did my hair, and put on makeup. I wanted to look my best for Matthew, but in an understated way. I chose a cotton sundress with a sunflower pattern. I wore my hair in loose waves and applied minimal makeup. I remembered something I had read years ago as a teenager. 'Good makeup should look like you aren't wearing any.' Although I love makeup and I love to experiment with colors, today, I took that advice and opted for a natural look.

I had spent the night before preparing for my guests. I had plenty of water bottles and healthy snacks. I bought extra sunscreen and mosquito repellent, just in case the kids needed it. When the coffee began to bubble up in the glass top, I took it off the burner. I poured it into my favorite mug and stirred in a little half-and-half. Then I stepped onto the cool cement of the porch, bare-footed as had become my Saturday ritual. I sat on the top step luxuriating in the coolness and the beauty of the morning, inhaling the steam from my mug.

Then in the distance, I smiled as I spotted the white Teen Harbor van carefully meandering up the bumpy driveway. It eventually came to rest under the big live oak near the boat. Doors eagerly swung open on all sides and teenagers began to tumble out, immediately straying here and there. Some admiring the boat, others making a bee line for the hen house, all chattering in unison. Girls cartwheeled and boys play-punched each other in the arms. They all seemed very young and I had forgotten how energetic groups of teenagers could be. Matthew quickly took charge and called all of the kids to gather round him. As a group, they walked toward me, stopping at the bottom step.

"Everyone, listen up," he said, projecting his voice for all to hear. "This is Miss Diana, and she is kind enough to let us come to her farm. So be sure to introduce yourselves, to thank her, and to be respectful of her property."

"Yes, Sir," they all recited casually. I could tell that Matthew was more of a friend than an authority figure to them, but I could also see how the kids held a great deal of respect for him and cared about his opinion of them. That is the best kind of leader—not the kind that leads by fear, but the kind that leads by agreement and respect. Otherwise, kids will just do whatever they want when the adult is not looking.

I walked down the steps to greetings from many of the kids. There were twelve in total, six girls and six boys. They all seemed excited to be on the farm and most were fascinated with the chickens.

"Noah and Bryan, you two can lead the group in unpacking the van. We've got coolers with drinks and snacks," Matthew directed.

"I bought extra water bottles too," I said to Matthew. "And I have healthy snacks inside, just in case you need them." He smiled his perfect blue-eyed smile at me and I promptly remembered. "Oh, and I have the best coffee in the world, if you would like a cup."

"The best coffee in the world is right here?" he asked, "Well, then this is my lucky day," he teased.

"I'll get it for you, so you can keep an eye on the kids. How do you like it?" I asked.

"You wouldn't happen to have half-and-half, would you?" he asked.

"Organic," I smiled, "only the best for the best coffee in the world. Do you take sugar?"

"No, thanks, just half-and-half is great." He smiled.

When I returned with the coffee, Matthew and the group were already clustered around the big old Wellcraft. It made my heart happy to know that it would be getting much needed attention after all this time. As I approached, Matthew was addressing the group on the subject of trouble spots—bare wood and peeling paint.

Not wanting to interrupt him, I simply approached and placed the cup in his hand. He accepted it smiling and offered an air toast to me as I nodded and walked away. I returned to my perch on the cool porch to finish my coffee while watching the group. Knowing that these kids had more than their share of heartache at the hands of adults, I thought it best to keep my distance until they felt comfortable with me. I noticed that they were surprisingly focused and did the work carefully as they were shown. I thought about the inner strength that each one of these children possessed in order to just get through each day. I thought about the girls growing up without a mother and was struck with how lost they must feel in this world. I suddenly felt lucky and blessed to have found my Goddess Tribe and I began to understand that these gifts that I was receiving were meant to be shared. At that moment, I began to consider applying to Teen Harbor to become a mentor for girls. I remembered Matthew saying that the background check was exhaustive and that most people did not want to put in the time required.

"Well," I thought, "if I start the process now, at least it's moving forward. The time will pass regardless of what I am spending it on."

With my coffee cup empty and my mind evaluating its decision, I went inside the house and grabbed my egg basket. As I passed the group, a young girl of about twelve years old abandoned her paint scraping duties and ran up to me.

"Hey, what are you doing?" she asked curiously, skipping beside me. I instantly understood that she was a high energy kid and was probably bored and desperate for anything else to do.

"I'm going to gather eggs," I answered. "Would you like to come along?" I asked. "I'm sorry, tell me your name again?" noting that she had not introduced herself earlier.

"Samantha," she replied quickly.

I looked over at Matthew to see if he knew that she had decided to split, and sure enough, he was looking at me too. I pointed to my egg basket and shrugged my shoulders. He, in turn, nodded and waved, silently stating, "Yes, that's fine."

"Okay, kiddo, have you ever gathered eggs before?" I asked her.

"No, but I like to eat eggs," she answered.

"The chickens usually lay their eggs in the hen house. But sometimes they hide them around the farm so that I won't take them," I instructed.

"I didn't know chickens were so smart," she pondered.

"It depends on the chicken," I laughed. "Kind of like people."

"So, first we'll get the eggs from the hen house, then we'll have to go on a hunt to find the rest. Luckily, I have learned most of their hiding places," I said conspiratorially. "Here Samantha," I said extending the basket, "you'll need this."

Samantha smiled and took the basket, stepping into the role of egg gatherer quite easily. She was small for her age, with long, blond hair and a sprinkling of freckles across her nose. Her large eyes were hazel, framed by thick, black eyelashes. She reminded me a bit of Ava. She wore a too big, blue t-shirt that read "Girl Power" and a pair of jeans that had seen better days. Her clothes were obviously handed down from one kid to the next until the center could not get any wear out of them anymore. I feared for a girl so pretty and small being so unprotected in this world.

As we entered the hen house, I pointed to the nests and instructed Samantha to gather the eggs carefully.

"Be careful not to crack them and if you see any poop in the nest, toss that straw out. We want our chickens to have clean nests, right?"

Samantha nodded as I spoke and gave me her full attention—a rare gift coming from a twelve-year-old.

While Samantha gathered the eggs, I grabbed the broom and swept the floor of the hen house. When all of the gathering was done, we returned to the house with a full basket of eggs.

"Can we cook some now?" Samantha asked expectantly.

"Did you miss breakfast?" I asked.

"No, but I don't like oatmeal, so I didn't eat," she responded.

"Oatmeal! I don't blame you! How do you like your eggs?" I asked.

"I don't know what it's called," she said thoughtfully. "My mom used to make them. They were fried, but not scrambled, and the middle was not runny. It was cooked in the middle," she replied, wrinkling her brow thoughtfully.

"My grandmother called that hard fried," I answered, "and that's my favorite too. Two hard fried eggs coming right up!" I said, turning toward the stove. Then I remembered what Matthew had said about the kids not having anyone to teach them basic life skills.

"And you, Miss Samantha, are going to be the chef," I said, handing her the egg turner.

"First of all, I use my grandmother's cast iron skillet. It makes the best eggs," I said. "And don't tell anybody, but I like to use butter flavor Crisco to oil the pan. I know it's not good for you, but we have to have some joy in life, don't we?" I laughed.

Samantha took note of my instructions, focusing intently on each detail—from cracking the egg to waiting for the perfect time to flip it.

"Ta-da! Perfect eggs!" I said as she slid them onto the plates.

As we sat at the table eating our eggs, Samantha's eyes suddenly became filled with tears.

"What's wrong, Samantha?" I asked.

She said nothing, and instead began to furiously wipe her tears with the back of her hands and then with her napkin.

"Nothing," she said. "I'm fine. I just need to go to the bathroom."

I pointed in the direction. "First door on your left," I called, as she hurried clumsily out of her chair.

"This is probably too much," I thought. "She misses her mother and the way she made eggs," I realized.

When Samantha returned, I remained in my seat, not wishing to invade her personal space.

I fought the urge to hug her, knowing that she would not be comfortable with that. I was, after all, just a stranger.

"Thank you for the eggs, Miss Diana," she said, refusing to look me in the eye, "but I have to go help with the boat now."

"Of course, dear," I replied. "Thank you for breakfast. You did a great job."

At that, she turned and ran out the front door and I watched her rejoin the group.

I busied myself with household chores for the remainder of the morning. Although it crossed my mind to go out to the boat, I decided to let them have their space—especially Samantha. Around noon, I headed outside to help them get ready for lunch. As I approached the boat, I noticed that they had made a great deal of progress in scraping away the peeling paint on the hull.

"Who's ready for lunch?" I asked.

Matthew turned to me, wiping his brow. By now it was hot outside and I could see that it was quitting time for the kids. He looked at me and smiled.

"Okay, lunch time!" He called to the group. The kids were all tired and slowly meandered toward the blankets and coolers that Noah and Bryan had unloaded from the van. In a surprisingly orderly fashion, they handed out sandwiches, chips, bottled water, and apples to eat under the big tree near the house. Matthew and I sat on the porch so that the kids could talk without grown-ups around and vice versa.

Smiling, he handed me a brown paper bag. "Your lunch order," he said "chicken salad on rye and kettle chips. Oh, one more thing!" he said. Then he turned and jogged down the porch steps to the cooler.

"And your iced tea," he said, handing me a red plastic cup filled with iced tea.

"Wow, that's service!" I laughed. "Thank you!" I said, smiling.

"So how did Samantha like gathering eggs?" Matthew asked.

"She did great and really seemed to enjoy it. She gathered a basketful of eggs from the hen house, found their secret hiding places, and she even cooked!" I said excitedly. "But then she got upset," I continued. "That's when she ran back to the boat."

"What happened?" he asked, concerned.

"I'm not sure," I said shaking my head. "She was fine, and then she started to cry while eating her eggs. She had mentioned earlier that her mother cooked eggs in that way. So, I think she had some memories of her mother that made her sad," I said.

"Oh," Matthew responded, slowly nodding in realization. "Poor kid, she's had a rough time."

"What happened?" I asked.

"Her mother—she was a young single mother," he began. "She was fifteen when Samantha was born and she didn't have any support. Her parents kicked her out when she got pregnant and the boyfriend—or whoever he was—was not in the picture. She never really had a chance. She got hooked on pain pills, then turned to prostitution to support her habit. She wound up overdosing on heroin in her apartment. Samantha was there at the time," he said sadly.

"Oh, that's terrible!" I said. "What about her grandparents? Can't they help her?" I asked.

"Unfortunately, they're unfit. They physically abused her mother. They both have a police record a mile long—child abuse, neglect, domestic violence, drug offenses," he continued, "So, no. Samantha is a ward of the state. Her grandparents are not legally allowed to come near her."

"Oh my God," I said, taking the full meaning of that statement to heart.

"Diana, the thing is that Samantha is not a unique case. Her story is all too common. In fact, Samantha is one of the lucky ones. She was not sexually abused or worse—trafficked," Matthew said, looking at me intently.

I gasped, physically revolted at the thought of someone harming her in that way. Then I looked out at the group of young people lounging contentedly under my tree. I now saw them with fresh eyes. These children had seen the worst that life has to offer, and yet, they were still resilient.

"They each deserve so much," I said. "They all deserve a happy and fulfilling life. Don't you think?"

"Absolutely!" he said, "That's why I do what I can."

"Matthew," I said, tentatively. "I've decided to apply to become a mentor for girls—at Teen Harbor."

"I think you should," he said matter-of-factly. "You're a good role model. You'd be really inspiring. They will assign you to one of the girls, to mentor her in—well everything—school, life skills, career choices, and just be a friend."

His belief in me made me smile. "I think we should plant a garden. This farm needs some great big sunflowers," I said, staring out at my vast yard. "What do you think?"

"I think the kids would get a kick out of it!" he said happily.

After lunch I took the group on a short tour of the farm and then we said our good-byes.

The teens piled into the van while Matthew and I stood talking.

"If you're serious about this, I'll email you the mentor application when I get home," Matthew said.

"Yeah, I'm serious," I said nodding. "I really want to do this."

"Well, as I said, I think you'll be great," he said, climbing into the driver's seat of the van.

"Thank you! See you Monday at work," I called.

"Oh," he said, scratching the back of his neck, "I'll be working in the Orlando office for a couple of weeks. They're short staffed on a big project."

"Well," I replied, trying to hide my disappointment, "when you get back, then."

I smiled and waved, then returned to my vantage point on the top step. As I sat back down on the cool cement and watched the white van drive away, I felt the tiniest twinge of abandonment. I tried to push it away, push it out of my mind. We had just enjoyed a wonderful Saturday morning together—although we *were* with a group of twelve teenagers. Still, I felt like our time had been awkwardly cut short. He didn't ask me to go out later, or even for tomorrow. He just left, informing me that he would be gone for "a couple of weeks."

"He was so nonchalantly non-specific," I thought, now getting annoyed. "Is he interested in me at all?"

I was very much aware that I was reading too much into this and again, I decided to just let it be. "If anything is there—a feeling, or a spark on his part—I need to just stand back and let it happen. There is no need to drive myself crazy trying to control the situation," I reasoned. "Anyway, I am the last person who needs to go rushing into a new relationship. Maybe he realizes that too."

A little later, I received an email alert from Matthew. As promised, he'd emailed me the mentor application packet which appeared to be about a mile long. The packet included pages and pages of personal questions, a list of references to fill in, and a background check form. Since I had already completed the background check for work, I could skip that part. After completing the packet, there would also be a series of interviews with the staff; and finally, a psych evaluation.

"Jeez," I thought. "I understand that it has to be thorough to keep the kids safe, but this is going to take months!"

I printed out the forms, sat down at the table, and began filling them out with a renewed respect for Matthew.

For the next two weeks, I immersed myself in either work or the mentor application. I stayed a half hour late at Web Synergy each day and gave more attention to little details. Jacob mentioned to me that he appreciated my effort in going the extra mile. Seeing an opportunity, I asked him if he would write a reference for me for the Mentor Program. He happily agreed and I had it on my desk before the end of the week. "One down, four more to go," I thought.

I also had Ava and Ian's visit to plan. They would be in town in a few weeks and it was important to me that I plan plenty of fun activities to keep us all busy. Ava was doing well in Savannah, but Ian was still having trouble adjusting and he held a lot of anger toward me for leaving him. My thought was that if I filled the time with activities, he would forget to be sullen and moody and just enjoy himself. I began to imagine all the possibilities for showing the kids a good time here in my new hometown.

"We can take a day to work in the garden with the Teen Harbor kids. They can meet Noah, Bryan, and Samantha—and, of course, all of the other kids," I thought. After learning their stories from Matthew, I had begun to realize that Ian really did not have it all that bad. Although I was permanently guilty in my own mind for all of the problems the divorce had caused, I knew on some level that this was not the end of the world. And that Ian was going to be just fine. "He, at least, has two parents who love and support him," I thought.

"Maybe we can take a little paddleboarding or kayaking tour—or both! Also, a walk through downtown Crystal River would be fun. And we can eat dinner at The Rusty Hook," suddenly remembering the first time I met Matthew. "I think the kids would really like that place," I thought.

Keeping busy made the next couple weeks fly by. Work was going well. My mentor application was almost complete, and I was looking forward to tomorrow's Goddess Tribe meeting. When I finally got home on Friday evening, I walked in the door, immediately kicked off my shoes, and made a bee line for my bedroom, tossing off my constrictive clothing, and settling into the plush magic of my robe. Next, I ritualistically put the tea kettle on, and retrieved my Goddess Tribe booklet from the coffee table. "Tomorrow is Wisdom and the color is yellow," I said aloud.

I took my teacup and the booklet into the bedroom and began to scan my closet for anything yellow. I had the yellow sunflower dress I had worn when Matthew came to the farm, but I didn't think it was dressy enough for the Goddesses. I continued to flip from hanger to hanger, knowing that I did not have anything else that was yellow. "I don't want to buy anything else until I lose this weight," I said to my closet. "Well, then," I said, "the decision is made. Yellow sundress it is."

That night, I had the same dream about Ma and the sunflowers.

Chapter Eight

I headed toward the church that morning with thoughts of Mammoth Sunflowers in my head. "I bet the Teen Harbor kids have never seen flowers that big," I thought excitedly, remembering how my own children used to stare in amazement at the size of our sunflowers. Living in Central Florida, I was pretty sure that as long as I got the seeds planted this month, they would grow just fine. I had only recently started planning our garden and held high hopes for it. Despite the heat, I did a little research and found that several vegetable varieties can do well with summer planting. As a result, I bought seeds for jalapeno peppers, bell peppers, okra, eggplants, and cherry tomatoes. I reasoned that we would learn while doing and expand to more exciting crops next year.

The air was still hot as I exited my car and clicked across the parking lot in my sandals toward the church. Fortunately, we had a pleasant breeze that day which blew through the oaks and swirled the Spanish moss. The sky was clear blue and a few wispy clouds floated lazily above. The only sounds were my shoes, the rustle of the breeze, and caws of birds. For the moment, it seemed that there was no one on Earth but me.

I entered the meeting room to the familiar burst of cool perfumed air and the tea-house decor. Remembering how reluctant I had been when Maymie dragged me in to my first meeting, I now felt excitement at each gathering and I loved seeing my Goddess Tribe friends dressed in the color of the month. Today was all yellow and sunshine as the ladies moved around the room, greeting each other and socializing until finally settling in their seats. As I approached the dessert table, I saw with surprise that someone had brought a basket of sunflower seed packets as take-home gifts. "What a great coincidence," I smiled, taking a packet of the Mammoth variety. Of course, the dessert for the meeting was Lemon Icebox Pie. There is just no denying the mood-enhancing power of yellow. That day, the room seemed to be the happiest place on Earth—even happier than usual, if that's possible.

I sat down in the only available seat next to a beautiful young woman with golden blond hair. She wore a wispy yellow chiffon knee-length dress and matching hat. The familiar scent of Chanel No. 5 hovered in the air around her. And somehow, she had even managed to find yellow patent leather Mary-Janes to complete her vintage look.

"Mind if I sit here?" I asked, already knowing the answer.

"Of course not. Please," she crooned in a heavy Southern drawl, gesturing toward the chair.

She had large blue eyes, creamy skin, and shiny golden hair, which poked out from under her hat, settling just under her chin. As I started to introduce myself, Maymie appeared at the podium, calling the meeting to order. Today, she was all fire and sunshine, in a bright yellow kaftan bedazzled with white sequins. The neckline and cuffs were ornately embroidered with gold and white thread, sequins, and pearls. Atop her head was an elaborately wrapped yellow turban from which dangled two enormous circular gold earrings.

"Welcome, ladies of the Goddess Tribe! You are all shining so brightly today! I can feel the love energy filling up this room and it fills my spirit. Yellow is a power color!" she proclaimed, extending her arms widely as the ladies clapped and cheered in agreement.

"Today we are going to talk about the Goddess Powers of Wisdom and Good Judgment," she announced. "But first, let us join hands in prayer."

I am Divine Wisdom, expressed in my thoughts, my words, and my actions.

I am Divine Judgment, carefully weighing the consequences of my behavior.

I am the Goddess Sophia, Keeper of the Old Knowledge.

Jealousy, foolishness, and strife do not enter my life.

I am Queen of Wisdom.

I willingly shine my light to others who come to me for prayer and advice.

I feel Divine Wisdom flowing through me like a river.

I lovingly pour my Wisdom onto the world.

And for this I am so grateful.

Amen.

She paused, gesturing toward the woman seated straight ahead of her. "Nancy will be presenting the Goddess Sophia."

Once again, everyone gave a welcoming round of applause as Nancy took the podium. She was regal in appearance, a tall, athletic-looking woman, with short blond hair and chiseled features. Rather than opting for the full yellow deal, as most of the ladies had, Nancy wore a white suit accessorized with a yellow scarf and yellow sandals. She wore gold tear-drop earrings and a thin gold bracelet.

"Okay, ladies," Nancy began, "Who in here could use a lesson on exercising good judgment?"

As expected, the group erupted into applause and buzzing in agreement.

"I'll take that as a yes," Nancy continued. "This is the Goddess Sophia, and her name is interpreted to mean knowledge, wisdom, and judgment."

Nancy was holding a poster of the Goddess, just as previous presenters had. The Goddess depicted was a beautiful woman with long, flowing red hair. She wore a red cloak and held in her hands, a golden chalice. Behind her flew the white bird of peace.

"Often in our lives, we find ourselves going through the motions without much thought to employing our collective wisdom or even using good judgment. If we feel it, then we just do it, without much thought or consideration to the consequences. I think the use of good judgment can be most colorfully illustrated in the areas of love and romance," she said, placing her poster on the easel. Has anyone . . . anyone here at all, ever exercised bad judgment in a romantic relationship?" Nancy asked jokingly.

Everyone in the room threw their hand in the air. As I looked around I began to consider my feelings for Matthew. We were just friends at this point, but I was fully aware that my feelings ran much deeper. I had just gotten out of a stifling twenty-year marriage and now I had developed a huge crush on the first man who had shown any interest in me. When I thought of it that way, I sounded needy and pathetic.

"Had I exercised good judgment when I married Jonathan?" I thought. The answer to that one was a resounding no. We had dated off and on in college and I honestly did not think we had much in common. When I found out during my junior year that I was pregnant, his parents pushed us to get married. They were relentless in nagging us. I had no interest in marrying Jonathan, and I told him so. Eventually, they resulted to bribery—paying our rent, our credit card bills, and my medical bills the duration of Jonathan's college term. I wound up dropping out of college, never to return. What Jonathan and his parents had offered me was safety and security. I felt totally alone in my situation. All my friends were preparing for graduation, careers, or grad school, and I was planning a baby shower. Being a clueless soon-to-be single mother at the age of twenty, I decided that marrying Jonathan was best for me and for our baby. Was any of this good judgment? No, it was not, but it was the best I could do at the time.

Reliving those painful memories, I had tuned out Nancy's presentation. When I finally snapped out of it, she was wrapping up with her closing statements.

"When we sit in meditation, we are able to tap into the Goddess within. The Divine Wisdom is already inside each one of us, but we must be quiet and listen in order to hear its voice," Nancy said, now looking right at me. "If you are not already practicing daily mediation, I invite you to try it this week. Each morning before your day gets hectic, take ten minutes to sit in the silence," Nancy said.

After her presentation, Nancy collected her poster and notes and Maymie took the podium once again.

"Thank you, Nancy, for that wonderful talk. Now, ladies, feel free to finish off that Lemon Icebox Pie and have some Goddess-ship time!"

Once again, the room was abuzz with a swarm of yellow. Looking at the group, I was reminded of honeybees circling something sweet.

"Nice to meet you, Diana. I'm Zelda. I've seen you at the meetings, but never had a chance to formally introduce myself," she said, daintily extending her hand to me.

"So nice to meet you too, Zelda. I love your outfit! You look perfect in it. It suits you," I said, smiling.

"Oh this, I've had it for years, but didn't have an occasion to wear it. Thank you," she said. I noticed that Zelda was very animated in her speech and mannerisms. She reminded me of Scarlet O'Hara or some caricature of a Southern Belle.

"Well, it's lovely," I said, nodding back at her.

"Oh good! Diana, you've met Zelda," Maymie said, walking toward us with Nancy beside her. "This is Nancy." Maymie chimed, placing her arm around Nancy's shoulders.

"Great presentation. I really enjoyed it," I said.

"You sure you didn't doze off just a little?" Nancy laughed.

"Oh no, I was thinking about using, or not using, judgment in my relationships. I was thinking about how I just let things happen to me rather than taking an active role in decision-making. That means weighing the pros and cons, and as you said, listening for my inner voice—sitting in the silence. I haven't done enough of that in my life. Thank you for the reminder," I said.

"The Goddess Sophia lives within you. She's speaking to you. Listen," Nancy replied, smiling.

I vowed to begin paying more attention to my own inner wisdom and good judgment. After realizing that I had not been playing an active role in my own destiny, I set the intention to listen to my inner voice and ask to receive the wisdom that I had gained from my many valuable experiences. I knew that the voice of wisdom was inside me, for I had used it as a mother in order to make the best decisions for my children. However, I had not used this voice very often for my own benefit. I decided to try meditation a few times a week, starting with five minutes per session. I searched the internet for meditation mantras and found one that I liked. Om Mani

Padme Hum, meaning Generosity, Ethics, Patience, Diligence, Renunciation, and Wisdom. I played the mantra while sitting quietly on my aunt's old floral couch, cross-legged. Although I did not have a spiritual epiphany, I found that my thoughts were clearer—less cluttered. And that it was easier to push negative thoughts, such as fear and guilt, out of my mind.

I knew that Matthew was back in town, but he had not reached out to me. Although my feelings were hurt by his lack of contact, I forced myself to put it into perspective. I was newly divorced and my kids would be visiting next week.

"What I need to do right now is focus on making myself valuable at work so that I can take care of myself financially. I also need to focus on being the best mother and role model I can be for my kids. When they visit me, I want to be fully present with them, not pining away for my crush like a high school girl," I reasoned.

"My relationship with Matthew is going to grow, one way or another, because we are both involved with Teen Harbor. He comes to my farm. We eat together. We flirt. What we have now is going to develop into something great because we are giving ourselves plenty of time to get to know one another as friends," I silently lectured to myself. Then, to my amusement, I recalled that I had given this exact advice to my own daughter over a year ago!

My week at work brought more responsibility and still more praise from Jacob. For the first time in my life, I was loving my job. I continued to focus on my own inner Wisdom and Good Judgment on every project that was assigned to me. As a result, I began to recognize those little gut feelings that I have as nudges from Divine Spirit, the Universe, or My Inner Goddess. I was not sure what to call it, but for me, those nudges were not to be ignored. They were my inner guidance system pulling me in the right direction—pulling me toward my destiny.

On Friday, I left work early in order to drive to Orlando to pick up Ava and Ian at the airport. I was excited and nervous about the visit because they had both been rather distant from me the past few months. Ava had busied herself in Savannah, taking summer school classes, while Ian made no excuses. He was angry with me and simply did not want to visit. I nervously drove around to the arrivals gate and my heart leapt as I saw Ian, tall and blond, standing next to Ava, his big sister, also blonde but about a foot shorter than him. I honked and waved at them and then slowly pulled up to the curb. Ian grabbed their bags and piled them into the back of the Volvo, while Ava hopped in the front seat.

"Hi, Mom!" Ava shouted, giving me a big hug. "Hi, Sweetie," I said, hugging her back. Ian then slid into the back seat. "Hi, Mom," he said less enthusiastically. "Can we go eat?"

I smiled silently, remembering that Ian was always hungry.

"Of course!" I said, "What are you in the mood for?"

"Can we get Mexican food?" he asked.

"Sure thing!" I replied, trying to think of a Mexican restaurant near home.

As Ava chattered on endlessly about college, life in Savannah, her friends, and her theater troop, I half listened and half panicked because I could not think of a single Mexican place that was on the way home. I wanted Ian to have a good time and desperately wanted him to be happy. Suddenly my entire day hinged on finding a Mexican restaurant between Orlando and Heritage Springs. Since I don't know Orlando very well, I wanted to find a place closer to home. On we drove while Ava chattered on.

"Ava," I finally interrupted, "Can you look up a Mexican restaurant in Crystal River or Heritage?" I asked.

"Sure, Mom!" she said and happily began researching restaurants on her phone.

"Hey, here's a good burger place," she said. "Burgers and Beers. It's top rated on Yelp."

"Ian, we can't find Mexican food," she called to the back seat. "Let's go to this burger place."

"Well, I don't really want a burger!" snapped Ian from the back seat. "Mom said we were having Mexican food!"

"Ian honey, we can't find a Mexican place near home. Let's just go there. What do you want?"

"Well, I wanted nachos, but they're not going to have them at a burger place, so forget it!" Ian yelled.

"Ava, can you please check and see if that place also has nachos?" I asked.

"Yes! They have nachos!" she snapped back at Ian. "So, there's no reason to be such a pain about it!"

"Okay, let's all just be cool," I said. "They have burgers, they have nachos, and they are close to home. Sounds perfect," I said, "Ava, can you put it in the GPS?"

I began to feel a familiar family dynamic kicking in—of me trying to please everyone, of Ian behaving like a spoiled brat, and of Ava behaving like a second mother to him. I had not ever allowed myself to look at my family this way. In my mind, we had always been the perfect little suburban family. But now, I could see clearly that we needed to shift our focus. Ian was a big boy at sixteen, but he was intentionally behaving badly and sucking up all the energy. I vowed to remain calm and not to coddle him. "He's got to learn to soothe himself instead of expecting me and Ava to baby him," I reminded myself.

We arrived at Burgers and Beers and were promptly seated in a burgundy colored booth. The air was thick with the smell of fried foods and grilled burgers. The place was packed with families, and chatter was quite loud. Ian slid in next to me and Ava sat on the other side facing us. A young woman in a white puff-sleeved top and a burgundy and white checkered skirt approached our table.

"Hi, I'm Suzy, and I'll be your server," chimed the young woman standing at the end of our booth. "Can I get your drinks?" she asked.

I really wanted to order a glass of wine, because my almost adult kids were starting to get on my nerves, but I realized that drinking alcohol would be a way of escaping and therefore, not being present. "Iced tea," I said flatly.

"Water," smiled Ava.

"Grape Soda," said Ian.

"Oh, I'm sorry," said Suzy seeming very concerned, "We don't have grape soda."

"Okay then, what do you have?" snapped Ian, slapping his menu down on the table.

"Iced tea, Coke," Suzy began, "Diet Coke, Sprite, Dr. Pep -"

"Eh, Eh!" Ian interrupted, holding his hand up. "I'll just take Dr. Pepper," Ian said loudly.

Suzy, seeming a bit dejected, turned and walked quickly to the kitchen.

I resisted rolling my eyes. "I hope he calms down after he eats," I thought. "Maybe he's just hungry."

The drinks arrived, and we finally placed our orders. A salad for me, a burger for Ava, and super nachos for Ian. Ava continued to talk happily about school and her theater group while Ian slumped next to me, engrossed in his phone. His eyes were glazed and his thumbs tapped furiously.

"Whatcha doing there?" I asked him.

"Video game," he replied, without looking up.

I smiled and raised my eyebrows at Ava across the table. I remembered the first Atari home video games when I was a child. Asteroids, Space Invaders, Breakout—pixelated black and white shapes on a nineteen-inch TV screen. Fortunately, they were not interesting enough to hold my attention past the age of ten or eleven. Ian seemed to have a serious video game addiction that I had hoped he would grow out of by this age.

"Food's here," chimed Ava as Suzy appeared at the end of the table holding a tray stand. Her fellow server helped her set the large tray on the stand and they began doling out the food.

"Super Nachos," she said to Ian, setting the largest plate of nachos I have ever seen in front of him.

"Good," I thought. "He'll eat, he'll have a full belly, and he'll be happy."

"So, Ian," I said, poking at my salad with my fork. "Are you excited about school this year?"

"Nah, I'm not going back," he answered matter-of-factly.

My eyes grew wide and my mouth fell open. I quickly tried to recover, knowing full well that he was going for shock value here.

"Oh?" I asked casually. "What, ah," I paused. "are you . . . ," I stammered. "What are your plans?" I finally asked.

"Oh, I don't know. I think I'll take the GED and then join the Army," he replied.

"What does your dad say?" I asked.

"He says it's a good idea," he replied. "He's tired of trying to make me go to class and do my homework and stuff. He said it's fine with him," he replied numbly.

"I see," I said, again raising my eyebrows at Ava from across the table.

"What is Jonathan thinking, telling him he can drop out of school?" I thought, feeling tightness in my stomach. "If he doesn't want to make him go to school, then he should make him move in with me," I thought, grinding my teeth. "But no! Ian can be a rude high-school dropout and a video-game addict, but heaven forbid he come and live with me!" I silently seethed.

Just then Suzy reappeared. "How is everything?" she asked. "Can I get you anything else?"

I looked at Ian, my potential high-school dropout, who was now shoveling in nachos with one hand while thumbing his video game with the other.

"House Chardonnay, please" I said, surprising myself with an uncharacteristically high-pitched voice, "make it a very generous pour."

When we arrived home, I went into my room to change, but instead sat down with my laptop and began a tirade to Jonathan in an e-mail.

Jonathan,

The kids arrived safely and all is well in that regard. However, over dinner Ian informed me that he is planning to DROP OUT OF SCHOOL, TAKE THE GED, AND JOIN THE ARMY! He also mentioned that YOU SAID THIS WAS FINE WITH YOU!!!!!!! WHAAAAAAT????

*On what planet is it okay that our son is a high school dropout???
Please tell me that he is mistaken and that you did not approve this
ridiculous idea.*

– Diana

The next morning, I got up early, as usual. I wanted to have
the house to myself for a couple of hours before Ava and
Ian woke up. As I walked into the kitchen, I was startled by
the sound of my phone vibrating. I picked it up to check the
incoming text message.

*Hey Diana, I know this is short notice, but is it okay if I bring
the kids out to the farm today? Our planned activity was cancelled last
minute. We can help you with the garden if you like,* read the text
from Matthew.

I smiled at the thought of them coming over to plant the
garden. I already had all of the seeds and I was eager to get
them in the ground. Also, I was relieved that I would have a
buffer between myself and Ian. "If other teenagers are here,"
I thought, "he might behave better."

I was also excited to finally see Matthew. I hadn't seen him
since he left to work at the Orlando office. We had both been
busy and I thought it best to just let things unfold with him,
rather than push.

*Hey stranger! Good to hear from you. Yes, you can come. My kids are
in town, so it should be fun for all :-),* I wrote, unsure if that was
actually true. I secretly hoped that Ian would not embarrass
me in front of Matthew.

I prepared my morning coffee and flipped on the radio.
Although my favorite station was '90s Alternative Radio,
there was a jazz show on Saturday mornings that I sometimes
liked to catch. I busied myself tidying up the kitchen to the
sounds of the radio and I suddenly felt as though I had traveled back in time to the 1930s. I had my old percolator on the
stove and jazz playing in my old farmhouse. I took my coffee

cup and snuck into Ian's room to check on him. He lay there sleeping peacefully. Although six feet tall, he still had a baby face when he slept. "My little sweetie," I said. Touching his hair, I remembered him as a little boy of three years old with golden curls and big brown eyes. I know it's cliché, but they do grow up so fast. They start out as your sweet little baby. They think that Mommy holds the moon and then they grow up to be big people with opinions and thoughts that differ from yours. They have goals and dreams that are not yours. They have the problems and baggage of their own generation, not yours. His hand went to mine and held it for about a minute or two before sleepily dropping away. Smiling, I crept out to my favorite spot on the porch. To my surprise, there sat Ava in the early morning light holding her coffee cup and gazing out at my favorite old live oak. The sun was just peaking over the horizon and dew was rising off the grass like fairy dust.

"Good morning, Miss Ava," I said, making a place beside her.

"Mama," she said and rested her head on my shoulder.

"We're having company today," I told her.

"Oh?" she asked, surprised. "I was hoping it would just be us."

"You'll like this kind of company," I said. "Remember how I told you I was volunteering?" I reminded her. She nodded as she listened. "Well the kids from the Teen Harbor group home are coming to help with the garden today," I said.

"What kind of group home?" she asked, concerned.

I told her all about the center and the stories of the kids who come to the farm with Matthew. And I told her about Samantha. She listened intently. "That's nice Mom. You're doing a good thing for those kids," she said.

"So," she said looking around, "where is the garden?"

"Nowhere yet," I laughed. "They're coming to help me start my garden. We'll put it behind the hen house. There's plenty of space back there. I thought we could make raised beds to help keep the bugs out," I said. "I've already bought seeds, extra dirt, and wooden beams, and well, this is a farm, so I think we should use it," I laughed.

We lingered for a while, leisurely sipping our coffee, then went inside to get ready for the day.

Around 9:00 a.m., I heard the familiar sound of the van tires on the gravel driveway, so I walked out onto the porch to greet my guests. The van came to a stop and the side door flew open. The kids hopped out excitedly and began to walk around freely and familiarly. I waved down at them and suddenly Samantha came bounding up the steps full of excitement.

"Hi, Miss Diana!" she said, "can we gather eggs today? Pleeeeease?" she asked, extending the word please for about five minutes.

"Hi, Samantha," I said, "it's good to see you. Sure, we can gather eggs after everyone is settled, okay?"

"Okay," she nodded.

Just then, Ava walked outside, her waist-length pale blond hair blowing in the wind. She was so fair—creamy skin, light hair, and bright blue eyes. My little starlet, I called her. But in reality, she was more of a farm girl than I would ever be. Ava loved animals of all kinds. She loved bird-watching, horse-back riding, and was fascinated with animal husbandry. As a pre-teen, she had requested book titles such as Pigeons for Pleasure and Profit: A Complete Guide to Raising Pigeons, The Horse Doctor is In, and Field Guide to Birds of North America. At age twelve, she had subscriptions to Chicken Fancy and Dog Fancy magazines, and was a member of the National Audubon Society as well as the Sierra Club. I, on the other hand, was intimidated by the amount of care that animals require, so I never had anything more complicated than a dog. Living on the farm, the chickens were handy for their egg-laying skills and after doing a little research, I found them to be pretty low-maintenance.

"Samantha," I said, putting my arm around Ava. "This is my daughter, Ava."

Ava smiled her big smile and extended her hand to the girl, "Hi Samantha, nice to meet you," she said.

"Oh," said Samantha shyly. She looked off to the side, rather than looking her in the eye and gave a half-hearted wave in Ava's direction. Then Samantha skipped back down the porch steps and joined the others. Once again, Ava and I were raising our eyebrows at each other in confusion. I guessed that Samantha was intimidated. She probably had not considered that I had a family.

When I turned to look for Samantha, I saw that Matthew was watching me with that same smile he had when I rode shotgun in his Jeep.

"Hi there!" I said, walking down the steps. "It's good to see you! I guess you've been busy, huh?" I said smiling, not wanting to give him the third degree.

"Yeah, it's good to see you too, Diana," he said smiling. He was tan, as usual, and today he wore a white t-shirt, faded khaki shorts, and his signature flip-flops.

"Did I forget how handsome he is?" I wondered.

"I ended up staying in Orlando longer than expected," he explained. "The job went over budget and extended past the timeline," he said, running his fingers through his hair. "I'm glad I'm not the Project Manager on that one! He's got some 'splaining to do," he laughed.

"Oh, wow," I said, "well, I'm glad you're back. I'm sure the kids missed you."

"Yeah, that's why I texted you on such short notice. No one at the center had planned anything, and I thought today was supposed to be a pool day. Anyway, our wires got crossed and the kids didn't have anything to do. Thanks for letting us come today—with your family in town and all. We really appreciate it," he said, running his fingers through his hair nervously.

"I'm glad you came. You're always welcome here," I said touching his arm. "I've got water bottles left over from last time, if you want to help me with them," I said, beckoning him inside. As he reached the porch, I put my arm around Ava. "Matthew, this is my daughter, Ava. She's visiting from Savannah, where she goes to college."

"Nice to meet you, Ava," he said, congenially extending his hand. "Savannah, huh? Great town. Best barbeque around!" he said smiling. "You go to SCAD?" he asked. Ava smiled and nodded. "Wow, good for you. That's the best art school you can find. They're doing some really cool stuff there, aren't they? Really transformed Savannah—buying up old buildings for the school."

"Oh yeah, it's amazing," Ava replied excitedly. "It's really challenging, but I love it there!"

"Well, it looks like we're planting a garden today, so I hope you and your mom have some pointers for us. Because, well, I don't know the first thing about gardening," he laughed. As he looked over at me, he shrugged his shoulders.

"I'm sure you'll do great," I said, inching inside the door. "The water bottles are just in here, in the kitchen. Matthew followed me inside to the kitchen and I suddenly felt butterflies in my stomach again. I hadn't bothered to flip on the light, so the room was dimly lit, with only the natural light

86

from the window. Being alone with him in my small kitchen made me nervous.

I opened the pantry door and bent down to pick up the case of water. It was heavier than I expected and when I turned around, I almost smacked him in the ribs with the large case of bottles.

"Oh, I'm so sorry!" I stammered, "did I hurt you?" I asked concerned. He didn't step backwards or seem startled. He just stood right there—unmoving.

"No, I'm fine," he said, grazing my forearms as he took the case from me. We were standing very close and I didn't know what to say. My heart was beating in my chest, yet I could scarcely breathe. I felt the electricity when he touched my arms. I could feel the energy in the air as I returned his gaze, looking into his blue eyes for what seemed like a long time.

"Mom, what are you doing in there?" I heard Ava call.

I suddenly remembered to breathe, inhaling deeply. His cologne was nice. It smelled like home. "Be right there," I called. Without a word, Matthew adjusted his grip on the case of bottles, and gave me a knowing smile. He turned, and I followed him outside.

We led the group to the spot behind the hen house where I had planned for the garden. As I looked out at the group, I saw that Ian had joined us and he was standing with Ava and Bryan, quietly chatting. I was relieved that he had joined in—and that he was being nice. I gave a short, yet obviously boring presentation on the benefits of constructing raised garden beds. The kids were starting to get antsy and to stray off into small groups here and there. I saw that this could easily unravel into chaos if we didn't do something quick.

I took a leap of faith and called out to the group, "After we get the garden planted, your reward is that we will go kayaking!"

Matthew looked at me with a surprised expression that said, "What the heck are you talking about?" All I could do was smile and shrug in response.

Luckily, the bribe worked for the moment, and the teens began to amble back to the garden area. After I explained the raised beds to Matthew, he showed the kids how to construct them. We made four raised beds, filled them with dirt and planted our seeds. Next, we added a simple chicken-wire fence around the perimeter to keep the deer out.

With so many hands, the work went quickly and it was quitting time before the temperature got too hot. We broke for lunch and Matthew and I sat down together on a picnic blanket to figure out how to make my hastily promised kayaking trip happen.

I knew from the Goddess Tribe that if I set the intention and had Faith, that it would come back to me. So, I held with the belief that the plan was already in motion and that it was going to work out.

"I've got two old kayaks in the garage," I said. "So, we won't have to rent so many." Matthew nodded, still thinking.

"We usually go through Heritage Springs Tours," Matthew said, "they give us a discount, but this is short notice," he said, scratching the back of neck. "Well, it doesn't hurt to ask, right?" he said smiling.

He made the call and I could hear the disappointment in his voice. "Nope, they're booked up today," he said.

"Okay, who else can we try?" I asked hopefully.

"I don't know. How about Rainbow Springs?" he replied thoughtfully.

I made the call to Rainbow Springs and explained our situation. "Thank you so much!" I said, hanging up. "Matthew, you're not going to believe this," I said happily. "Rainbow

Springs is donating free park admission and a kayak tour for all of us!"

The look on his face was complete surprise and without thinking, he put his arm around my shoulder and pulled me to him in a hug. "You're the best!" he said.

Although the hug was friendly and spontaneous, the connection with him felt electric. I felt tingles all over my body and I had to catch my breath. Something was different about Matthew today. I sensed a change in him. He seemed warmer—more relaxed, and more comfortable with me.

After lunch, Matthew made the announcement to the teens that we were going to Rainbow Springs. They would have to stop by the center for swimsuits and then meet us at the park. I changed into a yellow bikini, a little bit concerned about the extra weight. But over the past couple of months, I had lost a few. And I had at least gotten a tan. I pulled on a thin blue sundress and grabbed my backpack. Ava, Ian, and I loaded up the Volvo with coolers, beach towels, and sunscreen and headed for Rainbow Springs.

"This should be fun," I said, not wanting to ask Ian too many questions. "Yeah," Ian said, "I like Bryan. He's a cool guy. And he's joining the Army after high school, too."

"Oh, how 'bout that!" I said casually, noting that Ian had said "after high school," and not "after he drops out of high school."

We arrived at the park, driving through a canopy of live oaks draped with Spanish moss. Everything was an intense emerald green: the trees, the moss, the shrubs, and grasses along the road. As we reached the parking lot, we saw that the place was alive with tourists. Families casually blocked the road, sauntering across carrying brightly colored coolers, floats, and small children. Toddlers strayed here and there, causing me to clench the wheel and slam on the breaks in panic. Frazzled mothers were clueless to their children's peril. Pre-teens hopped and cartwheeled with no regard for our slow-moving vehicle. We finally made our way to a shady parking spot under one of the giant oaks.

After about ten minutes, I saw the van ambling toward us in the same panicked start-stop fashion that my passengers and I had just endured. I waved, seeing Matthew in the driver's seat and noticing me, he smiled and pointed to the spot next to us. I walked over a few feet and stood in the spot to save it for them.

After they had parked and unloaded, Matthew went over safety rules with the group of teens. A drill with which they were familiar and paid little attention to. Ian joined the group and was standing next to Bryan. I assumed that he would want to hang out with his new friends today. Samantha walked up to me and smiled. "Can I share a kayak with you, Miss Diana?"

"Sure, kiddo," I said smiling. "We'll ask for a three-person kayak, so that we can all fit," I said, gesturing to Ava. Samantha looked suspiciously at Ava.

"That sounds like fun," chimed Ava, nodding in encouragement toward Samantha as if to say, "I promise I won't bite."

"Okay," replied Samantha reluctantly.

When we arrived at the kayak launch, the park employees began assigning kayaks and handing out life jackets. Through the crowd, I saw Matthew approaching me.

"Hey," he said.

"Hey you!" I replied.

"Do you want to ride with me so we can keep an eye on the group? From the back? Like last time?" he asked, scratching the back of neck. He seemed to do that when he was nervous about asking me something.

I wanted to. I wanted to so badly. I longed to be near him and to feel his energy. But I had promised myself to be fully present with my son and daughter while they were visiting, so I knew that I had to say no.

"I would love to," I said wistfully. "But I've already promised to ride with Ava and Samantha. We've got our tour guide and it looks like Ian is riding with Bryan. So, if you and Noah ride together, we will have plenty of eyes on the group," I said, trying to smile.

He was visibly disappointed but being the sweet and happy guy that he was, he quickly recovered. "Good idea," he said smiling. "I'll see you after the tour."

The two girls and I donned our lifejackets and clumsily settled into the kayak. The water below was cold, about seventy-two degrees, clear to the bottom, and perfectly aqua-blue as we set out on the tour. Tall cypress trees lined the banks, heavy under the weight of Spanish moss. Palm trees, varieties of pine, and oaks all coexisted in this world where the tropic and the temperate mixed. Underwater plants swayed in the gentle current while small fish casually swam past. According to the park brochure, ancient people once lived here, built their homes, and bathed in the crystal blue springs. The air was alive with the calls of birds and the sounds of insects. Ava had brought her binoculars for bird-watching and she occasionally shouted out a bird spotting. Samantha suddenly seemed intrigued.

"Look, a red-tailed hawk!" Ava exclaimed pointing to the top of a cypress tree.

"Can I see it?" Samantha asked timidly.

"Here," Ava said, handing her the binoculars. "Up there, it looks like it's caught something."

Samantha held the binoculars over her eyes and tilted her head upwards. With her small frame and her blond hair, she resembled Ava at that age. Soon, she and Ava were passing the binoculars back and forth. Ava would make a sighting, then show Samantha the bird on the brochure, reciting its food preferences and migration patterns. I regarded Ava with pride. "She has grown up to be a smart, intelligent, and kind young woman." I smiled to myself as I leisurely paddled along the glassy surface of the water.

After our tour, we walked to the headsprings, where swimming was permitted. Ava left her binoculars in my backpack and eagerly dove into the cold blue water from the dock. Samantha lingered nervously on the dock, watching the others take the plunge.

"Aren't you swimming Samantha?" I asked.

"I'm not a very good swimmer," she confessed, kicking at the dock planks.

"The buoyed area is shallow. It's perfectly safe," I coaxed. "Here, I'll get in first and then I'll help you." I said reassuringly. Knowing that the water was going to be freezing, I braced myself for the shock and just dove in as Ava had. My body plunged into the shock of ice cold water. I opened my eyes and could see clearly as I dove downward. I playfully skimmed over the bottom, and touched off to launch myself upward. I gasped as my face hit the surface. Suddenly, I felt exhilarated and alive.

"Always worth it to just dive right in," I thought happily. I swam back to the dock and hung on the edge.

"Now you go over to the other side," I said and pointed, "inside the buoys and I'll meet you there." I enjoyed swimming, and even though I didn't mind helping her, I wanted to have a little time to swim in deep water. It was so cold and clear. It was magical and when I looked up again, I saw Matthew smiling at me from the dock. I waved at him, then swam toward the buoys.

As I swam, I watched Samantha walk around the dock to the shallow side. I ducked under the rope and swam to shore. Samantha was standing on the water's edge looking unsure.

"Come on in, it's shallow."

She slowly walked forward, gasping at every inch as she continued into deeper water. When the water reached her rib cage, she stopped.

"Far enough?" I asked. She nodded—eyes wide, teeth chattering, and lips blue.

"You'll warm up if you move around," I said. "Can you dog paddle?"

"What's dog paddle?" she asked.

"Dog paddle is like this," came a voice behind me. I almost choked when I turned to see that it was Matthew, dripping wet, and bare-chested. He had a small tattoo on the right side of his chest. His skin was brown and he was, as I suspected, in great shape. His arms, chest, and stomach were firm, and muscular, but not too big. It was clear that he took care of himself, but he didn't overdo it at the gym. To me, he was just right.

Matthew came closer and demonstrated cupping his hands and pushing down on the water to show Samantha the dog paddle. "Now you try it," he said.

Samantha, while standing, cupped her hands and paddled them on the top of the water as Matthew had shown her.

"Good job," he said. "Kick your feet while you're doing that. Your head stays above water," he instructed.

"Try it," I said, "I'll support you.

I put my arms out in front of me to support her. She clumsily splashed and thrashed, trying to get the hang of kicking and paddling at the same time. "You're doing great, Samantha," I encouraged, as she elbowed me in the face. "Keep going."

As she was thrashing around with my support, I instinctively scanned the area for Ava and Ian. I spotted them with the older kids. They seemed to be having a great time, so I continued helping Samantha. I showed her how to hold her breath underwater, and encouraged her with a game that I used to play with my kids. We had an underwater tea-party, where we sat on the bottom and pretended to set the table for tea while holding our breath. Matthew was hilarious pretending to have tea with us, and I kept laughing underwater, which caused me to come up coughing and gasping for air. Unfortunately, he couldn't stay with us for long, because he had to keep an eye on the other kids too.

Samantha was not able to master the dog paddle, so I recommended that she try swimming underwater. "I was never much of a dog-paddler either," I told her. "I learned to swim underwater first. It's easier and the movements are more natural. If you can hold your breath, you've got it!" I said. Before the end of the day, Samantha was comfortable swimming underwater. "Next time, I'll teach you how to tread water," I promised. "After you learn that, you can go in deep water. You'll be a mermaid in no time."

The sun crossed the sky and the long summer day finally came to an end. Exhausted and hungry, we gathered our group and headed to the parking lot. Matthew unlocked the van and the teens began to climb inside. Ava and Ian wearily got into the Volvo and immediately pulled out their phones. They were both a little sunburned and their blond hair was tangled and half dry.

I stood in the parking lot, rummaging through my purse for my lip balm, when Matthew touched my arm. Startled, I looked up to meet his gaze.

"Diana," he began, "Thanks for today," he said, taking my hand. "You really are amazing. I mean, I can't believe we put this together so last minute," he said, smiling at me.

"Yeah, we make a pretty good team, huh?" I said, teasingly.

But as I said it, he didn't laugh. Instead, he looked at me very seriously and ran his fingers through his hair. "Yeah, I think we do."

"Hey, you want to do something tonight?" he asked tentatively.

Yes, of course I wanted to do something with him tonight—and every night for that matter—especially after seeing him shirtless. But Ian and Ava were in town to visit me and I really needed this time with my family. I had to trust that this was the right thing to do and that Matthew and I would have our chance when the time was right.

"Matthew," I said sadly. "I would love to do something tonight. But I think Ian and Ava are tired and hungry. We're going to find food and then probably be couch potatoes for the rest of the night." I explained, struggling to find words that would not hurt his feelings. "They're going to be here for a week. But I would love to take a raincheck."

"Right, I see," Matthew said, looking toward the car in a moment of realization. "Of course, yeah, with the kids in town," he said, moving toward the van. "Another time," he said, attempting a smile.

My heart sank and suddenly I was worried that I had missed my chance. I waved feebly and got into the driver's seat. "What if he never asks me again?" I thought. "What if he meets someone else who doesn't have kids? What if he meets someone younger?" I questioned. My mind began to spiral out of control with thoughts of losing Matthew forever—our budding summer romance, dead in the water.

"Hey, Mom," called Ian from the back seat. "Can we go eat?" Fortunately, Ian startled me from my inner panic. I reminded myself that I was thinking crazy thoughts and falling into old patterns of self-doubt.

"Thank you, Ian," I said.

"For what?" he asked

"Reminding me that we need to go eat," I said as I drove through the canopy of live oaks and out of the park toward the nearest burger joint or Mexican restaurant.

The first place on the map was The Blue Gator Bar and Grill, so I pulled into the small parking lot. We entered to a sign that read "Seat Yourself," so we weaved through the small dining area to one of the rustic wooden booths. Above us, an alligator skin was nailed to the wall for décor.

"Did you have fun today?" I asked.

"Yeah," said Ian, "that place was awesome. I can't believe how blue the water is."

"It comes from an underground spring," I said. "So, what did you and Bryan talk about?" I asked, nonchalantly.

"Oh, he's joining the Army after high school and he told me that the Army won't take you unless you graduate high school. They won't take you with just a GED," he said.

"Oh? Is that right?" I asked, trying to sound unconcerned, "I had no idea."

"Yep," he said, "So, I guess I'll have to stay in school."

"Oh, okay," I said, still trying to play it cool, knowing very well that Ian often liked to disagree for sport. "Well, I'm sure it will all turn out fine," I finally said, seeing our server approaching.

She took our drink orders and to my relief, Ian was polite and ordered something that was actually on the menu.

"So, Mom," Ava suddenly said, "What's the deal?"

"Deal?" I asked. "What deal?" feeling confused.

"With that Matthew guy," she said accusingly. "What is the deal with you and him?" she asked.

"Oh, that." I said, trying to think of the words to describe our deal.

"Yeah, where do you know him from? How did you meet?" Ian asked.

"Well, let's see. The deal is that he's very nice and we are friends, although I honestly don't know him all that well." It felt strange saying those words, because they did not ring true for me, even if they technically were true. I felt that I knew him quite well and it seemed to me that I had known him for longer than I actually had.

"I met him through friends at work. We all volunteer at Teen Harbor, as part of a program sponsored by the company we work for. We earn paid time off for volunteer hours. It's a great program and it helps the kids a lot," I said.

"He likes you," Ava said matter-of-factly.

"What makes you say that?" I asked, surprised.

"Oh, I don't know, the way he was looking at you all day long. And every time you turned around, he was there," she said.

"What?" I said, feeling the need to defend him. "No, he wasn't. He had to keep an eye out for all of the kids. He's very responsible. He was not looking at me." I said, suddenly aware that I was protesting too much.

"Mom," she said abruptly, "It's fine. He seems like a nice guy. And he's not bad looking either," she said, clearly amused.

"Wait a minute. Wait a minute. Wait a minute," I quickly said. "There isn't anything to talk about because," I stammered, "there just isn't anything. We both volunteer at Teen Harbor, and that is it!" I said, now feeling the blood rising in my face and ears.

This conversation was not going my way and I felt as if she had me against the ropes. Instead of keeping my cool, I was completely blowing my cover. I would never have made it as an international spy, that's for sure. Good thing I didn't try that career path because I would be dead by now, my red ears having given me away. I needed to compose myself and take back control of the subject. I breathed deeply a couple of times and then I began again.

"Okay, here is the deal, Ava," I began. "Matthew is, as you said, a very nice guy and yes, he is very attractive," I continued, "BUT!" I emphasized, "I think it's too soon to jump into anything right now," I said, relieved that I had gotten my point across without turning red.

"Why is it too soon?" Ava asked.

"Well, don't you two think it's too soon? Wouldn't it bother you to have your parents start dating other people?" I asked.

"Dad's dating his therapist," Ian stated matter-of-factly.

"Oh!" I said, my mouth dropping open. I was suddenly quiet and needed a moment to process this news. "He sure changed his tune," I thought. "Just last month, he was asking me to come home—to come back to him! And he even mentioned her in the letter." I recalled. Even though I knew it was over between Jonathan and I, even though I had wanted it to be over, I couldn't help but feel a tinge of jealousy hearing that he had already moved on as if it were no big deal. I wondered if was easy for him to have another woman taking my place, sitting in the car where I used to sit, sitting at the kitchen table across from him. Had he just replaced me with a new model?

"Well, how do you two feel about that?" I finally asked.

"Fine," said Ian. "She seems nice."

"I haven't met her," said Ava, "but it's fine with me. I mean, I'm in college, so . . . ," she trailed off. "I'll be on my own soon."

"But Mom," Ian said, "you shouldn't be alone. I don't like the thought of you out there on that farm all by yourself—going gray, getting all old and wrinkly, eventually dying all alone with no one but your chickens to mourn your passing . . . ," he continued dramatically. "Of course, we'll be alerted, about a month or two later; after the animals have gotten to you."

"Ian, gross!" Ava shouted.

"I'm not old! Good grief!" Once again, the conversation was out of my hands. "And you saw today, that I do things. I volunteer. I work. I'm not just rotting on the farm! Jeez." I snapped.

"Ian, stop being a jerk," Ava snapped. "Mom, what we're trying to say is that we think it's fine if you start dating again."

Just then, the server arrived with our drinks. As she handed me my iced tea, I handed it back to her.

"Can I trade this for a Chardonnay, please?" I asked.

Chapter Nine

On Sunday, I took Ava and Ian to the Crystal River Archaeological State Park, a sixty-one-acre site located within the Crystal River Preserve State Park. I was interested in seeing the ancient burial mounds and I thought the kids would enjoy the natural scenery. I brought my recently purchased Nikon DSLR camera, which had set me back a pretty penny. But with all of the natural beauty in Crystal River, I was hoping to get some great shots. We shared a day of bird watching peppered with a little history lesson. I had always loved learning about ancient civilizations and was pleasantly surprised to learn that this large site was nearby. The park had once been sacred ground where Native American people travelled from as far north as the Great Lakes to engage in rituals, burial rites, and trade. It is believed that they all may have shared a common religion with the native people of Mexico and South America. Amazingly, the site had been an active center of community for thousands of people from about 500 B.C. to around 1400 A.D. For reasons unknown to us, the site was abandoned after that time.

As we strolled through the park along the paved pathways, we passed several small mounds neatly covered in green grass. Inside these were the ancient remains of people—whose families had traveled far and wide to bring them to this sacred final resting place. As with much of Crystal River, the area was lush green, canopied with Florida hardwoods whose ancient branches drooped with Spanish moss. Sabal palms intermixed with pines and live oaks made a diverse landscape above which bald eagles were known nest.

We lazily approached the midden area, which was a large raised area, ceremoniously shaped in the form of a crescent. This area was a sacred landfill of sorts, where discarded objects were deposited to eventually become part of the landscape. Oyster and turtle shells, the bones of ancient deer, and fish had lain there for a thousand years, alongside broken arrowheads and ornately designed pottery. The ceremonial shape of the garbage dump led me to think of the crescent moon and the lunar cycles' relation to the divine feminine, or Goddess. The burial of the dead and the sacred landfill, made me wonder if the ancient people were drawing a parallel between the death of people, the death of animals, and the death of useful tools. I realized that they must have been truly thankful for everything that they had. Loved ones, the animal spirits who gave their lives so that these people could live and feed their children, and the tools they needed for life. They even honored art—beauty was held sacred in the discarded broken pottery—within the ceremonial moon shape.

"Smile, you two! I want some nice pictures of today," I said, holding my camera expectantly with one hand, while waving for Ava and Ian to stand closer together.

They both moved closer together, smiling, and as I snapped the picture a strong breeze blew Ava's hair all about, slapping it into both of their faces.

"Okay, one more," I laughed. They groaned and got into position again. This time the picture was perfect.

Near the river's shore on the south end of the park, stood the tallest of the mounds, a thirty-foot-tall mountain made of shells and now covered in grasses and foliage known as the Temple Mound. A modern wooden staircase led to the top because the original staircase had been destroyed by a construction crew before the area became a State Park.

As we approached the mound, I stopped to snap a few pictures of the mound in the distance. When I looked through my view finder, there atop the Temple Mound, stood a woman gazing out at all that surrounded her in the vast emerald landscape below. However, her presence there was not what caught my attention, what did was the way she was dressed. She wore an enormous blue, red, and green feather headdress. As I zoomed in, I could see that the headdress was decorated with a red and black tower-shaped center piece that was etched with white crescent moon shapes. She was bare chested and her skirt was also made out of the same style of red and black tower-shaped pieces, also etched with white crescent moon shapes. As she turned in my direction, I could see her prominent gold nose ring—a thick bar that pierced her septum. Then as I watched, bewildered, she touched her first two fingers to her lips and slid them downward to the center of her chest, painting an oily path of dark brown from her mouth to her heart. Suddenly, I felt a jolt of energy go through my entire body as I realized that her bright green eyes were staring directly at me. Startled, I dropped my expensive camera onto the grass. In my sudden panic, I lunged for it. Then, realizing that it was intact, I quickly turned my attention back to the Temple Mound. She was gone.

"Kids, did you see that?" I asked in a frenzy.

"See what?" asked Ian casually. "You dropping your new camera? Be careful."

"No, not the camera," I stammered, "The Temple Mound," I pointed.

"Yeah, that place looks cool," he said. "We going up now?" he asked curiously.

Confused, I clutched my camera with the hope of having photo evidence.

"I took a picture, didn't I?" I mumbled.

I scrolled through my pictures again and again, frantically searching for the photo of the Temple Mound, but it was not there. The last photo saved on the camera was the one I had just taken just Ava and Ian, before we headed toward the Temple Mound.

I was shaken by the vision of the woman—the Priestess. Yet as I tend to do, I began to question myself. And I began to wonder if I had actually seen anyone up there at all. However, even in my skepticism, I could not erase the chilling image of her green-eyed gaze, as she wiped mud down her face and neck.

We climbed the steps to the mound and took in the view that my apparition had just enjoyed. The area below was lush and verdant with grasses, trees, mangrove islands, and salt marshes. The calls of birds filled the air as the breeze rustled through the trees. I imagined what the complex must have been like two-thousand years ago, bustling with hundreds of visitors preparing to participate in rituals—ceremonies of the moon, planets, and stars—that the Priestess oversaw. Suddenly, my arms were all gooseflesh. On the way home, I stopped at a bookstore and picked up a book on Native American mythology and totems, determined to uncover the mystery of my priestess.

Chapter Ten

The first Saturday morning in September, I leisurely laid in bed with a tinge of melancholy that no one was coming to the farm for a visit. Ava and Ian were safely back in school and focusing on their studies. I was relieved that Ian had taken Bryan's advice to heart and was now doing better in school. I was also grateful that our relationship had healed somewhat. We were moving on from the hurt that can become so comfortable to hold on to. I was letting go of it in exchange for possibility.

With my kids back home, I had hoped to pick up with Matthew where we had left off when he had asked me out at Rainbow Springs. Sadly, those plans had fallen through when he was asked to return to the Orlando office for another project. Although Orlando was not that far from Heritage Springs—only about two hours—a first date at his hotel was not going to work for me and I appreciated that he thought enough of me not to ask. Not to mention the drive there and back would amount to four hours in total. I did not want to start a relationship that way. It felt . . . wrong. Matthew was special to me and I wanted him to value me. Call me old-fashioned, but I still believe that men like a little bit of a challenge and there is just no challenge involved when a woman gladly drives four hours for a first date at a hotel.

I silently walked to the kitchen and found my trusty percolator waiting for me. When my coffee was ready, I headed back into the bedroom to lay out my clothes and choose my nail polish for the Goddess Tribe Meeting. I was looking forward to my outfit today because I had finally gone shopping for something new. The last pink dress I had worn had been to Ma's funeral. Before she passed, she had asked that everyone wear pink—even the men. It was her favorite color and it was meant to convey a celebration of her life. At her memorial service, all of her loved ones gathered to celebrate her life, surrounded by flowers, her artwork, and a sea of pink. I delivered her eulogy in a pale pink sleeveless linen dress. I was not sure how I was able to stand in front of so many people and recount the story of my grandmother as I knew her. I can only say that I was propelled to do it by some force inside me. I did not keep the dress. Unwilling to donate it, but not wanting to have it as a reminder of loss, I had left it in the closet when I left Jonathan.

The End-of-Season Sale at Macy's turned out to be a lucky break. I was fortunate to find a rose-pink Ralph Lauren wrap dress—knee-length with three-quarter sleeves—on the clearance rack. When I took the size eight into the dressing room, I was pleased as punch to see that it fit me in the most flattering way. It was fitted, constructed of a stretchy blend which included something called elastane. Whatever it was, the elastane worked just great to hold my waist in while creating a curvy silhouette.

Now, carefully selecting the pink dress from my closet, I laid it on the bed and instinctively went to get my jewelry box. I smiled as I saw the large heart-shaped pink stone sparkling up at me on its setting of rose gold. "How perfect is that?" I asked the empty house.

As I reached the church narthex, I eagerly entered the room feeling the welcoming scent of roses and instantly began to smile. Where I had once resented and feared churches, I now felt like this particular church—at least on the first Saturday of the month—was my home. I loved the Old Southern Teahouse feel of the yellow striped wallpaper. The décor, accompanied with coffee and dessert really brought me back to my grandmother's house. The whole place was comfort food—real food, as well as food for the weary soul.

Today, all of the ladies were delightfully clad in various shades of pink. Since the topic was Love, they all seemed to have put some extra panache into their wardrobe choices. Their decorated hats, bright floral scarves, and glistening pink gemstones brought images of fairy godmothers to mind. I remembered the wand fight that the fairies had in Sleeping Beauty and how the colorful magic dust had burst out of the chimney, alerting the spying raven.

"Welcome back, Sugar," Zelda crooned as she approached. She was dressed in pink chiffon ruffles and she wore a pink bejeweled headband to match. "Don't you just love dressing up?" she asked, smiling.

"Let's go get us some pie before they eat it all," she insisted, grabbing my arm and leading me to the table.

"The topic today is love. So what do you think, Diana? You got a beau?" she inquired.

"I'm working on it," I smiled. "I have my eye on one, anyway."

"Oh, my goodness! That's so exciting. Tell me about him," she said, fidgeting with energy.

"Well," I began tentatively. "His name is Matthew and he's tall and very handsome. He's smart, funny, and caring. He volunteers for those in need. And he's just a great guy."

By then, many of the group had stopped their chatter and I had an audience.

"Go on," said Lil, smiling her pink lipstick smile. "What does he do for a living?"

"He's an application developer at the company where I work," I answered.

Several of the ladies chattered in agreement that the job was a good one.

"Has he asked you out yet?" asked Margie, her large eyes questioning. Today, she was a vision in a pale pink suit.

"Well, sort of . . . ," I trailed off.

Suddenly Maymie was standing right next to me. She was a show-stopper in her signature chiffon kaftan. Today, the light airy fabric was covered in bold pink roses. She wore a matching turban, as usual, and on her earrings and bracelets were large enamel roses.

"What's 'sort of' asking you out?" demanded Maymie, maternally.

"Well, we spend a lot of time together platonically, but we haven't been on a date date yet," I said apologetically. "We've been trying to get together, but he's been working in the Orlando office quite a bit lately. In fact, we were going to go out last week, but he got called back, last minute. That's where he is now," I said regretfully. It was clear that my dating story was disappointing them. It was kind of disappointing to me too. After Ava and Ian left, I had hoped to take Matthew up on that raincheck. Instead, he was called back to Orlando to troubleshoot a problem on the weekend. Being short staffed, they asked him to stay for a couple more weeks—just until they could hire someone locally.

"We will talk about this later, Honey," Maymie said, patting my hand. "For now, we've got to get this show on the road," she announced as she made her way toward the podium.

I quickly cut two slices of strawberry cream pie and plopped one onto Zelda's awaiting plate, and one onto mine. Then we hurriedly rushed to our seats like a couple of school kids who were late for class.

"Ladies! My word! You all look so bright and beautiful today! And I can already feel the Love filling up this room!" She declared, her arms outstretched. "Now today, we're going to talk about my favorite subject—Love! But first let's go into prayer together. Won't you all join hands?" Once again, Zelda took my hand.

Today, I affirm that Divine Love is all around us.

Divine Love dwells inside all beings,

Connecting us all in oneness.

There is no separation, no fear, and no strife.

For all creation is Love.

And all Love is creation.

Anything else is an idea that we have the power to deny.

Love lives in us and works through us at all times.

And for this, we are so grateful.

And we give thanks.

Amen.

"Our presenter today is Miss Virginia and she's going to introduce us to the Goddess Kuan Yin and the Goddess Power of Love," Maymie said, looking up from her prayer.

A petite woman with shoulder-length, light brown hair proudly stepped to the podium. Then she quickly stepped from behind it, noting that it was too high for her. She was dressed primly in a light-pink cardigan and skirt. She wore a strand of pearls around her dainty neck with matching pearl earrings. She smiled brightly, her pink lipstick illuminating her white teeth as she addressed us from in front of the podium.

"Welcome Ladies! I'm Virginia and I'm fixing to tell you all about Love and the Goddess, Kuan Yin," she began.

Virginia held up her poster displaying a beautiful Asian Goddess, setting it carefully on the easel. Kuan Yin was pictured seated in the lotus position with her palms together in the Anjali Mudra. Upon her head, she wore an elaborate silver crown covered in pink jewels. Her black hair was pulled up and pinned with matching silver clasps and held in place with intricately carved hair sticks. She was loosely draped in pink and gold fabric so that her navel was showing and a pink lotus sat upon her lap. She wore silver and pink bejeweled arm cuffs and earrings. From her neck to her navel hung a huge silver necklace which was covered in large pink and green jewels.

"This beautiful lady is the Goddess Kuan Yin," Virginia began confidently. Although Virginia was petite, I could tell that she had a very strong energy.

"Kuan Yin is also the Divine Mother and as such, she is the Goddess of Mercy and Compassion. I have chosen her to represent the Power of Love because both compassion and mercy share the Power of Love at their core. Kuan Yin represents the qualities of the Divine Mother in that she provides comfort, healing, and guidance to those who ask. She is the Daughter of the Phoenix and she helps those rising from the ashes of defeat to claim their power. She embodies the feminine gifts of creativity, compassion, and love. She is infinitely caring and merciful; a comfort to all who seek her help.

"Now, most of you have probably been thinking of Love as the romantic kind. And while romantic love is wonderful, the Goddess Power of Love is so much more than that. Love is the foundation of our world. Love is the creative force that brings all things into being. Think about it, ladies. Anything that is born, built, or made comes first from love. A mother loves her baby and shows her infinite compassion; an architect loves her vision for a building and shows it infinite patience; a writer loves her story and shows it infinite wisdom; a philanthropist loves her charity, showering it with infinite abundance. I could go on and on. Love is a creative power and, as women, we are the keepers of it. Women are builders of good things. We build families. We make our houses into homes. We raise our children. We give of ourselves for the greater good. We are, at our very core, creators. And as such, we are the keepers of Love," Virginia proclaimed.

"I want you all to know, that I love my new wedding cake business," she said, smiling happily. "In this venture, I have combined several things that I love. I love weddings, I love baking, and I love cake-decorating. I love seeing the happy faces of the bride and groom when they see their cake. My business was built from love and I knew that it would be successful, and sure enough, it is!"

"Now ladies, tell me, what do you love?" she asked.

As expected, hands flew up the air. The ladies were excited to share all of the things that they love.

A woman with long flowing ringlets and a large straw hat began waving her hand excitedly. She wore a pink, burgundy, and blue floral kaftan. The fabric was richly decorated with tiny flowers and paisleys. It reminded me of an Indian or Asian print. Around her neck hung a rose-pink mantra mala with a burgundy tassel. Her long black ringlets were intermixed with a few strands of silver. She wore teal and blue peacock feather earrings which set off her sparkling green eyes.

"Yes, Francie," Virginia said.

"I love gardening, and I have made my backyard into a haven with beautiful flowers, herbs, and fruit trees. I sit in my hammock every day and luxuriate in the peace and beauty that I have created," Francie announced proudly. "I even planted a butterfly garden, so my yard is alive with fragrance and beauty."

"That's wonderful, you've created a space of peace and beauty for yourself and your guests," Virginia replied, then turning her attention to another raised hand.

"How are your sunflowers coming along, Diana?" Francie asked, turning to look at me.

"How did you know?" I asked quizzically, "Oh! You brought the sunflower packets!" I said, putting my palm to my forehead.

Francie nodded jovially.

"They're growing surprisingly fast," I answered. "It must be the rich soil on the farm. But yes, they're doing great. They'll be blooming very soon, of that I'm sure," I nodded.

"I'm Francie," she said, extending a hand to me. When I reached out to shake her hand, she grasped mine with both hands and smiled a big smile. "You are a ray of light, my dear. Such a beautiful soul," she said, still holding my hand. "What a blessing to have you in our Tribe."

"Oh, thank you, Francie," I said. "I love this group. You all have done so much for me in just a few months. I can't imagine where I would be if I hadn't stumbled upon this place."

"Destiny and Divine Order, my dear. You are exactly where you need to be at all times."

"Tell me, Diana," she asked. "What do you love?"

"Well, I haven't thought about it much. Honestly, I never ask myself that question," I replied apologetically. "I love my kids," I said, pausing to think if there was anything else.

"Yes, we mothers, we love our children!" Francie agreed. "What else?" she prompted.

I got the feeling that she was trying to get me to delve deeper, to ask the questions that I never ask.

"I love a clean and comfortable home. I love an amazing dinner prepared with love," I said tentatively.

"So, you like to cook?" Francie asked.

"Yes, I love to cook and I love dinner parties filled with friends and family. I love sitting on my porch with my coffee in the morning. I love the first time I need to pull on a sweater in the crisp autumn breeze. I love seeing the magic of the first flowers blooming after a long winter. I love springtime on a college campus. I love walking in the forest in the rain. I love snuggling in front of a roaring fire with a glass of wine. I love the satisfaction of a hard day's work and a job well done." I said, surprised that I was able to come up with so many things to love.

"All wonderful things, Diana." Francie said, patting my hand. "All love is creation. All creation holds possibility. Such is the beauty of everyday life."

After the meeting, I hurried home, buzzing from the coffee and the promise of the day. My boss, Jacob, had asked me to attend a leadership seminar with him in Orlando. I was flattered by his confidence in me and secretly hoped that he was eyeing me for a promotion—or at least a raise. Since the kids had left, I had done little else but focus on my career and my mentoring application. After all of the excitement of the past month—with Matthew and Teen Harbor, along with the visit from Ava and Ian—I was feeling lonely. And I looked forward to weekend plans, even if they were work related.

When I arrived home, I went hastily into my bedroom to change out of my pretty pink dress, but then I thought about it and decided, "No, I think I'll wear this. It's brand new and it's really flattering," I said smoothing the dress in the mirror. "Anyway," I said aloud, "Leaders can wear pink!"

Jacob was a handsome man—about six feet tall with a similar build to that of Matthew. But where Matthew was sunny and bright, Jacob had a darker disposition. He had closely cropped dark brown hair and chocolate brown eyes. His skin was slightly olive, although he did not appear to go out in the sun much. He always kept his appearance immaculate and seemed to be all business. A bit of a workaholic, he never accepted invitations for Friday Happy Hour.

The plan for the afternoon was that he would pick me up and we would ride together to the Leadership Conference. Although I was the slightest bit nervous about riding two hours in a car with my boss, I was determined to make a good impression. The night before, I had reviewed several client accounts so that I could fill him in on them during the drive. At 4:00 p.m. on the dot, I heard a car honking in the driveway. I looked out the screen door to see Jacob in his black BMW. I quickly grabbed my bag, which contained my notepad, wallet, a bottled water, pens, and lip balm, and hurried to the car. I opened the passenger side and slid in to the smell of new leather.

"Nice car," I said, not believing my own comment. The new smell was somewhat overpowering and I began to have pain in my sinuses that travelled up to my forehead. I silently wondered if he used new car smell air freshener.

"Hi, Diana," he said, smiling. "We're right on time. With no traffic, we should even have a few minutes to spare," he chimed. "I hate being late." He frowned, scratching his head. "I thought that afterward we could have some dinner and talk about the conference," he said. "Review our notes," he said reassuringly. He then hit the gas and flew down the driveway, bumping me out of my seat all the way to the road.

"Gravel road, huh?" Not so great for my car," he said, shaking his head.

"Not so great for my backside," I thought.

When we finally reached the highway, the drive went smoothly, although Jacob drove faster than I preferred. As we talked about work, I filled him in on my clients and he nodded in interest, seeming to appreciate my intimate knowledge of each one. Traffic was light on Saturday, which, combined with Jacob's lead foot, landed us at the conference early. I was relieved to get out of the car, so as I exited, I headed for the hotel coffee shop, and assured Jacob that I would meet him in the ballroom.

I followed the smell of coffee to a small café nestled just beyond the large hotel lobby. Although Jacob was nice enough, I was relieved to have a moment alone to decompress after the drive. At the counter, I placed my order for a large iced coffee, black. It was evening, and I really needed a pick-me-up in order to stay focused during the conference.

"That'll be $5.50," chimed the barista happily, "do you want your receipt?" she asked as if five-dollar coffee was the most normal thing in the world. As I reached for my wallet, a large hand went over my shoulder and presented a credit card to the barista.

"I'll get that," said a familiar voice. As I turned around, my eyes grew wide when I saw that the hand was attached to Matthew.

"What brings you to town, pretty lady?" asked Matthew playfully. He was standing very close to me, and not having seen him in a while, I was feeling butterflies again.

"Leadership Conference," I managed to say, "it's in the hotel. Are you staying here?" I asked feebly.

"I am," he said. Pausing, he ran his fingers through his hair. "What about you?" he asked, his blue eyes gazing intently at me.

"Oh, no," I stammered, "I'm only here for the conference. We're leaving tonight."

He looked at me quizzically.

"Jacob invited me to come," I blurted. "Suggested that I come," I corrected myself. "For career development," I continued.

For a split second, I noticed a look of concern pass over Matthew's face. Then his sweet smile returned.

"Can I take you to dinner later?" he asked, his blue eyes fixed on me. "I still owe you a dinner," he smiled.

I was ready to melt into his arms, until I realized that I was going to have to say no to this invitation too.

"Matthew, I would love to, but I rode here with Jacob, so I really can't stay after the conference. This is a work thing for me," I said apologetically. Although I was aware that, as an adult, I had every right to make plans in Orlando with Matthew, I was concerned about my career and I wanted to make a good impression. Cancelling on Jacob would have been unprofessional.

"I will be back home by ten or so," I said. "Why don't you call me later?"

"Diana," he began, shaking his head, "I can't pretend that I'm not disappointed. We just can't seem to get our schedules straight. But sure, I'll call you later." Then, stepping even closer to me, he leaned forward, putting his arms around me and resting his hands on the small of my back, "I don't like having to work over here so much. It takes me away from what's important to me. I'm going to figure this out. I promise," he whispered.

I couldn't breathe. I could barely move. I closed my eyes and rested my head on his warm chest.

"Diana, I've been looking for you. The conference is starting," came a voice from behind.

Startled from my trance, I turned abruptly to see Jacob standing nearby looking stricken. "What's that look for?" I wondered.

"Got to go," I whispered to Matthew. As I walked away, he grabbed my hand and did not let go until it slid out of reach.

As I entered the ballroom, I realized that I had forgotten my coffee. As predicted, with thoughts of Matthew now taking up permanent residence in my brain and no coffee to help me stay focused, I found the conference to be torture. We were divided into teams and invited to participate in various team-building activities. It seemed to go on for much longer than scheduled. Then, when it was finally over and we were saying our good-byes, Jacob recommended that we take our team to dinner.

I had hoped to grab a quick bite closer to home, so that I would be available when Matthew called; his phone call now being the most important thing in my world. Instead, I was piling into a shuttle with my new teammates and field-tripping to the nearest steakhouse. Dinner dragged on due to a large number of talkers in our group—Jacob being one of them. When I finally glanced at my phone, I saw that it was five minutes to ten and we had not even left Orlando.

I was feeling a mixture of frustration and disbelief. "Why is it that we cannot get any time alone?" I wondered. "He has now asked me out three times and we have not been able to be alone together one single time," I pondered, worrying that if I cancelled our phone call, he was going to throw his hands in the air and finally give up on me.

Instead, I texted him discreetly while the team was chattering away, enjoying their steaks and red wine, and having a great time. *I'm stuck at dinner with my team members. Jacob insisted. Haven't left Orlando yet :-(*

Then I carefully put my phone on vibrate and held it on my lap just in case he texted back. I waited five minutes. Nothing. After ten minutes, he still had not responded. Then after twenty minutes, still nothing. My heart sank. "He's tired of chasing me," I thought miserably. This thing with Matthew, that I had insisted so many times was nothing, was now the most important thing to me. "Why didn't I try to see him here?" I questioned. "It's really not that far. My stupid old-fashioned ideas about dating are getting me nowhere and now I might lose him," I thought to myself sadly.

When dinner finally came to a close, we took the shuttle ride back to the hotel and Jacob and I got into his BMW. I thought about Matthew alone in his hotel room upstairs. "All I have to do is call him and tell him I'll stay," I thought.

"Let's get going," Jacob announced enthusiastically. Then he proceeded to lead-foot it all the way back to Heritage Springs. Although his driving made me nervous, I was grateful to be home an hour earlier than expected. Exhausted and disappointed, I thanked Jacob for the conference and for dinner.

"Diana," he called as I stepped out of the car. "Thanks for coming along. I enjoyed . . . ," he paused, "having some company," he stammered. "I mean you're a great addition to the team," he said blushing.

"Thanks again," I called. Although confused by his sudden nervousness, I was too tired and frustrated to ask questions or delve deeper. "Drive safe," I said, thankful to be outside, in the cool night air. I could hear the familiar calls of frogs and the chirping of crickets beyond the trees. I breathed a sigh of relief as I walked up the steps to my cozy and welcoming old farmhouse.

I put the tea kettle on the old stove and turned the radio on to my favorite '90s alternative station. Then, drained from the day, I went into my bedroom where I hastily threw off every stitch of my now uncomfortable clothing. After wearing the stretchy pink dress all day long, my perception of it had changed drastically. It was no longer comfortable and flattering, it was a cage I needed to escape. I tossed it into the hamper and enswathed myself in my oversized gray robe. "Ahhh, that's perfect," I said to the house; and forgetting the tea kettle, I hopped onto the four-poster bed. Luxuriating in the comfort of my soft bed and my plush robe, I dozed for a moment.

Suddenly, I was awakened by the whistling of the tea kettle. I wandered sleepily to the kitchen and hurriedly took it off the burner, confused by the amount of water that had sprayed out onto the stove. Then, as I turned to go back to bed, I was startled by a knock at the door. Fear gripped me as a thousand images of burglars, escaped convicts, and gangs of ruffians assaulted my thoughts. I was frozen, trying to think clearly. It was all going to come down to this moment.

"Think, Diana, think!" I whispered. My dad had given me a rifle for the specific purpose of shooting burglars, convicts, and ruffians, so I was in luck. I grabbed my purse off the table and slung it over my shoulder. Then, I silently made my way to the hall closet where I carefully took the rifle and moved quickly, but quietly, into my bedroom, securing the lock. I was now locked in my room with my purse, car keys, phone, and gun.

"If they break in the front door," I whispered, "I'll climb out the bedroom window and make a beeline for my car—shooting only if necessary." I then took out my phone to call 911. However, after punching in my pin, I was alerted that I had four messages. I quickly touched the message icon and saw that they were all from Matthew! I breathed a sigh of relief, thinking in my drowsy state, that I could call him to come check on me. "Wait, he's in Orlando," I remembered. Then, confused, I read the messages.

I drove from Orlando. I needed to see you.

I'm outside your door.

Hey, I just need to talk, can you please answer.

I heard the tea kettle whistling for like ten minutes, are you okay?

Finally understanding the situation, I carefully put the rifle under my bed and ran to the front door. I looked out the window just to be sure and there, under the oak tree, sat Matthew's Jeep Wagoneer. My heart leapt as I hurriedly fumbled with the locks and yanked open the door. My pulse, still racing from the burglar scare, the sight of Matthew standing on my porch only made it more intense.

"You okay?" he asked, concerned. "I knocked and you didn't answer, but when I heard the tea kettle boiling over, I got really worried."

"I'm fine," I said, breathlessly, "You just . . . " I breathed. "You just gave me scare." I paused, placing my hand at my heart. "I fell asleep and I didn't know it was you at the door."

He was looking at me with what appeared to be a mixture of amusement and concern.

"Come in, come in," I said, waving him inside. Still catching my breath, I walked over to the sink and poured myself a glass of water. I took a long drink and stood for a moment, breathing deeply as I tried to calm my nerves.

Matthew sat down at the kitchen table, calmly watching me, his hand supporting his chin. We were quiet for a few minutes and I liked that about him; He didn't need to fill every moment with talking. Finally, I finished my water and I set my glass down on the counter beside the sink. I casually stood there leaning against the sink, gazing at Matthew expectantly. I did not ask him why he had driven to my house that night, because I already knew the answer. He looked down at his hands, clasping his fingers. Then he looked back at me, his blue eyes returning my gaze.

Having made his decision, he rose from the table and slowly walked toward me. I felt the energy in the room as my breathing quickened again. Neither of us said a word as he touched my face, lightly running his fingers along my cheekbone, then to my ear, and then my neck. He then gently moved the collar of my robe, exposing my bare shoulder, and softly began to kiss from my shoulder, to my neck, and back to my cheek. I dreamily moved my hands to his back, feeling his warmth through the cotton t-shirt. I lifted his shirt to finally touch his bare skin; and in so doing, I felt the electricity of our connection. I breathed deeply, breathing him in, and I knew that I would have no regrets about this night, no matter what.

I awoke just before sunrise, as blue light began to gently illuminate the sheer lace curtains in my bedroom. I extended my right arm and felt the solidness of Matthew's bare chest next to me. Comforted, I scooted closer, laying my head on his chest, feeling the rise and fall of his breath. Sensing my presence, he put his arm around me, resting his hand on my hip. I could not fall back asleep. I was too enraptured with the man sleeping so peacefully next me to. I ran my index finger around the tattoo on his chest. I touched his neck, his cheek, and his ear, wanting to memorize every detail of him. I gently picked up his hand and examined his long fingers, his perfect fingernails. To me, everything about him was perfect. I sat up in bed and felt around the covers for my robe. Not finding it, I decided I had better dig around in my nightgown drawer for something else. Suddenly, Matthew's arms were around me.

"Where are you going?" he asked, pulling me to him.

"I couldn't sleep and I didn't want to disturb you," I confessed. "I'm going to go make coffee."

"No, stay," he said, holding me closer. "You're not disturbing me."

"Alright, I'll stay," I said, snuggling against his chest.

Soon Matthew was sleeping peacefully again, so I carefully got out of bed and pulled a royal blue silk robe out of my nightgown drawer. I had only worn it once in my life, one Christmas morning with Jonathan and the kids, but this seemed like as good a time as any to recommission it. Tying my new robe, I crept into the kitchen to make coffee. My eyes grew wide at the site of my big gray robe curled up on the kitchen floor. As I hastily gathered it in my arms, I smiled just a little at the thought of my wanton behavior the night before. I piled it in a chair and put the percolator on the stove. Then, I trekked down the hall and hung the robe in the bathroom. Returning to the kitchen, I poured myself some coffee and quietly opened the front door, stepping onto the cool porch to greet the morning.

As I sat there in my favorite spot, sipping my coffee, I heard the screen door creak open and slam shut. I turned to see Matthew walking out in my big gray robe with a cup of coffee. It fit him perfectly, if a little roomy, and I smiled at the cuteness of him.

"Nice robe," I laughed. "Thanks, it's my girlfriend's," he said sitting down next to me.

"His girlfriend," I thought, hearing the words in my head. They sounded nice and they put my mind at ease. I was feeling fragile this morning after breaking my own dating rules with him last night. Frankly, I half expected him to be gone this morning.

"I thought you were asleep," I said.

"I kind of was, but I'm awake now and I wanted to come sit with you," he said.

"Diana," he paused, looking away for a moment. "ever since we met, I've wanted nothing but to be with you. Your laughter, your bright smile, your gorgeous hair," he said, touching my morning tangles. "But it was never the right time, or we had a bunch of kids with us . . . I was always making excuses to see you, to spend time with you. But I never told you that," he said taking my hand. "You've just been through a difficult divorce and you're still dealing with the aftermath. And I know how it is. So," he said, thinking of the right words, "I didn't want to rush you. I didn't want you to feel like I was pressuring you," he said, touching my hair again. "I've missed you and I . . . I'm sorry. I never should have agreed to take that project in Orlando. And seeing you with Jacob yesterday, that scared me. I was afraid that I would lose you if I didn't do something to let you know."

"So," he continued, "I got you a little something yesterday," he said, reaching into the pocket of his robe. He then carefully pulled out a small burgundy box and placed it in my hand.

"Oh, how sweet!" I said, accepting the gift. I opened it to reveal a silver charm bracelet. "Oh, Matthew, I love it," I said.

"Look," he said excitedly, "I picked charms for you, to mark the time we've spent together. Here's a little silver octopus, for the first time we met at the Rusty Hook and you talked me into eating grilled octopus," he said, touching the tiny charm. "You looked so pretty in that green dress, I would have done anything you said," he laughed.

"Next, for when I asked you to come paddleboarding with us, just so I could see you again," he said, touching the miniature paddleboard.

"And this one is an anchor, for the only excuse I could think of to spend more time with you—by pretending that I wanted to fix up your boat!" he said smiling.

"Pretending!" I said, laughing. "You're fixing that boat, mister, you already promised me," I said nudging him.

"And this is the day that I knew that I was in real trouble," he said, pointing to the silver mermaid charm, "Swimming at Rainbow Springs, I couldn't take my eyes off of you. You were just like a mermaid," he said, kissing me.

I held out my wrist and he attached the clasp. "Matthew, this is the most thoughtful gift I have ever received. I will wear it always. Thank you," I said.

"So, I was thinking," he said. "It's Labor Day Weekend. We finally have some time alone together. I want to take you somewhere, just you and me. No kids," he said smiling.

"That sounds perfect. What do you want to do?"

"Have you ever been scalloping?" he asked.

"No," I said, "but I've eaten my share of scallops. Sounds like fun! Let's do it."

"I have a friend who lets me borrow his boat. I'll arrange that with him," he said cheerfully. "Do you have a mask and snorkel?"

"That, I do have," I replied proudly.

"If you want to get ready and get your stuff packed, I'll let my buddy know that we need the boat today," he said. "Then we'll have to swing by my condo so I can change."

As I walked into the house to shower and pack my things, inwardly I was still processing everything that had just happened. I was excited about getting to know him better and about seeing his home. I recalled Matthew saying, "We're finally together." "So sweet," I thought, stroking the charm bracelet. I turned the water on so that the bathroom became hot and steamy. I stepped into the shower and let the hot water splash over me; savoring the feeling on my skin, as my mind relived every moment of the previous night.

Chapter Eleven

I slipped into my teal green bikini, pulled on a white mesh cover-up, and propped my sunglasses atop my head. Then I packed my faded blue beach bag with sunscreen, snorkel, mask, towels, and other necessities. Matthew had been so complimentary about my shape, that I was not the least bit self-conscious as I walked into the living room to greet him. He was sitting on my aunt's old floral couch, dressed in the same t-shirt and jeans from the night before. I could see a shadow of stubble along his jawline and his sun-streaked hair was disheveled.

"The boat's all set," he said, blue eyes smiling. He rose from the couch to put his arms around me. "You look like you're ready for a day on the water, pretty lady. What are you doing with a guy like me?" he asked jokingly.

"Right now, you're ruggedly handsome, but I imagine that you clean up nicely too," I said, smiling up at him.

We got into the Wagoneer and drove to his condo which was in a newly constructed Spanish style building. I was taken aback at how upscale and modern it was. There was a fountain in the front, a circular drive, and the building itself was located on the riverside.

"This is nice," I said, impressed.

"Well, it's convenient anyway. My buddy keeps the boat docked here. We split the dock rental fee, so I get to use the boat too," he said, holding the door for me.

We took the elevator to six, which was the top floor. The hallway carpet and paint looked shiny and new compared to my farmhouse.

"How long have you lived here?" I asked.

"Oh, not long," he said as we reached his door. He opened the door to reveal a lovely modern apartment with a full view of the river. The furniture was masculine, a brown leather sectional, big screen TV, a rustic, nautical-looking trunk served as a coffee table. University of Florida football paraphernalia was scattered here and there.

"Make yourself at home," he said, kissing me on the cheek. Then he disappeared into the bathroom. I sat down on his leather couch, and looking around at his things, I realized that I did not know him as well as I thought I did. Although the condo was lovely—clean and new—it felt . . . cold; and unlike my cozy old farmhouse, it did not feel lived in. "But then," I thought, "he's in Orlando so much that it probably hasn't really been lived in yet. My attention then turned to the balcony, so I slid the heavy glass door and walked outside. The air smelled coastal and the breeze was still cool as I marveled at the magical river view. Down below, I could see the gated swimming pool area and the boat dock. "This is why he's tan all the time. The mystery is solved," I thought, smiling to myself.

A little while later, Matthew appeared from the bathroom, clean-shaven, and wrapped in a towel. "Can you download your fishing license while I get dressed? I'll pay for it," He said, winking at me. I followed him into his bedroom, where he pointed to his computer desk. I sat down in his office chair as he typed in the password over my shoulder. I could smell his clean skin and I longed to be in his arms again. While I searched for the Florida Fish & Wildlife website, I could hear Matthew behind me getting dressed. I turned, but he was already right behind me again, his face close to mine as he reached for the keyboard. "Just fill in the information and use my credit card," he said, pointing to the online form.

"Here you go," he offered, putting his card down in front of me.

I thought about saying no. There was no reason for him to buy my fishing license. It was inexpensive, and I could afford it, but he was clearly making a kind gesture, and I wanted to graciously accept the gift. So instead of protesting and making a fuss, I simply said, "Thank you," and kissed his arm which was still supporting him as he leaned forward.

"Okay, we're all set. Let's go catch dinner," he said brightly.

We anchored the boat in the bay on a perfectly clear day. The water was flat. I sat atop the ladder adjusting my mask, clumsily slipped my feet into my fins, and prepared to jump into the cold green water.

"You'll need this," Matthew said, handing me a mesh bag, "for your catch," he said, smiling.

I hooked the bag around my wrist and jumped into the water.

The water was clear and cool, but not cold. To the left of me, I could see the green patches of sea grass swaying gently in the current.

"This is where you are supposed to look," I thought, remembering Matthew's brief lesson.

I drifted leisurely with the gentle waves, just above the seagrass, letting my arms stretch out in front of me. The sunshine from above illuminated the grass beds in bright yellow. As I floated, suspended above, my eyes caught a glimpse of a tiny blue sparkle. I swam to the grassy bottom to investigate, and as my hand reached out to grab, the little scallop suddenly came to life, clumsily dancing in a confused zig-zag to evade my clutches. Hundreds of tiny blue eyes had seen my encroaching hand, and the little mollusk began to pump furiously, opening and closing its shell as it propelled itself from my grasp. Unfortunately for the scallop, it tired quickly, and I was able to pick it out of the seagrass as it drifted to the bottom like a balloon losing air. I popped it into my bag, now feeling a tinge of guilt, but also knowing that although this mollusk had fought the good fight, they really don't live that long anyway.

"I'll become a vegetarian someday, but today is not that day," I thought to myself.

Suddenly, I felt a tugging on my foot, and turning, I saw Matthew silently waving at me and pointing to his almost full bag. I laughed into my snorkel, noting that after much soul-searching and mental advocacy for the little scallop, I had only managed to bag one. "I'd better get moving", I thought.

And feeling a rumbling in my stomach, happily forged ahead to catch my dinner.

In the late afternoon, we returned to the dock sun-kissed and loaded down with scallops. The day on the water with Matthew had been absolute heaven. We decided to cook bacon-wrapped scallops for dinner, so we drove to the store to pick up bacon, white wine, and salad fixings. When we entered the cold grocery store, I realized that I had nothing to wear, but my damp bikini and mesh cover-up.

"Matthew," I said, "I think I need some clothes."

"No, you don't," he said jokingly. "You look fine to me."

"I mean dry clothes, silly. I'm cold." I smiled back.

He put his arms around me in the store. "I'll warm you up," he said, rubbing my arms.

"No, I mean I think I need to go home and pick up some clothes. This is all I have," I said.

"Well," he said, "in that case, why don't I go pick up some clothes, and we'll have dinner at your place?" he said. "I love your house. It's got a good vibe," he said.

I smiled in agreement. We finished our shopping and stopped at Matthew's place for his things. He came out of his bedroom carrying a duffle bag, and we drove back to the farm.

I felt comfortable cooking in my own kitchen and I was happy to have Matthew there with me. After longing to be near him for months, I finally had him all to myself. I busied myself wrapping bacon around scallops and placing them on a baking sheet. Matthew turned on the radio and poured two glasses of wine. "I'll make the salad," he proclaimed, handing me a cold glass of Sauvignon Blanc. We clinked glasses and went back to our tasks. After I popped the tray into the oven, I went over to the sink to wash my hands. A familiar song came on the radio. I hadn't heard it in so long that I had forgotten how much I liked it, and how happy it was. Matthew came up behind me and put his arms around my waist, happily swaying to the music. He turned me around and we danced in the kitchen while the scallops baked.

After dinner, we spread a blanket on the grass so that we could watch the stars. We propped ourselves on pillows, brought an extra blanket, and the rest of our wine.

"This is nice," I said. "So peaceful."

"I like that about you, Diana," he said kissing my hand. "You're peaceful."

"What do you mean?" I asked curiously.

"You're peaceful and calm," he said. "And steady . . . like a river."

"That's sweet," I replied thoughtfully. "I never really thought of myself that way."

"Diana, there's a lot I haven't told you about me," he said quietly. "Stuff I don't like to talk about. But I want you to know. I want you to be the person I tell it to."

"Okay," I said, sweeping a stray hair from his face. "You can tell me whatever you like."

"I know I can. And I know that you won't judge me because that's not you. You're a very warm person. You're open-hearted and kind."

"I think you'd better spill it, Matthew. I'm beginning to think that you're a serial killer or something," I laughed squeezing his side.

"No, no, it's nothing like that," he said, "But," he paused, "my wife, Amy—we never got divorced."

I suddenly felt a pain in the pit of my stomach as if I had been punched. I felt heavy, like I was being pushed into the ground and sucked under the soil. "Of course this is too good to be true," I lamented silently. "He's married, meaning that I have just slept with a married man. How could I be so stupid?" I wondered. "But wait, why didn't Monique or Shyla know? This doesn't make any sense."

"Okay?" I said with nervous expectation.

"It wasn't that simple. It's much worse than that," he said pausing. "I didn't tell you because, well, it was just easier to say the divorce was difficult—and it was. And honestly, I didn't know what, if anything, was going to happen with you, with us. But now that I do, I want to tell you everything," he said, taking hold of my hand.

"She died from a drug overdose. And it was my fault," he continued, staring blankly at the sky.

"Oh no, I am so sorry!" I said, shocked. "That's terrible! What happened?"

Gazing up at the star-filled sky, he spoke quietly. "Amy and I dated in college and you know how it is—everyone we knew partied. It was no big deal back then. But after college, we all got jobs, had responsibilities, and we stopped acting like college kids. Everyone stopped partying except for Amy. I should have recognized the signs, but I was only twenty-five and I just didn't think her drinking was that bad. We had dated in college and then we moved to Houston together after graduation. The next logical step was to get married, so we did."

"Yeah, a lot of us did that," I said, touching his arm.

"Amy had a lot of demons. I found out after we were married and away from our college friends. She had trouble coping with her job and she had bouts of depression. Her childhood in foster care really started to haunt her. In the evenings after work, it wasn't unusual for me to come home and find that she had already finished a bottle of wine by herself. One bottle turned into two. Next, she started drinking on her lunch break. When she got busted for being drunk at work, she had a choice—either go to rehab or get fired. She chose to go to rehab; an inpatient program because her body was toxic from the amount of alcohol she had been ingesting. I supported her totally. I wanted to help her get better. When she got home, we both thought that everything was going to be bright and sunny—smooth sailing. But it wasn't. The same problems that had caused her to drink in the first place were still there. She still suffered daily. She still got depressed. She still had difficulty holding a job. I became more of a parent to her than a husband," he said sadly.

"I always thought that I would get married and have kids. But understandably, Amy didn't want kids. She put me off at first, said she wasn't ready. Finally, she told me that she thought that she would be a terrible mother. She was afraid that she would abuse our kids, the way that she had been abused," he continued.

"Anyway, we had some good times, when she was taking care of herself. But for the most part, our marriage was not a happy one. Over time, I threw myself into work and I really had a great career in Houston. I was moving up in the company and doing well financially. Amy got sober for a while and started going to therapy and AA. But then, five years ago, she was in a car accident. It was a fender bender, but she had back and neck pain that wouldn't go away. So, she asked the doctor to prescribe her pain medication. However, the doctor didn't know about her history.

Having an addictive personality, she took that bottle of pills and then asked for a refill. Once again, I didn't see the signs until it was too late. Amy became addicted to oxyco-done. I just couldn't cope with her by this time, so I called her family for help. They asked us to move here so that Amy and I would have more of a support system. They were helpful and understanding, and I really needed them at that time. But moving here completely derailed my career. I got the job at Web Synergy, thanks to Amy's family putting in a word for me. It's a good job, but the opportunities are not the same as what I had before. It was like what you said, 'that your wings were clipped.' That's how I felt too. This time when she went to rehab, I started seeing a therapist. He told me, basically, that I had had to put myself and my needs on the backburner because I was constantly worrying about my wife. He told me that I needed something else, something besides Amy's addiction. That's why I started volunteering at Teen Harbor. Amy had been terribly hurt by the foster care system. She was eventually adopted by amazing people, but before that, she suffered horrific abuse that, as an adult, had changed the course of both of our lives. I wanted to do my part to keep that from happening to another kid," he said.

"Oh, Matthew, I had no idea," I said, touching his face.

"So, after moving here, I kind of started to detach from Amy. I relied more on her family to pick up the pieces," he continued, exhaling.

"About three years ago, when she could no longer find a doctor in the state of Florida to prescribe oxycodone, she started buying them on the street or using the cheaper alternative, heroin. When she started that, I said, 'That's it. I'm out.' I offered to send her to rehab one last time. When I dropped her off at the clinic, I drove straight to a lawyer and I filed for divorce."

"When Amy got out of rehab, she tried to talk to me. She wanted to come back home. I told her that I had already moved her belongings into her brother's house and that was where she needed to go. I was heartless. I was emotionally numb," he said quietly.

"Amy's brother found her the next day, when he got home from work. She'd overdosed on a drug called fentanyl. It's more potent than oxycodone, even more potent than heroin. She bought it off the street from some drug dealer," he recounted, shaking his head.

"Anyway, her family still blames me for her death. For being so cruel to her when she needed me. But I just couldn't go on living that way. I just couldn't . . . ," he trailed off. A tear streaked his cheek and he quickly wiped it away; just as Samantha had done when she didn't want me to see her cry.

"Matthew, I'm so sorry," I began. "And, no, I could never judge you for that. You did the best you could for her. You tried," I said. "Do you ever miss her?" I asked.

"Not in the way that you think," he said, "We were together for a long time. She was my family. My parents were older and they both passed away about ten years ago. I didn't have anyone else. But no, I don't miss the relationship we had. In some ways, I feel responsible."

"Matthew, please don't blame yourself. You are so wonderful. You are sweet and kind and caring and you're a perfect gentleman," I continued. "She was lucky to have you."

"Now, I'm lucky to have you," he said, kissing my hand. "Sometimes I just wish that I had done things differently."

"Don't beat yourself up," I said, touching his cheek. "We're all here on this Earth to find happiness—to embrace happiness," I said, quoting Lil.

"I'm embracing it right now," he said quietly, "here with you and the stars."

"Me too," I said contentedly.

"Diana, wake up," I heard Matthew whispering. The air was damp and chilly. I realized that we must have fallen asleep outside.

"Look over there," he said pointing. Just a few feet away from us were three deer grazing: a buck, a doe, and a fawn.

I quietly sat up, leaning against Matthew and pulling the blanket closer. We watched as they casually strolled around the front yard in the dewy darkness, until they caught our scent and sprang toward the forest. We could see their white tails disappearing into the mist. "Forest Spirits," I said, "the Native Americans believe that the deer invite us to change our way of thinking—to have a fresh perspective," quoting my book.

"I think being with you is giving me a fresh perspective," Matthew said. "I'm glad I'm here,"

"I'm glad you're here too," I said, leaning to kiss him. "You, showing up on my doorstep was the best surprise ever,"

Achy from sleeping on the ground, we gathered our blankets and returned to the house, thankful for each other and the soft warm bed.

Chapter Twelve

M onday morning was Labor Day and we slept until 10:00 a.m. As I awoke to the sun shining in the windows, I thought it must be so late. I was reminded of how, when I had first moved here, I slept late as often as possible. I felt sad thinking of that past picture of myself. I wanted to hug her and tell her that everything was going to be okay in time. "Just trust," I would say to her. As I lay on my back, looking over at Matthew sleeping next to me, I was so thankful for all that had changed in my life in just a few months—and just a weekend.

"Hey, sleepy head," Matthew said, turning toward me and placing a hand on my hip.

"Good morning," I said, moving closer to him. He was so much bigger than me that he completely enveloped me in his embrace, and I loved that. I felt soft and small, and protected.

"What do you want to do today?" he asked.

"Oh, I don't know," I said, "I'm pretty happy right here."

"Me too, but I thought I should ask," he said. "Some friends from my building are having a cookout today at the pool.

It doesn't start until 1:00 p.m., so we have plenty of time. Interested?"

I thought about it for a moment. We were having a wonderful time just the two of us and I was relishing it. I was learning so much about Matthew. Last night, everything he said about Amy and all of the sacrifices he had made for her. It told me quite a bit about his character—caring, responsible, and loyal. But then, I had already seen that in him with Noah and Bryan. In fact, I had learned a lot about Matthew just from spending time with him, not talking at all. However, meeting some of his friends might reveal another side and I wanted to learn all about him. I wondered how he would introduce me.

"Sounds like fun," I said. "I would love to meet your friends."

We arrived at the cookout at 2:00 p.m. which passes as right on time according to the phenomenon known as "Florida Time". As we entered the gated pool area, several people turned to wave at us. Matthew waved hello, while keeping one arm around me. We approached one of the umbrella tables where a few guests were seated. Introductions began, Matthew smiling, shaking hands, and still keeping one arm around my shoulders. He politely introduced me to everyone there. Ron and his wife, Kristi, lived down the hall from Matthew. I was pleasantly surprised to see Mike from work. He, his wife Mayra, and their two kids lived in a three bedroom apartment on the first floor. Then there was Jeff and Cindy, a young couple from Ohio who lived on the fourth floor, and Steve, Jen, and their three kids who also lived on the first floor. In all, there were fifteen of us there. Everyone seemed happy to see Matthew, and a few of the women pulled me aside and said that it's great that Matthew had found someone. I felt a little bit scrutinized, but I understood why, guessing that everyone there knew about Amy.

The kids played in the pool while their mothers watched, occasionally calling them out to reapply sunscreen. The guys gathered around the grill, swapping stories and drinking beer. I sat down in an empty chair at one of the umbrella-shaded tables and contentedly watched the scene, occasionally sipping from my water bottle. Although a few months ago, I would have felt lonely and sad without my kids, today, I felt free and unencumbered.

"Diana, right?" I heard a woman's voice.

I turned to see that Mayra, Mike's wife, had taken a seat too. Mayra was a petite Indian woman with long wavy black hair and pretty face. She wore an aquamarine colored swimsuit cover-up and sipped occasionally from her bottled green tea.

"Yes, hello, Mayra. It's good to finally meet you. I work with Mike," I said.

"Yes, he told me," she said, smiling "Is that how you know Matthew too?" she asked probingly.

"Yes," I said, not giving her much to go on. Having gotten more than my share of the third degree about Matthew, I knew that I needed to take control of this conversation now.

"How do you know him?" I asked.

"He and Mike have been friends since college," she said. "We decided to move here on Matthew's suggestion. We were looking for a safe, sleepy town to raise our kids. We found it!" she said, laughing and extending her arms to indicate all that was around us.

"This building is lovely," I chimed. "It's new?" Now I was doing the probing.

"Yes, it's five years old. Matthew and his, er, wife were some of the first to buy here," she said uncomfortably.

"It's okay," I said, reassuringly "I know all about Amy. Matthew told me."

"Oh," Mayra breathed, relieved, "Well, I think you two are great. I've felt so bad for him, you know, with everything," she stammered. "It was just awful. Just so sad," she continued. "I mean, you have no idea how torn up he was," she said, scowling and shaking her head. "I mean, can you imagine?" she said, adding emphasis.

"Poor Matthew," I said, feeling her words. "No, I can't imagine."

"So, you knew Amy?" I asked.

"Yes, but not well. She wasn't very easy to get to know. She was kind of closed off," Mayra recounted. "To me, it was clear that she was deeply troubled," she said, scanning the pool for her kids. "I felt bad for both of them, but I think Matthew thought that he could fix her. You know, be the knight in shining armor," she continued. "He's a good guy . . . But you can't save anyone who doesn't want to save themselves," she said.

"He's a great guy," I said. "I know that I'm very lucky." I smiled.

"What are you two talking about," came Matthew's voice right behind me.

"Oh, we were talking about you," teased Mayra. "I told Diana all of the embarrassing things you used to do in college."

"That's good," he laughed. "Fill her in. She doesn't know what she's getting in to," he said, putting his hands on my shoulders. Then he planted a kiss on my cheek and went back to talking with the guys.

By evening, our bellies were full and we were both a little sunburned. We said our goodbyes and got into Matthew's Jeep to head back to the farm.

"So, how was that?" Matthew asked. "Not too painful?"

"No! I had fun," I laughed. "I like your friends and they're all really nice people. They seem . . . protective of you," I said.

"What? Was anyone rude to you or anything? I'll have a word," he began.

"No, nothing like that. They were great. I could just tell that they care about you," I said.

"Well, I'm glad I got the chance to show you off," he smiled. Then he got quiet for a moment.

"Diana," Matthew said seriously. "I have to go back to Orlando tomorrow, but I'm going to tell them that this is it. After this project is finished, I can't travel for work anymore." He reached over and squeezed my hand.

"Aw, I would love that," I said, "if you're sure."

"I'll come back Friday night," he said. "If that's okay with you."

"Yes, please!" I said, smiling at him. "You're always welcome on my doorstep."

We got back home and Matthew and I spent one more night together before he had to go back to Orlando. I snuggled close to him so that our bodies were touching all night. I wanted to feel his energy, to soak him in if that's possible. So much had changed since Saturday morning, when I was unsure if we would ever be together. Tonight, I felt closer to him than I had ever felt to anyone in my life. I knew that we were here together because of the Goddess Tribe—because of all of the positive changes I had made for myself. I thought of Amy and her depression. And I wondered if I could have slipped so far if Maymie hadn't pulled me out with her boldness and her insistence that I bring the key lime pie. The thought both frightened and embarrassed me. Matthew said that I was steady like a river. I hoped that was true. I so wanted to be the Diana he saw.

The 5:30 a.m. alarm was the worst sound in the world that morning. It meant that our weekend together was over. I put on my blue robe, leaving the big one for Matthew and I went into the kitchen to make coffee while he showered and dressed. I poured myself a cup and sat down at the kitchen table. As soon as I did, flashes of Saturday night appeared in my mind: of Matthew on my front porch; of Matthew gazing at me from this vantage point; of the song that played, magically fitting for the moment; of his touch. My hand automatically reached for my bare shoulder.

"Coffee smells good," Matthew said, walking down the hallway toward me.

Startled from my trance, I replied, "Yeah, I made the good stuff, just for you."

He swung by and planted a kiss on my cheek as he headed for the cupboard. He was right out of the shower and he smelled so clean. I smiled at how comfortable he was in my kitchen now. He knew where the mugs were kept. He poured his own coffee and got the half-and-half out of the refrigerator without asking or feeling shy. He whistled as he popped bread into the toaster. And now he was leaving me.

"Diana, what's wrong?" he asked, picking up on my sadness.

"You know," I said. "Just . . . ," I paused trying to get the words out without crying. I don't like crying in front of anyone. There was a time, when I was young, that I would cry at the drop of a hat, but after being married to Jonathan, I stopped. For a time, I could not feel anything. And I had refused to cry at all. Now that I felt the tears coming, I became panicked that I would seem needy and overly emotional.

"It's just been so . . . nice having you here," was all I could manage.

"Aw, Diana, it's been amazing," he said, hugging me from behind. "I'll be back Friday night. I promise. And I'll take you somewhere really nice," he said, rocking me reassuringly. "I'll call you. I'll call you every day, okay?"

I could only nod my head in agreement. So that's what I did, biting my lip to keep the tears back. Then, just as Samantha had done, as soon as he let go, I made a beeline for the bathroom and washed my face and waited until I was calm. When I came back out, Matthew was right there, enveloping me in his arms. I felt his smooth cheek against mine as he whispered in my ear, "I love you, Diana." We embraced tightly for a long time, not wanting to let go. Then, after I watched his Jeep amble down my bumpy driveway and then out of sight, I retrieved the gray robe from his side of the bed and put it on. I curled up in it, letting it envelop me, and I dozed off for another hour dreaming that he was still beside me.

When I awoke, the house felt totally empty. It's strange how the absence of one person can create such a void. I showered and got ready for work as usual, but I did not feel usual at all. I felt like I was free falling with no parachute and no safety net. I went through my day, trying to focus on work, but thoughts of my weekend with Matthew kept cropping up—his scent, his eyes, his touch. Thankfully, around 1:00 p.m., Monique came by and asked me to lunch.

"Yes, I'll come," I said, desperate for the distraction of conversation.

We went to Salad Stop again and waited in line for our orders, then zig-zagged through the chatty herd of fellow salad-eaters, to join Shyla and Paul.

"So," asked Shyla casually "how did you spend your long weekend," addressing the table.

"Oh, Marco and I worked in the Flower Shop on Saturday," said Paul, "Then we went out for dinner Saturday night—to that new place, Café Marnier. It's really nice, great food, great atmosphere," he raved. "Then we just lounged around at home the rest of the weekend. It was nice. Restful," he said dreamily.

"That sounds nice," said Monique. "I really want to try that place. How's the menu?"

"Oh, it's amazing! You have to go!" Paul intimated, leaning forward, "And don't skip dessert. It's totally worth it."

"Well, my weekend was good. I went to Tampa to see some friends," said Monique. "We were at the beach pretty much all weekend. It was a welcome break," she agreed.

"Tampa! That sounds nice," Shyla began. "I drove over to Jacksonville and spent the weekend with family. Lots of food! I'll be dieting for weeks," she laughed.

"What about you, Diana, you're quiet over there," Shyla observed. "What did you do over the weekend?"

"Well," I said, clearing my throat. They all looked at me with concern.

"I, um," I started to say, but then I began choking on my iced tea. This went on for longer than normal and it was difficult for me to compose myself. Paul jumped up and began furiously smacking me on the back as if to dislodge a foreign object, but there was nothing to dislodge. He finally gave up and sat back down.

"Okay," I breathed, finally recovered. "I spent the weekend with Matthew."

Their eyes grew wide and their jaws dropped simultaneously.

"Or rather, he spent it with me—at my house," I corrected, shrugging my shoulders.

"Oh. My. God! No, you didn't!" yelled Shyla, so that once again, the other salad-eaters were staring in our direction.

"Ssh," said Monique, moving her hands downward to gesture 'everyone chill out.'

"Okay," Monique began. "Now what did you say?" she asked, cocking her head slightly to one side.

"Well," I paused, "Matthew and I spent the weekend together at my house. We also went scalloping in the bay, and he took me to a cookout with some of his friends," I said shyly. Then adding quickly, "And Mike was there, so I figured you would find out soon enough anyway. So, yeah, that was my weekend."

There was a pause, as they looked at me, stunned.

"Well, hell yeah! Go Diana!" Paul said, smiling brightly.

"Oh gosh, you guys," I said, burying my head in my hands.

"He's smokin' hot!" said Shyla. "You go!"

"Yeah, I think he's pretty hot too," I said, smiling. "He's also really great. He's sweet, attentive, polite, caring . . . He's just the best," I said, closing my eyes. "And now he's back in Orlando and I miss him so much. It's silly, but I do."

"Aw, that's so sweet!" said Monique. "Does he know how you feel?"

"I think so. He's coming back Friday night," I said.

"Oh, Diana, you poor thing. What are you going to do with yourself this week?" Monique asked.

"Work, and finish my mentor application," I said. "I need something to keep my head straight."

"Hey," Monique began. "Why don't you come with me to yoga tonight? Class starts at 8:00 p.m. I go to Soulful Yoga, the studio across the street from the office.

I thought about the offer and could not come up with a reason to say no. I used to love going to yoga class or working out several days a week. Now was a good time to get back in the game.

"Why not?" I said. "Yoga is a great mood booster and I could really use a stretch. I feel all crunched up and tight," I said rubbing the back of my neck.

"Deal!" said Monique happily.

"So, after this week, he's finished in Orlando?" Shyla asked.

"No, he's coming back for the weekend," I said, "to stay with me and then he has to go back until this project is done. Then, he said that's it. No more traveling."

"What!" Shyla exclaimed loudly, "do you remember when you said he wasn't interested in you? Oh my god!" she said shaking her head.

"Diana, that's so sweet," Monique chimed. "I'm happy for both of you. You're so cute together."

"Thanks, I'm very happy," I began. "Or at least I will be on Friday."

That night, I retrieved some of my yoga clothes from my long-neglected workout-wear drawer. I put on a black tank top and yoga pants and twisted my hair on top of my head. At 7:30 p.m., I headed over to Soulful Yoga for my first class.

What a gift Monique had given me in reminding me that I needed to take care of my physical body. I had been engaging in quite a bit of introspection thanks to the Goddess Tribe, but self-care includes moving and working the physical body too. This month's theme of love was not just about romantic love, I reminded myself. Love is love for one's self and for others. My problem, I realized, was that I had not been showing myself much love since leaving Jonathan. I was feeling guilty and punishing myself. When I got home that night, I felt so upbeat and motivated, that I set my alarm an hour early, planning on going for a run. Then I poured my cup of tea and got into bed with my Goddess Tribe booklet.

Suddenly, I was surprised by the vibration of my phone.

"Matthew," I said, happily answering his call.

"Diana," he said, "it's good to hear your voice."

"You too!" I said happily. "I miss you already."

We chatted for a little while about our day. Then Matthew reiterated that he would be back on Friday and that we would go out to dinner.

"As promised," he said, "I'll take you somewhere nice. Got a place in mind?"

"Funny you should mention that," I said playfully, "I do have a place in mind. It's new and it's called Café Marnier. I think we need reservations."

"Okay, if that's what you want, then I'll take care of it," he said.

"Matthew," I said, "I can't wait to see you,"

"Yeah, I'm ready to be there right now," he said, sounding weary. "I'll be glad when this project is over."

"Hang in there," I encouraged.

"I will. Don't worry," he said. "But I'm thinking of you—a lot. Just trying to keep from going crazy."

"Hey, I went to yoga tonight, you should go too. It's very relaxing," I said.

"Oh, I would feel silly doing that. I'm not very flexible. You'll have to show me how to do it this weekend," he said teasingly.

"You have a deal," I said.

"I could spend more time in the gym, though. I guess I should anyway. There's not much else to do living in a hotel all week," he said regretfully.

"Let's Facetime tomorrow, I miss your face."

"And I miss yours," he said quietly.

We talked for a little while longer, until I grew too sleepy to keep my eyes open.

"It's only three more days," I said.

"Yep, one down," he said, "Goodnight, Diana."

The next morning, I got up early and dressed for my run. The air was a cool and breezy seventy-two degrees, and smelled green, like freshly cut grass. I inhaled deeply, happy and grateful that the weather proved perfect for outdoor exercise. Although I felt out of shape, I managed to half-walk, half-run a full two miles. I was pleased with that as a starting point, but more importantly, taking a jog in the morning quiet was a great way to organize my thoughts for the day. Jogging along the roadside was peaceful and meditative and being out in the country, not a single car came by. I could only hear the clicks of the cicadas and the calls of the birds as I traveled down the lonely two-lane road. As I returned home, I felt light, motivated, and happy.

"Why did I ever stop doing this?" I asked myself. "It feels so good, and it improves my mood so much." Remembering how low and depressed I had become only a few months ago, I realized that I was scared for myself. I vowed to keep up with my exercise routine and never let it lapse again.

That week at work went by slowly. However, since I had added running and yoga to my routine, my outlook was much brighter. Not only did I feel good, but I looked better. I noticed that in the mornings, my eyes were clear, rather than bloodshot, and the usual puffiness in my face was not there. In the evenings, after yoga, I slept like a baby. I also filled my time with finishing up my mentoring application. By Friday, I finally had it completed. I had gotten references from Jacob, Paul, Monique, Shyla, and of course Matthew. The next step would be the interviews and the psych evaluation. Eager to get started, I called the center to schedule for the next available time slot. After work, with thoughts of seeing Matthew, I absent-mindedly gathered my things and walked straight for the door.

"Diana," called Shyla, "aren't you coming to Happy Hour with us?"

"Oh, I totally forgot," I said apologetically. "Matthew is coming back tonight, so I kind of spaced."

Then, looking at my watch, I realized that I had plenty of time. "Sure, I'll come for a little while. I'll just get a club soda."

We walked to Jake's, where Monique, Mike, and Paul were already waiting. To my surprise, Mayra, Mike's wife, had joined the group.

"Mayra!" I said, walking over to greet her. "I'm glad you're here."

"Yes, me too!" she said happily. "My mom is picking up the kids today. So, we're going to have a well-deserved date night. What about you? Where's Matthew?" she asked, concerned.

"Oh, he's on his way back from Orlando, as we speak," I replied. "We're going out later, but I wanted to stop in before heading home to get ready."

"I'm glad you did. Let's get together sometime soon—for lunch or a double date or something," Mayra said.

We exchanged numbers, I said my goodbyes, and I eagerly drove home thinking only of Matthew. Counting the minutes, and the hours until I could be in his arms again. When I arrived, I hurriedly jiggled my key in the old lock, and ran inside to get ready for our date. I wanted to look my best. I wanted everything to be perfect. I showered quickly, spritzed perfume. Then I dried my hair and wound it around large rollers to give it some extra lift.

"What to wear? What to wear? What to wear?" I mumbled as I rifled through my closet.

"Shit, why didn't I buy something? What was I thinking?" I asked myself accusingly.

In fact, my plan of keeping busy all week had worked so well, that I had not given any thought to what I would wear tonight.

"Oh boy," I sighed. "This means only one thing . . . ," dreading the prospect "Shapewear."

Since I had been exercising all week, I thought that I could probably fit into one or two of the cute dresses in my closet. However, it was going to be a tight fit. Reluctantly, I reached for my shapewear slip from the back of the closet. Midnight-blue satin lycra with black lace, "How could something so dainty and pretty behave so much like a medieval torture device," I asked the garment. The exquisite piece of intimate apparel was heavily reinforced with double-stitching, thick lycra panels, boning throughout, and a padded, push-up underwire bra. The affect was stunning—a perfect hourglass figure; high round breasts with enticing cleavage, narrow waist and a perfect curve along the hip. But, the pain was real . . . very real. And the fight to get the thing on lasted over ten minutes. In the end, I was victorious. The pay-off was that I could now choose any dress in my closet, knowing that it would just slide contentedly over the shapewear, with no argument.

I chose a dark blue knee-length dress with a sweetheart neckline and empire waist. I accessorized with silver hoop earrings, a silver chain and the silver charm bracelet that Matthew gave me. Next, I opened Ma's jewelry box to choose a ring. I picked the sapphire ring which featured a trio of blue sapphires, accented with small diamonds. As I regarded myself in the mirror, I realized that this was the most 'dressed up' that I had been in a long time. I was happy with my appearance, and I was excited to see Matthew. I imagined what he would say, never having seen me this way.

Then out of nowhere, it hit me—an overwhelming sense of guilt and shame. "What is happening to me?" I wondered. Feelings of guilt over being happy, going out to dinner, spending money, and starting a new relationship, all came crashing down on me at once. I crumpled on the floor, feeling deep despair and began to weep uncontrollably.

"Why can't I just be happy?" I wondered. "Where is this guilt coming from?" I asked myself, realizing that I felt as though I had no right to feel frivolous joy. I had no right to go out on a date and just have fun. I had no right to appreciate my appearance in this sexy blue dress. I had no right to revel in being pretty and flirty and feminine. Although I had made progress, deep inside, I still felt that I ought to punish myself for leaving my family; for not being there to help them live their lives; for not being there for Jonathan. I sat on the floor for a few minutes, pondering the origin of this deep sense of guilt. Why do we, women feel the need to martyr ourselves day in and day out? I didn't know the answer to that, but it was certainly something that I wanted to bring up with my Goddess Tribe next month. This month, however, the theme was Love and that, I reminded myself, includes self-love—a healthy dose of it, in fact.

I stood again, in front of the mirror and I told myself, "Diana, I love you. You know what? You're a pretty awesome lady. Here is what I want for you. I want you to go out and have a blast tonight! Drink wine, eat dessert, kiss Matthew in public. Just have a great time. Drop the martyr shawl and embrace life, Sister. Love yourself, you Goddess, you!" I thought for a moment on what Ma would say to that, now that she had passed into spirit. Remembering the twinkle in her eye, I felt confident that she would agree.

Now running short on time, I splashed cold water on my face, dropped some eyedrops into my eyes and applied my makeup. When I was ready, all I had to do was wait for Matthew. Thinking about him driving up, I suddenly became nervous and my thoughts started to spin out of control again.

"What was I thinking spending all last weekend with this man I barely know?" I asked myself. "What if he wants to stay this weekend too? I'm jumping in too quickly. This is a stupid mistake. I need to be working on my own problems right now, not fixating on him. Clearly, I'm crazy!"

I got myself into such a state that I began to feel queasy. Just then, I heard Matthew's car in the driveway.

"Oh shit, oh shit, oh shit. I need to calm down. I need to drink some water," I thought.

I walked quickly to the kitchen, opened a water bottle, and downed it. Out the window, I could see Matthew opening his car door and getting out. I began to breathe deeply through my nose and out my mouth. "Calm the heck down, calm the heck down," being my mantra. Then came the knock at the door. My stomach jumped and I felt so nauseous that I was afraid I would be sick. Hands shaking, I smoothed my skirt, stood up straight, and smiled. Then I casually walked to the door and opened it.

Blue eyes smiling back at me. "Ah, that's why I spent last weekend with him," I reminded myself.

"Wow," Matthew said slowly, looking me up and down. Then without a word, he took me in his embrace and kissed me.

"That too," I thought, when I recovered, "that is another reason why."

Chapter Thirteen

We parked in town and walked hand in hand in the cool evening air along the crowded sidewalk to Café Marnier. The sky was sapphire blue and a pleasant breeze blew my hair and rustled the trees. The romance of the street lanterns and the live oaks dotting the sidewalk was reassuring to me and I smiled, taking in the scene. Although I was still nervous, I was feeling a bit more relaxed. I squeezed Matthew's hand as we approached the restaurant. The evening breeze and the street lanterns reminded me of that summer evening I had set out to have dinner alone, only to be surprised by Matthew, Monique, and Shyla. The coincidental meeting that night had certainly changed my life for the better.

The smell of good things cooking permeated the air and we saw a long line of people waiting to be seated. Hopeful diners stood on the sidewalk and filled up all of the nearby benches. The restaurant entrance was open to the street, allowing the evening breeze to blow through, with tables in the front that had a street view and another dining area further inside. Matthew led me through the crowd, holding my hand as we approached the hostess desk. He gave his name and we were seated inside, in a cozy candlelit booth in the corner.

"Good call on the reservations, Diana," Matthew said, taking my hand. "I had no idea it would be so busy."

"Good call on making the reservation. Thank you," I said, happily taking in the atmosphere and the airy feel of the place. The walls were brick painted white. Greenery and vines spilled down the walls from a high planter that encircled the inside of the dining area. Strings of white light bulbs hung from the high ceiling, providing the only source of light. The result was enthralling, as if we had entered a mystical land that also happened to serve good food.

"It's new and everyone's talking about it," I said, picking up my menu. "Paul said to be sure to save room for dessert. According to him, it's amazing."

The server came by with sparkling water and Matthew ordered us a bottle of wine. It didn't slip past me that he ordered the same white wine that I had chosen last weekend. When the server poured it, the lights twinkled off of my wine glass and cast a soft glow onto the white tablecloth.

"To a bright future," said Matthew, raising his glass.

"A bright future," I agreed, clinking our glasses. As I did, I remembered myself earlier that evening, collapsing in a heap and feeling guilty for what? For just wanting to be happy. As I sat there with my glass of wine, in that beautiful restaurant with Matthew, I realized that I was so very happy; and at that moment, I did not feel guilty at all.

After dinner, we took a stroll along the sidewalk, window shopping the small boutiques along the way. Matthew slowed in front of a window display of silver jewelry and charms. "Hey, let's go in here," he said, pulling me inside the doorway.

"Matthew, I don't need anything," I protested.

"Who said anything about need?" he asked, touching my cheek. "I want to buy you a charm for your bracelet."

We walked to the case that held the charms. Matthew asked the sales person to pull out the velvet case so that we could have a better look.

"Which one do you want?"

I looked down at the black velvet case. It held shiny silver charms of all kinds; unicorns, peacocks, dogs, golf clubs, tennis racquets, soccer balls, stick-figure children, musical notes. And then I saw a fat little silver heart. "That one," I said, pointing. "I'll take the heart. It looks so full and it will remind me of how much I love this night."

The next morning, although lingering in bed beside Matthew was tempting, I decided to get up as usual and go for my morning run. I knew, especially after yesterday's meltdown, that I needed to keep up with my exercise and self-care. I wanted to be the best me. I wanted to be the Diana that Matthew saw—peaceful and steady. I also had fears of losing myself in this relationship as I had done with Jonathan. Jumping in to a relationship with Matthew had been wonderful, and I wanted to do this differently. I wanted to have an equal partnership, and I wanted to create something between us that would help us both to grow in ways that would not be possible alone. As I jogged down the quiet country road, I considered the questions of guilt. Why did I feel unworthy of joy? Why did I feel unworthy of love? If one were to look up the word "guilt" in the dictionary, the definition would allude to the commission of a crime; a person who has been found guilty. So why then, did I feel guilty? What crime did I commit?

Chapter Fourteen

Although it was eighty degrees outside, my thoughts were alive with visions of autumn, my second favorite time of year (spring being the first). The first days of autumn, with their cool mornings and long shadows, serve as a harbinger for the coming holiday season. I smiled as I remembered how I used to cook like crazy from November through New Year's Day. And my family always looked forward to the big dinners and the unexpected homemade surprises that I would whip up on any given night. I realized that I missed cooking for a group, and the joy of bringing the family to the table together. I missed the excitement and the chatter. I missed the kids filling their plates to overflowing. "Your eyes are bigger than your stomach," Ma used to say. "Not anymore," I laughed.

Today, I chose a stretchy plum-purple wrap-dress from my closet. I applied matching autumn colors to my eyes and lips, pretending that the air-conditioned house reflected the outdoor temperature. Next, I reached for Ma's jewelry box, taking from it my favorite ring, the pear-shaped amethyst. I reverently slid it onto my finger and admired how it sparkled in the light. "Thank you, Ma," I whispered.

There is a Power in autumn. The Power to change the color of the landscape. The Power of the autumn breeze to knock the colorful leaves off of the trees and usher in the frosty winter-like mornings. In Florida, we have a few varieties of trees that would change color, but most of the trees on the farm were live oaks. Although I loved the Spanish moss, I couldn't help but feel a tinge of sadness at the absence of a real autumn season. As I walked outside, I noticed with pride that our sunflowers were in full bloom. I stood before the row of huge sunflowers, each at least seven feet tall with blooms as large as dinner plates.

As I walked into the Goddess Tribe meeting, the rose-water air was accompanied by scents of cinnamon and hearth. The room was a sea of purple, plum, and lavender. I casually walked across the room, smiling and greeting the ladies who I now regarded as my friends. I poured my coffee, basking in the aroma and went over to admire the dessert.

"Wow, that looks amazing!" I gushed, regarding the black-berry and plum cobbler.

"Thank you. I made it from a family recipe," chimed a soft voice nearby.

I looked up to see a tall woman of about thirty-five with long, wavy, strawberry-blond hair and bright blue eyes. She was delightfully covered in freckles and she was wearing a purple chiffon knee-length dress. The top had a square neck-line and long puffed sleeves. The waist was fitted and the skirt was flared and flowing, perfect for twirling.

"Hello, Diana. I'm Iris," she said, smiling easily. "So nice to see you here every month."

"Thank you. I really look forward to every meeting. I learn something new, meet someone new, and," I hesitated, "these meetings feed my soul and give me strength." I said, embarrassed that my eyes were getting teary.

"We each have something to add to these meetings which makes what we take away so much greater," Iris said.

Just then, I heard Maymie addressing the group.

"Ladies of the Goddess Tribe!" Maymie called. "You all look like Goddesses in purple, the color of royalty. I can just feel the energy in this room. It fills me up and revives my spirit," she continued. "Please help yourself to coffee and the wonderful cobbler which Iris made for us. We will begin our meeting in just a minute." she proclaimed.

Iris and I made our way to two empty chairs and sat down. I was happy to see Zelda sitting in the chair to my left. She was always so bubbly and entertaining with her dramatic mannerisms and archaic way of speaking.

"Today, our Goddess Power is Power! And I will be presenting. But first, let us join together in prayer."

"Of course, Maymie should present Power. She is the embodiment of it," I thought.

Each meeting, I looked forward to seeing what Maymie would wear. As usual, she did not disappoint. Today, she wore a royal purple Moroccan kaftan that was heavily embroidered along the neckline and sleeve openings with gold thread, beads, and jewels. The patterns were gold laurels and stars. A starburst design was ornately embroidered at the center of her bosom. She also wore her signature matching turban—royal purple with a huge purple, pink, and gold bejeweled pendant from which an enormous tear-shaped amethyst hung at the center of her forehead. Her green eyes sparkled as she spoke.

"Ladies, please join hands and take my words into your hearts," she began.

I am the Goddess in expression, creating my life with my very thoughts.

I am the Universe becoming self-aware, Start-Dust, Magic, and Infinite Power.

I am the Power of Love, spreading my arms around the Earth.

Bringing Love where there is Hate,

Hope where there is fear.

As I join my sisters in Goddess Mind,

Our collective thought has the Power to change the World.

Knowing this Power,

I keep my thoughts pure, centered in Love at all times.

I reject ideas involving fear and hate,

Embracing only Love and my Infinite Power

To make the world a better place.

And so, it is.

Amen.

"Our Goddess this month is the mighty Isis," Maymie said.

Suddenly, I had a vision of the 1970s TV show that I used to love as a kid. The heroine of the show was a school teacher who used an ancient amulet to transform into 'The Mighty Isis' in order to help teens out of dangerous situations. I quietly giggled at my childhood memory and Zelda looked over at me quizzically.

"Isis is our Power Goddess, as her crown symbolized the power of the Pharaoh," Maymie began, placing her poster on the easel for all of us to see.

Her poster depicted a beautiful Egyptian Goddess with an elaborate headdress—part bird, part throne. She had long flowing black hair, brown skin, and dark eyes. Her arms were spread to reveal colorful wings. Her form-fitting dress was blue and gold. Around her neck, she wore an ornate cuff necklace of multi-colored gemstones.

"Isis's crown is in the shape of the Egyptian throne and she carries the ankh, or Cross of Life. In fact, her name, Isis, means throne and she is the omnipotent Divine Mother. Isis wields her power as protector of the weak and downtrodden. She is also the Goddess of health, marriage, and wisdom—all areas where she expresses her feminine Power," Maymie said lovingly.

"Feminine Power is a Goddess gift that we all share. We have the Power to shape our world and to make it a more caring place. We, with our divine thoughts and actions, can create a world centered in Love, Creation, and Imagination. We, with our divine thoughts and actions, reject ideas based in hate, destruction, and fear. We give our Power to what is good, and give no credence to that which does not serve us," she continued, extending her arms toward the group.

"When we choose to use our Power to embrace what we Love, we take all of the energy away from the problem and put that energy into the solution."

"When we engage in language such as 'War on Drugs,' 'Fight Terrorism,' 'Fight Obesity,' we are giving the problem all of our divine energy," she said.

"Now ladies, do you know that since these terms were popularized, each problem has grown exponentially?" As she asked the question, we all nodded in agreement.

"Why is that?" she asked. "It is because we all on this Earth are giving our divine energy to the problem rather than the solution," she stated matter-of-factly. "We have within us, the ability to solve all of our problems by giving our divine energy to what we Love, not what we hate," she continued.

"So instead, use your Goddess guided thoughts to say, 'I want to help those who are suffering.' Let us say, 'I want a world filled with Peace, Prosperity, and Harmony.' And let us affirm, 'I want happiness, health, healing, and wholeness for all of my sisters and brothers.'"

"The Dalai Lama, himself, prophesied the Power of women when he said, 'The world will be saved by the western woman,'" Maymie proclaimed.

"You are that woman," Maymie said, pointing at me.

"And you are that woman," she continued, pointing at Zelda.

She continued in this way, until she had pointed out each one of us.

"And I am that woman," she said, pointing to her heart.

"Together, ladies, we have the Power to create the world we want if we stay focused on the one true Power in this Universe and that is Love."

Throughout Maymie's talk, I began to think about how I could use my power to create change in the world. Working with the kids at Teen Harbor was a start. "They are impressionable and have seen so much negativity. Now is the time to introduce some positive ideas to them," I thought, remembering how much Matthew had helped Bryan and Noah. "They also have no home life, to speak of. They live in a group home, but that's so institutional," I thought. As I pictured ideas of home-life, I, of course, thought of the holidays and the big deal I used to make when I lived with my children.

"Diana," said Maymie, picking up on my thoughtful expression, "do you want to tell us how you're going to use your Power to create change?"

"Not quite," I replied sheepishly. "But I want to help the Teen Harbor girls to realize their power. I'm not sure how just yet."

"That sounds like a wonderful way to use your divine power, Diana. You love kids. And you're a powerful role model for girls. I think you need to step into your power and realize that. You are someone who forges her own path. Young women will look up to you in whatever way you choose to help," she said and smiled.

After the meeting, Maymie took me aside and asked me about Matthew.

"So, Diana, at our last meeting, you mentioned a new man in your life. Did he finally ask you out for real?" she asked jokingly.

"Yes, he did—a few times. But things didn't start out the way I had planned," I said, pausing.

"What do you mean, Sugar?" she asked, with a look of concern on her face.

"Well, we're moving much faster than I thought . . . ," I said, feeling uncomfortable. "Than I thought I should? Or that I would? I'm not sure," I pondered.

"I wanted to make sure that our timing was right; That we didn't rush in to a relationship too quickly. And Matthew felt the same way. He told me that he didn't want me to feel pressured," I continued. "And I didn't," I insisted. "Not one bit. If anything, I felt like I was holding myself back from something that I wanted very much—something that I trusted was a good thing for me. Matthew is sweet, kind, caring, and compassionate. He encourages my dreams. He's strong and comforting. He's the best man I've ever known," I said, looking into Maymie's bright green eyes.

"Well, Diana, it sounds like you've got yourself a winner!" she exclaimed.

"Don't get so hung up on rules and proper timing. Just let it unfold naturally like you have been. That's the best way. I think you're worried about protecting your heart, aren't you, Sugar?"

"I don't know. Maybe," I said, considering her suggestion. "I guess I was so hung up on rules and what was appropriate and when, because I . . . ," I paused to find the words. "Because I cared how Matthew perceived me. I wanted him to know me as a person and to value me for who I am."

Maymie smiled and nodded understandingly. "Nothing wrong with that, Sweetie," she said, patting my hand. "You're a smart lady. As I said earlier, I know a few who could take a lesson from you," she said.

"But I know that he does. He does value me, so much. And I value him. I think I was afraid of falling too hard. Matthew is the type of person that I could easily lose myself in. Lose my goals and dreams and just focus on him. I've done that before and I don't want to do that again. I want this relationship to be . . . ," I paused, "a partnership, where we help each other reach our goals, not a one-sided situation. I want to lift him up and, well, I want to be lifted up too. And I already know that Matthew does that."

"He sounds like your perfect match—a soulmate—Diana. We meet many in a lifetime, but don't always recognize them," Maymie said, touching my arm.

"Oh, Maymie, I'm in love," I said smiling.

"Oh, I can see that, Sugar," she said. "Sounds like you're one lucky woman. I'm so happy for you, Diana."

I smiled back at her, but then remembered the guilt and shame that I had felt in the midst of utter joy.

"But there's one thing I wanted to ask you," I began, looking into her wise green eyes. "If I am so happy, why do I feel so guilty about it? Why do I feel like I don't deserve happiness?"

"Guilty?" Maymie repeated forcefully. "Well, Sugar, exactly who did you kill?" she asked matter-of-factly. "Who did you shoot, stab, or abuse in whatever way?" she continued. "Whose war did you start? What bomb did you drop? What bank did you rob? Whose Christmas presents did you run off with?" she asked.

"No one. No one's," I stammered.

"Then you're not guilty of anything, my dear. And as far as happiness goes, every soul on this planet deserves to be happy, Diana. That includes lovely women who give up everything to raise their children and who just want a taste of love and joy for themselves too. That includes you," she said, hugging me tightly.

"Now," she said, placing her warm hands on my shoulders, "stop being so darn silly and embrace joy! Haven't you learned that yet?" she said teasingly.

That meeting on Power affected me as deeply as the first meeting had. I had never felt powerful. I had never considered that I might have the power to change a person's life, much less to change the world. But as I began to take stock of my life and the people in it, I realized that I did, in fact, have the power to change lives.

"I have the power to raise two children. I have taught them right from wrong to the best of my ability. I am not perfect, but I am a good mother. I have the power to impact those around me—younger women in my life—Monique and Shyla. I have the power to be a mentor to Samantha. I have the power to spread joy, to be a good listener, to help other women claim their power. And I am a steady and peaceful presence for Matthew. I have the power to quiet the noise of a stressful week, and be a safe harbor for myself." And I realized too, that my guilt was stupid and wrong-minded. "If I am to claim my power to be all of the things that I want to be and to be all of the versions of Diana that other people see, then I must have joy in my life. I must take care of myself absolutely first as a number-one priority. How can I hope to have anything to give this world if I am empty?" I asked myself. "This is especially important now," I thought, "with Matthew coming home tonight," vaguely aware that as usual, the Goddess Tribe topic for the month could not have been more fitting.

Late that night, I was awakened by the sound of the rattling and clanking of the old farmhouse door. I heard footsteps, and the bumping of a suitcase with one bad wheel in a tired-out procession down the hallway. The bedroom door creaked open revealing a sliver of light. I rolled over to see the silhouetted figure of Matthew sitting on the edge of the bed. I smiled groggily, reaching for his hand and said, "I'm glad you're home." When he leaned forward to enfold me in his embrace, I felt the familiar feeling, the warmth and the safety, that I had not fully realized was missing until that moment.

"Home," he repeated, exhaling as he hugged me tighter.

Happily together at last, with no worry of the Orlando project or any other taking Matthew away, we rode to work together on Monday in Matthew's old Wagoneer. I loved the smell of it and the sound of the motor and the enormous front seat. Everything about Matthew was as comforting and familiar as visiting family after a long absence.

As we pulled into the parking lot, I noticed that Monique was right behind us, but I didn't care. I was too happy to worry about what other people thought. Anyway, Monique already knew, and she was very happy for us. "So what if she sees us in the same car," I thought. "She already knows and thinks we're great together. Anyway, Matthew and I are in different departments, so according to the employee handbook, we're golden," I reminded myself a little nervously. As we got out of the car and walked together toward the building, Monique called out

"Good morning, you two!" and gave a friendly wave. "Yoga tonight?" she called. "Definitely!" I replied, smiling back at her. Matthew and I both waved to her casually and continued into the building. "See you later," Matthew said, planting a kiss on my cheek before strolling past the sea of cubicles toward the IT department. As he did so, my eyes lazily drifted across the room, landing on Jacob. Jacob's eyes met mine as his expression suddenly became that of someone who had just felt the first painful rumblings of food poisoning deep in the pit of his stomach. He looked away abruptly, pretending he wasn't looking, but his expression remained pained.

"Yikes, what's his problem?" I thought, searching my mind for a clue. "Matthew and I are in different departments. We can date under company rules. It's a non-issue," I thought as I continued to scan my memory. "I wonder if he's jealous?" I pondered, as I remembered the sudden awkwardness when he dropped me off after the Leadership Conference. "Could he have been trying to ask me out?" I wondered. Him being my boss instantly made that idea totally inappropriate. "Maybe that's why he was acting so strangely," I thought. "He couldn't ask me out unless I agreed to move to another department. That would certainly be an awkward situation to be in," feeling a glimmer of understanding and empathy for him.

Although I felt bad for Jacob, I was glad that he had not asked me out, because I would have said no, remembering how I had yearned to be with Matthew in his hotel room that night; how I had gone to dinner and ridden in the car with Jacob in order to appear professional. All the while, he was trying to figure out how to ask me out. Jacob, not understanding how much I had already fallen for Matthew, would have been embarrassed and humiliated. I would have said no to a date with him, and we would have shown up at work, pretending it never happened, thereby creating an even bigger awkward situation. "It was all better left unsaid," I reasoned. "I'm sure his disappointment will blow over in a day or two."

For the next few weeks, Matthew and I were inseparable. We rode to work together. Each morning, I would wake up early for my run, and come home to find Matthew waiting for me in the kitchen, with breakfast made. I went to yoga a few nights a week with Monique, while Matthew preferred the gym. Afterward, he would pick me up at the juice bar next door. We usually cooked dinner together unless we were feeling too lazy. Nights like that called for take-out or sandwiches in front of the TV. He went home to his place a few nights a week. Often, I would end up there anyway. Together, we fell into a blissful routine. I felt comfortable in my new life. I felt right as rain.

One day, while I was working on a new social media account, Jacob came by my cubicle. "Diana, can I see you for a second, please?" he asked, gesturing toward his office. I felt queasy as I immediately fell into "what did I do wrong" mode. I ran through a mental list of possibilities as I followed him to his office, but I couldn't come up with anything. I had been doing a pretty good job in the months since my first Goddess Tribe meeting and I felt that Jacob was generally happy with my performance.

"Have a seat, Diana," he said, gesturing to the empty chair facing him. I sat down and primly folded my hands in my lap, not knowing what to expect.

"Diana, we're a relatively small firm, but we're experiencing steady growth," he began excitedly. "Now, we've just today brought on a big client," he paused for effect, "a very big client." I nodded my head and leaned slightly forward in order to appear more interested than I really was. "It's Florida Innovative Energy Resources!" he proclaimed with pride as a wide smile overtook his usually serious expression. "Oh, that's great," I smiled, continuing to nod at him, while making a mental note to Google this company ASAP.

"I believe in rewarding hard work," he continued, raising his eyebrows, "And Diana, I've got to say that you've been doing a great job for us. You're really heading in the right direction," he said, giving me two very nerdy thumbs ups.

"Thank you, Jacob. I appreciate that," I said, wondering where this was going.

"So, I've decided to turn the account over to you to manage," he said, clapping his hands together.

"Oh wow, thank you!" I said, genuinely appreciating his confidence in me. "And of course, this is going to mean an enhanced work load for Diana, so it's only right that this comes along with a raise," he said, smiling and handing me a document to sign.

"An enhanced work load for Diana," I thought, "who talks like that? He's very handsome, but bless his heart . . . all the charm of a turnip."

I smiled at the figure, aware that this would help a great deal with Ava's college tuition, not to mention, repairs to the farmhouse.

"Thank you, Jacob!" I said, smiling.

"Just one more thing," he said tentatively, "I need to ask you to stay a little late tonight to go over the analytics. Shouldn't be too late, and we'll order dinner!" He said 'dinner' in an upbeat way as if eating takeout in the office was a great reward.

"Okay, sure, I can do that. And thank you, again," I said.

"Congratulations, you deserve it," he said, shaking my hand as he guided me out of his office.

That evening when I returned home, I pulled a letter from the mailbox. It read:

Dear Ms. Davis,

Thank you for your application to the Teen Harbor Mentor Program. Here at Teen Harbor, we encourage hard-working, creative, and spiritually-minded adults like yourself to use your gifts to mentor children and young adults in need. In order to move forward in approving your application, we ask that you participate in a group interview and psychological evaluation.

Your interview is scheduled for:

October 20th at 10:00 a.m.

Please allow several hours in order to complete the process. Most candidates find that the evaluation takes about five hours.

Thank you and we look forward to meeting you in person!

Sincerely,

The Teen Harbor Evaluation Team

If I'm being completely honest, I'll admit that I wasn't very excited about getting the letter at first. Matthew and I had settled into a pleasant routine together, and I liked my freedom. I was enjoying having no commitments outside of work, and now with the new account and the raise in salary, I was going to be very busy. "Maybe too busy to volunteer at all," I considered.

"Hey, that's great! It's about time. I was beginning to think they'd forgotten about you," Matthew said, reading over my shoulder.

"They're really understaffed. It's a wonder they can be so thorough," he said, shaking his head slowly. "But it's a good thing. It's important to check for crazies! You have no idea the kind of nut-jobs that are out there wanting to work with kids. I'm talkin' Craa-zy!" he said, raising his eyebrows and wiggling his fingers above my head for emphasis.

"You're looking pretty crazy to me right about now. I don't think their process is thorough enough." I teased, putting my arms around him and resting my chin on his chest.

"A few of us slip through the cracks," he smiled. "That's how I know they'll take you." He laughed, kissing my forehead. I rolled my eyes and pretended to try to wriggle away from him. He held tight, pinching my side, right where I'm most ticklish. I giggled and squirmed and poked his ribs. This exchange quickly degenerated into laughing fits and mushy smooching in the kitchen. Anyone watching would have barfed, but it was my idea of heaven. Such is love.

"But seriously, Diana, you're doing a good thing. I'm proud of you. The girls at the center really need role models. Smart, powerful, gorgeous women like you," Matthew said, resting his hands at the small of my back. There was that word again—"Power"—and I knew that he was right. "I can be a role model. I have the power to help girls in need," I thought to myself, remembering Maymie pointing to me and saying, "you are that woman," when she told us that we all had the power to change the world. "And I am that woman," I thought to myself.

"You're the best," I said, "How did I get so lucky?"

October 20th was a Saturday, so it was no problem setting aside five hours for the evaluation. Although there were many ways in which I would have preferred to spend my Saturday, especially with my enhanced work load, I understood the importance and was eager to complete this last step in the mentorship process. However, the day I received the letter, a little voice inside my head began whispering, "What if I fail? Matthew will know, and I will be totally humiliated." Day after day, it continued. "They'll be judging me. They will ask about the divorce. They will ask about my children. They might even ask if I've had bouts of depression." The nagging little voice was relentless. I tried to quiet it through yoga and meditation. That worked for a few hours, but it always returned with more scenarios for me to worry about.

I imagined a panel of doctors in white coats. All men, seated stiffly behind a clean white rectangular table. They would all wear glasses with which they could look down their noses at me while asking embarrassing personal questions. I would be seated alone in the middle of the room in a cold, rickety, metal chair.

"Now, Ms. Davis," the first one would ask, "when was the first day of your last period?"

"What's that got to do with . . . ," I would begin.

"Please just answer the question, Ms. Davis," he would interrupt.

I would give my best guess and he would scribble notes in a white notebook.

"Are you 100 percent sure about that?" he would ask accusingly, looking up from his scribblings.

"Um?" I would try to think, furrowing my brow.

"What about bowel movements, Ms. Davis? Are they regular?"

"Mostly?" I would reply, confused.

"Irregular bowel movements can be a sign of drug abuse, Ms. Davis. Are you a drug addict?" The next doctor would ask, leaning forward.

"Uh? No," I would then stammer.

"Are you having sexual relations with one of our other mentors, Ms. Davis?" the third would ask probingly. In my imagination, this one would have a strong southern accent.

"Fraternization can lead to drama. We don't like drama, Ms. Davis," he would drawl, raising an eyebrow and shaking his head disapprovingly.

The vision always ended the same way. The last of the doctors would then take out a giant stamp and ink pad from under the table. His sole purpose was to, very theatrically, stamp "REJECTED" on my file and point to the bright red exit sign which illuminated the door.

Fortunately, the reality was much less frustrating. I arrived in the reception area and gave my name to a smiling young woman behind a polished wooden desk. She was young and stylish with a hipster afro and tortoise shell cat glasses. She wore a white V-neck t-shirt underneath a blue button-down with the sleeves rolled up, faded pedal pushers, and flip-flops. Upon the desk were family pictures, a potted African Violet, and a little wooden plaque which read "Everything Begins with a Dream." A silver Buddha figurine sat in the corner upon a stack of bright pink sticky notes.

"Welcome to Teen Harbor, Diana. We're really happy that you applied to the mentorship program," she chimed. "I'm Taylor Welch," she said pointing to her name badge. "I'm a social worker and I'll be on your evaluation team," she said extending her hand to shake mine. "I'm not sure if anyone's told you, but the first step is the psychological evaluation. It's an online multiple-choice evaluation," she began. "Follow me and I'll help you log on to the test site," she said as she led me into a sparsely furnished office with one small desk, a chair, and a computer. A large plastic fern sat forlornly in the corner.

"Have a seat, Diana," she said. As I sat down, she reached over me and began typing in the login information. "Okay, Diana, now answer everything as truthfully as possible. You may notice that many questions repeat, just continue to answer truthfully and you'll do fine," she instructed.

"Okay, thanks," I said.

"Oh, and one more thing," she remembered. "This test can last hours, so if you need the restroom, it's that door there," she said, pointing to the shabby gray door directly across from me. "And don't worry, you will be the only person in this room after I close the door. When you're finished with the test, click the "send" button and then come get me. I should be at my desk," she said. "Any questions before you get started?" she asked, her golden eyes wide with expectation.

"No . . . thanks," I smiled feebly, dreading the hours to come.

As I began the test, I noticed that the questions seemed to be targeted at specific disorders—anxiety, bipolar disorder, substance abuse, violence—and a section on depression. They asked, "How often have you experienced these symptoms in the past six months?" I was not bipolar, did not have a problem with substance abuse, or with violence. But when I came to the section on depression, I knew that I should lie. I had gotten out of my fog about four months ago. So technically, I should answer yes to those questions. But would doing so disqualify me from the program?

"How often were you very anxious, worried, or scared about a lot of things in your life?"

"How often did you feel fear, guilt, shame, or blame yourself?"

"Have you lost interest in activities that you used to enjoy."

"Have you experienced significant weight gain or weight loss?"

I had been lost, anxious, worried, scared, and guilty. I had stopped doing all of the things I loved. I had gained fifteen pounds in a very short period of time. But reducing what happened in my life to a few multiple-choice questions was not a fair assessment of me. After meeting my Goddess Tribe, I had done a complete one-eighty. Remembering my sad self, shuffling around my messy farmhouse in that big gray robe, when the little old church lady knocked on my door relentlessly. That turned out to be one of the best days of my life. Another would be the day that I met Maymie.

"No, I am not perfect," I thought, "but I have gifts to share and I am going to share them. I am not depressed. In fact, I was never clinically depressed. I was sad. That's what I was—sad, because I had good reasons to be sad. I will not be labeled or diagnosed for feeling sad. Too often in our society, people are told not to be sad. If a loved one dies, if a loss is experienced, if you get divorced—sadness is a part of life. There is a beauty to sadness. Moving through it, really letting yourself feel it; letting yourself sob, if that is what's called for. Experiencing a broken heart and then to come out of it on the other side. There is strength in that; in making it through and pulling yourself out to see the sun again.

"I am healthy and whole, right now," I said to myself, "I have come out of sadness to be better for it. This multiple-choice assessment can kiss my butt," I thought and checked the box marked "Never, in the last six months."

After a couple of hours, I had finally finished all of the questions. I clicked "Send" with a sigh of relief and laid my head on the cold keyboard. I was now actually looking forward to the panel questions.

"Taylor?" I said, as I turned the corner into the reception area.

"All done?" she asked. "We're just about ready for you," she said grabbing a folder and making her way around the desk. "We'll just be down the hall in the conference room if you want to follow me," she said, gesturing to the hallway. "Diana's here," she said as we passed the kitchen. The three people who had been chatting casually by the coffee machine slowly sauntered out and followed behind us.

Once we were all seated, I was offered coffee or water. I chose water, noting that caffeine would probably make me jittery and I did not want to appear jumpy or nervous. The panel was decidedly different from the one I had imagined in my self-imposed nightmare. First of all, they were all much younger than I had expected—probably all in their twenties or early thirties. Secondly, they seemed like nice people. I'm not sure why I was expecting mean judgmental people to be the type to want to work with homeless teens. "Of course, they're nice," I thought, quietly amused at my earlier panic.

"Hi, Diana," a young woman at the head of the table began, "I'm Sylvia Nash and I'm the psychiatrist on staff here. I basically oversee the Teen Harbor program." I noted that Sylvia Nash looked very young to me. It seems that as I get older, people in their early thirties start to look like teenagers. She was tall and fair with large brown eyes framed with thick eyelashes. She wore her light brown hair lazily twisted on top of her head with a hair clip. She wore a green button-down shirt and jeans.

"Diana, thanks for coming in and devoting such a large part of your weekend to this process," she continued. "But it's of the utmost importance that we screen every adult who enters the mentorship program."

In all, the panel was made up of one man and three women. After Sylvia's initial remarks, they went around the table and introduced themselves. Taylor, whom I had met earlier, Amber Richey and Dillard Tompkins were recent college graduates with degrees in social work.

"So, Diana," began Sylvia. "We already know that you have passed the mental health evaluation. The results of that test are immediate and more of a formality than anything. We've read your application, references, and background check. We know about you on paper," as she tapped her long fingers on the folder in front of her, "But we want to hear from you why you want to be a part of the mentorship program," she said looking up from the folder expectantly.

Quietly relieved that I passed the mental health assessment, I began to formulate my answer in my mind.

"Well," I began, "I want to work with the teenage girls in order to guide them in their school and career choices and to help them claim their power as young women."

"Claim their power?" asked Dillard, "What does that mean?" Dillard was about five feet six with a slight frame. He reminded me of some of Ian's teenage friends. He was textbook hipster, his fashion icons being a cross between the Vikings and the Lumberjacks. He sported a red flannel shirt, skinny jeans, and a gigantic beard. Perched atop his head was the inevitable "man bun," a lone lump of hair resting sadly above the shorn sides.

I smiled at him. "Bless his heart. He'll hate himself for that hairdo one day," I thought.

"It means that women have a tremendous amount of untapped power. Most girls do not feel powerful at all. I would imagine that would be doubly true with homeless teenage girls," I said matter-of-factly, "and I want to help them to realize it. To realize and tap into their power, and to be proud of who they are."

"That's so important," said Amber sincerely, moving her glossy dark hair off her shoulders. "It's very common for girls at risk to be influenced by . . . bad people. People who see their vulnerability as something they can exploit. That's often how women wind up in prison. A bad guy scopes them out. In their eyes, he seems to be the first person to love them, to tell them they're worth something. By the time he shows his true colors, it's too late: sex trafficking, drug dealing, theft—the girl is set up and she can't escape."

"It's our mission to keep these kids safe from people and situations like that—to give them hope, and," she paused, clearing her throat, "a future."

"Tell us more about how you can empower girls, Diana," said Sylvia.

"By teaching them their worth and being a role model for them. Feminine Power lies in Faith, Strength, Judgment, Love, and Imagination. It lies in the ability to cooperate versus compete. I want to teach these girls to have compassion rather than fear, to find peaceful solutions rather than fight for supremacy, to negotiate rather than confront, to create rather than destroy. Women are caregivers, life-givers, and home-makers. And by homemaker, I don't just mean someone who does not work outside of the home, I mean that women make a house into a home, no matter what they do professionally. Women make homes." I paused, knowing I had become a bit too passionate but also that I had meant every word.

The four of them quickly looked at each other. After a few quiet remarks, Sylvia turned back to me and said, "Welcome to Teen Harbor! We look forward to having you here."

Chapter Fifteen

November in Heritage Springs Florida is a pleasant time of year, with temperatures lingering in the 70s. Preparations for the upcoming holidays were on my mind. I was looking forward to cutting a real Christmas tree with Matthew, a ritual I had not enjoyed since childhood. With Jonathan and the kids, it was just easier to use the same artificial tree year after year. We had a nine-foot Balsam Spruce and a six-foot white pine. We had fun with decorations, though. One year, I decorated the white tree with blue lights and baby blue ornaments. It was magical and frosty, and I loved it. It served as a second tree and stood in the hallway upstairs, illuminating the night with its blue glow. Today's color for the November meeting was light blue. I scoured everything all the way to the back of my closet, finding my powder-blue chiffon halter dress with a fitted waist and flared skirt. It was ultra-feminine, hitting just below the knee, and it was also a size six. I had not worn it in over a year, but it was all I had in light blue, so I put aside my hesitation and decided to try it on. I was pleasantly surprised that it fit. It was tighter in the bust line than it had been before, giving me a curvier silhouette, but I was happy with the result. Although I hadn't specifically set out to lose weight, just getting back into life, exercising, and making an effort to eat healthier had helped.

I felt pretty and feminine and I was suddenly glad that Matthew would see me leaving wearing this dress. He and the kids were already outside working on the boat and I could hear their chatter and laughter from afar. I grabbed my purse and car keys and walked out on the porch. I could see them beside the old boat, sanding and scraping, laughing and joking, with Matthew supervising. "He is so good with them, such a kind and compassionate soul," I thought, as I watched them from my vantage point on the porch. Just then, Matthew looked up and saw me watching him. He smiled a big smile and waved before he started walking in my direction.

"Wow," he said as he approached, "someone looks awful pretty," he said, as he reached the bottom step.

"Why, thank you, sir," I said, smiling. As he came closer, he put his arms around my waist and I wrapped my arms around his neck and he easily lifted me down to where he stood.

"Where are you headed, pretty lady?" he asked.

"I have a meeting the first Saturday of every month. I told you that. Don't you remember?" I responded.

"Oh, right, you did tell me. I just can't think of anything but how pretty you look," he said, leaning in for a kiss. "Are you free later? We could do something for dinner. I'll take you wherever you want to go."

"I was thinking that I would cook tonight. Why don't you come by for dinner around seven o'clock? You can bring the wine," I said, gently touching his face.

When he smiled his eyes got those adorable crinkles at the corners and I couldn't help but kiss him again.

I drove to the meeting thinking of Matthew and little else. We were still in the early stage of a romance where everything is nerves and butterflies, thinking of the other person incessantly, dreaming about them, imagining that everything you do throughout your day would be better if you could just share it with them. If that were a permanent state, the human race would be clinically insane by now. I imagined people in high-pressure careers like astronauts and brain surgeons going through their day, queasy, constantly checking their texts, and dreaming of their beloved.

"Oops," the astronaut on the International Space Station, would say dreamily, "looks like I've killed us all. Better send one last selfie to my boyfriend before we explode. I just love him."

I walked into the meeting room to the scent of apple cinnamon and caramel. Scented candles were lit to commemorate autumn, and the room was decorated with purple, lavender, and light blue flower arrangements. Today, the place was a sea of beautiful ladies in powder blue. It was a perfect color for the Goddess Tribe. Chiffon, silk, and linen twirled and fluttered around the room. Light blue pill box hats, gloves, pearls, earrings; they really pulled out all the stops for these meetings. And that's part of what made them so much fun. I loved seeing what the ladies would wear.

I noted that the dessert for today was blueberry cheesecake. I took a small serving, paying more attention now that I was magically able to fit into my size six dress again.

"Hello there, Diana," said Zelda "This is Sarah. I don't believe you have met," she said gesturing toward a petite young woman to her left.

"Nice to meet you, Sarah," I said, smiling.

"A pleasure to meet you, Honey," she responded. Sarah looked like a China doll. She had smooth golden skin, rosy cheeks, and long wavy black hair, which was tied loosely at the base of her neck with a blue satin ribbon. Her large blue-green eyes were fringed with thick black eyelashes and her lips were rose pink. She wore a light blue cotton dress with a wide satin sash, and flared skirt. She had tied her glossy black hair with a matching bow. She reminded me of the Victorian China dolls that Ma used to buy for my doll collection.

"How's the cheesecake?" Sarah asked, her large eyes gazing expectantly.

"Oh, it's amazing," I complimented. "Did you make this?"

"Why yes, I did, Diana, and I'm so glad you like it," she said, smiling.

"I think I'm going to be doing some cooking for the holidays," I said. "Can I have the recipe?" I asked.

"Well," said Sarah thoughtfully, "It's a family recipe. My mother was very protective of her recipes," she continued. She paused, considering my request. "But I guess it would be alright if I share it with you—as long as you promise you won't share it with anyone else," she said, "unless you have a daughter," she said, moving toward the chairs, "that would be okay too."

"Ladies in blue!" called Maymie loudly. She wore a light blue and silver kaftan with a matching turban. On her ears, she wore large silver hoops and, on her wrists, dozens of silver bangles. "You all look so lovely today and I can see that this is going to be a very special meeting." She paused to allow the chatter to quiet down.

"Make your way to your seats because we are going to be talking about one of my favorite Goddess Powers and that is the Power of Imagination," Maymie continued.

"That's right, take your seats, ladies," she said looking at Patsy and Virginia who were still chatting near the dessert table. "Let's all get ready to join in prayer."

Patsy and Virginia, giggling, quickly hustled to the two remaining open seats just in time to join hands in prayer.

I am The Goddess Power of Imagination.

Divine Spirit dwells within me, blessing me with a boundless ability to visualize all good.

With my strong Faith, I open my mind to visualize the world as it should be,

A world filled with Peace, Love, Prosperity, and the birthing of Divine Ideas.

I reject all thoughts of hate, fear, and lack.

For these thoughts do not serve me and they do not serve our world.

Instead I focus my Goddess Energy on all that is good.

I use my imagination to see my world ruled by the Power of Love,

And for this I am grateful.

Amen.

"And now Lil is going to tell us more about how we can use our Goddess Power of Imagination to shape our world," Maymie said, nodding to Lil as she took the podium.

"Good morning ladies," chimed Lil. "Y'all know that I'm presenting the Power of Imagination. But I bet you don't know who the Goddess is," Lil smiled, placing her Goddess poster on the easel.

A beautiful Hindu Goddess wearing a gold crown sat smiling happily on the poster board. She had brown skin and her long black hair was adorned with pearls. In her hands, she held an ornately carved sitar. A peacock sat contentedly at her feet in the idyllic river valley as the sun set over the mountains.

"Saraswati is the Goddess of music, the arts, and learning. Since all of these activities spring forth from imagination, as well as feed the imagination, Saraswati is the perfect Goddess to represent The Power of Imagination. Saraswati literally means 'she who leads to the essence of self-knowledge.' So, how can we get to the essence of self-knowledge through our imagination? Well, as creators, we use our minds to form thoughts. As we allow our minds to drift, to expand, and to explore, our imagination becomes boundless.

"As we practice quieting our minds through meditation, we gain the ability to control our thoughts, bringing forth only good thoughts. We practice imagining the life we want and the world we want. As we practice imagining, we begin to visualize. When we visualize what we want in great detail, we send a powerful message into the Universe that will be reflected back at us. Now, would anyone like to try a visualization exercise?" Lil asked.

Predictably, all hands flew up. I slowly raised mine, too, and was immediately called on.

"Diana! Great! I'm glad you volunteered," Lil cheered.

She then asked me to relax, focus on my breathing, and close my eyes so that she could guide me through a visualization.

"Diana, describe a scene that makes you happy," she said.

I thought for a moment and was immediately blocked by mental chatter. I began to worry about Jacob and deadlines and managing my time. Ever since Jacob had given me the new account, I had been going in early and staying late. My exercise routine was thrown off, and my free time was now filled with Teen Harbor commitments.

Then suddenly, an idea sprang forth and it would not quit. I saw it all clear as day.

"I think that I would like to start my own business," I said dreamily.

"Okay, Diana, tell me, what does that look like?" Lil asked.

"I am in my own office and I am wearing a business suit," I said.

"What kind of business suit?" she asked.

"It's—it's light gray, a gray jacket and pants and a white top.

"What does your office look like?" Lil asked.

I began to describe a floor in a refurbished old building downtown. It was all sort of modern shabby chic. The walls were exposed brick that had been painted white. The light fixtures were large, oddly-shaped industrial-style exposed bulbs—one round, one oval, one elongated, etc. The desks were long white tables and there was a large whiteboard on the wall. Everything was white—white computers, white coffee pot, white mugs. The floor was gray and white distressed hardwood. Next, Lil took me through a visualization of talking with a client, assigning tasks to employees, and then scheduling a meeting in my imaginary office. Everything was so real that I felt like I was already working there.

"Now, Diana, how do you feel?" Lil asked.

"I feel excitement. I feel motivated. I feel as if I am already there," I said.

"That's exactly how you should feel, Diana! And now that your mind has experienced it, you will live it. You have sent your vision out and it will come back to you. You have the power, through Imagination, to shape the substance of the universe," Lil said. "You can open your eyes now. You did great!"

After visualizing my own business, I began to visualize the month ahead. I realized that I missed big family holidays. The thought began to formulate of me happily hosting a big

Thanksgiving feast at my farm. I couldn't wait to get home and tell Matthew all of my new plans.

Thanksgiving morning, the farmhouse kitchen was all business. While I prepped the turkey and ham, Ava and Ian skillfully took care of the side dishes. With family recipes that we knew by heart, the kitchen ran like a well-oiled machine. Years of practice had made my kids into excellent cooks. I can't think of anything more gratifying than passing traditions that I love on to my kids and knowing that they love them too. We made a variety of Ma's dishes. Cheese and potato casserole—a very fattening family favorite—contained cubed potatoes, sour cream, sharp cheddar cheese, and loads of butter. Shredded sharp cheddar and butter squares were added to the top for crisping under the broiler. Next was sweet potato casserole. With brown-sugared pecans, marshmallows, and the obligatory butter squares placed on top for browning, it was as sweet and delicious as a dessert, but had passed for a side dish for decades. I made Southern Ambrosia, a decadent fruit salad of pineapple, orange, grape, cherry, coconut, and pecans. But it's hope of being remotely healthy is dashed by the delicious addition of whipped cream, and yes, sour cream. Of course, we had traditional mashed potatoes, loaded with heavy cream and butter and blended to fluffy perfection with Ma's old Kitchen Aid mixer. I also made skillet cornbread for the stuffing.

"It's called dressing—turkey and dressing," Ma used to scold us teasingly. We grandkids had somehow been corrupted by modern media into calling her beloved "dressing" by the word "stuffing", a term that was for Yankees and was just plain wrong. This act was almost as traitorous as requesting a Pepsi rather than a Coke.

Samantha watched us, wide-eyed, from her seat at the kitchen table. Teen Harbor had appointed me her mentor, so she was happily spending most weekends on the farm. She loved the peace and quiet, the silence of nothing at all but the occasional coo from the chickens on a warm afternoon. She enjoyed gathering eggs and taking long walks around the property. She loved reading books in the hammock.

I had given her the job of folding the burgundy cloth napkins into fan shapes and tucking them decoratively into each glass. This was a job that Ma had given me when I was her age. Although twelve years old is plenty old enough to cook, Thanksgiving Day is not the day for lessons. We were on a tight schedule. The guests would be arriving soon and there was still a lot left to do. With such a large crowd, I did not have enough matching plates to go around. So instead I chose a few plates from each of Ma's many sets for a mix and match, shabby-chic look.

Matthew, Noah, and Bryan tidied up the front porch and moved the large wooden picnic tables together. Seating for fifteen would only fit outside, so I had asked that they set up under the big oak tree. Luckily, we were blessed with perfect weather: seventy degrees, breezy, and a crystal blue sky. The farm was the ideal setting to join together with family and friends for a dinner of giving thanks.

The guests began to arrive as the last of the dishes came out of the oven. The house was warm from the oven and fragrant with the smell of Thanksgiving turkey, ham, and all the fixings. Mike and Mayra, with their two children, brought a huge pan of macaroni and cheese with a toasted breadcrumb topping. I took the heavy dish from her grateful hands and placed it on the buffet table.

"Wow, Mayra, that looks amazing! I can't wait to try it," I said.

"Me too! But I'm so nauseous, I don't know if I'll want any," she said miserably.

"I'm so sorry to hear that. Are you coming down with something?" I asked, concerned.

"Yes," she said, placing her hand on her abdomen. "I'm coming down with my third child," she smiled.

"How exciting!" I exclaimed! "When are you due?"

"The end of July," she said, smiling meekly.

"Well that is just such great news! I can't wait to meet him or her," I said, hugging her.

"What's this about a new baby?" Matthew asked cheerfully shaking Mike's hand.

"Yep, number three and also our last," Mike laughed. Matthew patted him on the back jovially, but when he looked away, I saw his expression change for the briefest moment.

Paul and Marco showed up shortly afterward with a large flower arrangement featuring yellow sunflowers and burgundy mums.

"Thank you, Paul, these are gorgeous" I exclaimed.

"Thank Marco," he said, smiling in his partner's direction, "this is all his work. But, I made the apple pie," Paul said, proudly placing it on the counter. The golden top crust was expertly embellished with a braided edge and tiny leaves.

"Wow, you really went all out on this! It's too pretty to eat," I said.

"Oh, we're eating it!" laughed Marco. "I've been looking forward to apple pie *a la mode* all week."

Well, we have lots to choose from," said Ava, but the good news is that you don't have to pick just one. You can try them all," she said, pointing to the array of dishes covering the counters and buffet table.

Just then, Shyla came in holding a pecan pie, and behind her, Monique with the pumpkin pie. "Hey, I passed the boat on the way in. It's looking good, Matthew," said Monique.

"Tell the boys. They've really been working hard on it," he said. "They're looking forward to taking her out on a fishing trip. It's all they talk about," he said, nodding in their direction. Noah and Bryan smiled good-naturedly, began punching each other in the arms, and then ran back outside. Rough-housing, as Ma used to call it. When we grandkids got too big to play boisterously in the house without breaking something, she told us to take our rough-housing outside.

We set the outdoor tables and placed the pans and platters overloaded with an array of delicious foods on the long gold table runner. Matthew carved the turkey as we watched with expectation. It truly was a Thanksgiving feast. Then we each took turns saying what we were thankful for. Mostly, we were thankful for each other, for family, for friends, and for the blessing of the perfect day. "This might be kind of cheesy," said Matthew, "but I wanted to give you something to mark our first Thanksgiving together," he said, handing me a small burgundy box. "Thank you so much," I said touching his cheek. "But I didn't get you anything."

"You have given me everything," he said, suddenly very serious.

Inside the box was a tiny silver cornucopia charm. "How cute!" I exclaimed. "I'll put it on my bracelet right now," I said giving him a kiss.

Just as we were ready to dig in, a bright yellow butterfly landed right on the end of Samantha's nose. I quickly snapped a picture. "this will go in my new family album," I said thankfully. "It's just as I imagined it would be, but better."

Chapter Sixteen

The first Saturday in December, I woke up early for my run. I stepped outside to the new day, reveling in the cool morning air. As I embarked on my usual route, I was happy that I was now able to cover more distance and that my body was getting stronger. The silence of the morning was nourishing as my only focus was the tempo of my shoes rhythmically hitting the pavement and my breathing. When I walked into the house, sweaty and breathless, Matthew was waiting for me in the kitchen.

"You're up early," I said, happily.

"Hey pretty lady, how was your run?" he asked, walking over to kiss me.

"It was great," I said breathlessly. "Beautiful morning! I was just about to start my meditation. Would you like to join me?" I asked hopefully.

"Sure, can I drink my coffee first? Is that allowed?" he asked with a child-like smile.

"Of course, I think I'll have some too after I shower off," I said.

We sat outside and sipped our coffee, just like we had, that first morning together, and I couldn't help but recall how far we had come together in just a few months.

When our coffee cups were empty, we walked into the living room and sat cross-legged on the rug.

"What do you do?" he asked.

"You sit in silence."

"What do I think about?"

"Nothing. If you can, anyway. When thoughts come up, bless them and release them and go back to focusing on your breath," I instructed.

"It is when sitting in the silence that divine ideas come to you. Listen," I said.

"Okay," he said, "I could really use some divine ideas."

I set a timer for fifteen minutes—a long time for a beginner, but I knew that Matthew was comfortable with silence. So, I figured he would be a natural.

During my meditation, ideas of starting my new business floated in and out like feathers on the breeze. "My time would be my own," I thought. "No more late nights at the office with Jacob." I smiled at the thought. "I would have the freedom to bring Samantha to the office and more time with Matthew. Maybe eventually Matthew will come to work with me in a partnership." I thought about that and how it would look and how it would feel. I smiled in the silence, knowing that it all felt very right.

As I approached the church , Maymie threw open the door to greet me. She stood there regally, like an Egyptian goddess. She wore a long flowing dress of yellow gold silk georgette, embellished with metallic bronze and gold leafy vines. It was beaded, sequined, and bejeweled in gold; made to sparkle and shine on the outside as much as Maymie sparkled on the inside.

Today, instead of her signature turban, she had set her hair free; dark mahogany corkscrew curls flowed wildly this way and that way down her back. She had braided gold silk ribbon into her hair in the form of a headband. I had never seen her hair before and she was truly beautiful with her gold leaf earrings, she sparkled from head to toe. Her cheeks and eyelashes glowed with the finest hint of gold glitter powder, illuminating the gold flecks in her bright green eyes.

"There's my Diana!" she said warmly as she embraced me in a big hug. As I hugged her back. I felt comforted, like a girl being enveloped in the embrace of her mother.

"I'm so glad to see you," she beamed. "And how is your friend? What was his name? Matthew?" she asked.

"You remembered!" I said with surprise. "He's great." I smiled. "We're great!"

"I am so happy to hear that, Diana. You deserve it. You know that? This is your time!" she chimed.

"Come on in here, let's get this show on the road!" she said, taking my hand and leading me inside.

As I entered the room, I was completely transported to a different place and time. The tea room was decorated for Christmas with abundant embellishments of gold. Gold ribbon and glittering gold ornaments were woven through the garland. A red and gold tablecloth covered the dessert table atop which was a golden candle centerpiece encircled with balsam and red bows.

The room smelled richly of balsam, pine, and cinnamon with a fresh Christmas tree glowing warmly in the corner. It was adorned with red, gold, and green ornaments and lit with the warm glow of gold lights. The topper was a gold angel, which, to my amusement, resembled Maymie. "Whomever bought that must have just had a fit when they saw it," I laughed to myself.

All of the ladies were dressed in varying interpretations of gold. I, not actually owning a gold dress, had chosen a beige polished cotton halter dress with a gold belt, earrings, and bracelet. On my finger, was the engraved gold band from Ma's jewelry box. Luckily, I also owned a pair of gold sandals to complete the look. As I beheld the breathtaking scene, I saw Isabel approaching. She was a vision in a gold satin sheath dress and gold strappy sandals, her glossy black hair hanging loose down her back.

"Hello, Diana, so nice to see you today!" she said warmly, touching my arm.

"Isabel, you look beautiful . . . as always," I said, giving her a peck on the cheek.

"I made the caramel flan today, Diana, so you have to try it. Es . . . ,", she paused, trying to find the words in English, "Is the recipe of my grandfather, so I know you will like it!" she laughed as I followed her toward the beautifully decorated table.

There stood Francie and Nancy smiling at me. As I approached them, I noticed that although they seemed nothing alike, they were about the same height and build—both tall with similar features, but different coloring. "Maybe they're cousins," I thought, "In small towns, families stick together," remembering Lil and Patsy.

"Hi Diana, so nice to see you," said Francie, "How does your garden grow?"

"It's doing well." I smiled. "We planted jalapeno peppers, bell peppers, okra, eggplants, and cherry tomatoes. It's my first attempt at Florida gardening, but more importantly, the kids are learning life skills. Growing your own food is very empowering," I said.

Francie smiled and nodded back. She was wearing a long flowing gold chiffon kaftan embellished with green and brown flowers and butterflies. While Nancy looked like a fashion model in her signature pantsuit. Today she was a stunner in gold polished cotton. The pants were tapered at the ankle flattering her shiny gold pumps.

"Ladies, we're doing something special today, so we've got to get started. Please have a seat so we can begin," Maymie announced. "Please join hands in prayer."

Today I affirm Divine Understanding.

Together in Divine Understanding we see

The Goddess within each of us

We see

The Divine being sitting next to us

I AM

The Divine being sitting next to you.

I understand and know the Goddess Spirit is inside me

Is a part of me,

Is me.

Is you.

There is no separation.

Only oneness.

Through Divine Understanding

I receive Divine Inspiration

I know my purpose.

I know what I must do.

And for this I am so grateful.

And so it is.

Amen.

"As you know, our power today is Understanding, presented by Iris. And let's also take a moment to thank Isabel for the wonderful dessert," Maymie said, smiling from Iris to Isabel.

Iris reached the podium with her Goddess poster and quickly set it on the easel.

"Hi, everyone," she said sweetly, her strawberry hair framing her fair face. "Today I'm going to introduce the Goddess Concordia," she said, gesturing toward the poster. "Concordia is the Roman Goddess of agreement, understanding, and marital harmony. She is a beautiful golden goddess with long flowing golden hair. She wears a gold toga and she loves her jewelry," Iris laughed. "She wears a gold grape leaf arm bracelet and a gold caduceus necklace," she said pointing to poster.

Concordia wore a necklace that looked to me like a medical ID necklace. "I've fallen and I can't get up," I thought, stifling a giggle.

"Actually, the caduceus is the symbol of peace," Iris said, smiling at me. I wondered if my thought had been aloud, but no one else seemed to notice.

"She also holds a cornucopia in her left hand, as a symbol of prosperity and an olive branch in her right, which signifies peace or reconciliation."

I was taken aback to see the cornucopia symbolism after receiving that odd little charm from Matthew. "What a coincidence!" I thought cheerfully. I always seemed to have strange synchronicities surrounding the Goddess Tribe.

"Concordia represents divine understanding in that she represents agreement and understanding. However, divine understanding is a little bit different from what you are probably thinking. As in Maymie's prayer, we see that divine understanding is our own understanding that we are divine beings. That I am a divine being and that each of you are too. That means that there should be no strife—only peace because we are one in divine spirit. If I fight with you, I am fighting with myself. If I am rude to you, I am rude to myself. If I wage war on you, I am waging war on myself. So, in our divine understanding, we see that Peace is the only way and that Love is truly the answer. As a divine being, your speech should always be positive and uplifting because your words have great power. When you are angry and lash out with angry words, all of that bad energy will circle back around and guess who it will hit? You, that's who," she said, looking around the group.

"Do you understand that in your daily lives, you are a divine being?" she continued. "That your annoying boss is also a divine being? Or that your ex-husband's new wife is a divine being. The politicians you see on the news are divine beings—although they may not know it. Do you see the divinity in all? And how do you remind yourself?" she asked the group.

Hands flew up with great zeal as they usually did at these meetings.

"Francie, how do you remember your divinity?" Iris asked.

"I meditate in my garden every single morning. It centers me and helps me to control my thoughts throughout the day," she said enthusiastically.

"Prayer and meditation are both key to accessing the Goddess within. Does anyone start the day with gratitude and prayer?" she asked.

All hands flew into the air, except for mine. I had started to meditate in the mornings, but I had not been as committed to gratitude and prayer.

"Isabel?" Iris called.

"I start my day with gratitude for my home, my family, my health and all of the blessings that I have. I pray and I say 'thank you' for everything that I can think of. I thank the workers who made the products that I use. I thank the inventors who created life-changing machines. And when I feel gratitude, I feel that I am on a better vibration—a frequency of love and abundance. Gratitude has changed my life," she said.

After Iris' presentation, Sarah stepped up to the podium.

"And now ladies, we have something a little different today. We are going to do a short meditation, just breathing in the silence. So, let's all take a cleansing breath in," she said, breathing in deeply, "and out," she said, slowly through her exhale. "Just relaxing in the silence. Focus on your breath. Thoughts may come and go, just return to your breath if your thoughts become unruly," she said as she breathed deeply.

In the utter silence, I breathed in and out. My mind began to wander, as I saw myself walking through my sunflowers. I began to pick the large flowers, one by one. As I reached the end of the row, I saw Ma there. "You're all weighted down, Sugar Plum," she said. "You need to let some of that stuff go." As she said the words, I realized that my arms were empty and the sunflowers had turned into monarch butterflies and were now flying up and up and out of view. I suddenly felt as light and free as the butterflies.

"Now, when you're ready, open your eyes," I heard from my reverie.

I looked around sleepily at the ladies in the room as we awakened from our collective trance. Just then, Maymie approached the podium.

"It's Christmas time, a time for divine understanding. This is the time when we affirm Peace on Earth, and goodwill to all. We exchange gifts of love and we take special time for our loved ones," Maymie said. "So of course, we have gifts of love for each one of you ladies," she said, smiling. "The gifts are now on the back table. Just go and think on it, the gift you choose is guaranteed to be the right one," she smiled, gesturing toward the table.

We moved slowly toward the table, each woman carefully selecting a box wrapped in shiny gold paper. When I reached the table, I closed my eyes and moved my hand over the remaining gifts. I felt something drawing my hand downward, and I carefully touched the box, then took it in my hand. When I unwrapped the box, my eyes grew wide in astonishment. There, just as in my daydream, was a monarch butterfly—a gold stained glass ornament, tied with a silk ribbon.

Christmas on the farm was going to be quieter and more reverent than our enormous Thanksgiving feast had been. After the Goddess Tribe meeting, I decided that the peaceful and reverent mood was what I needed for this traditionally stressful and hectic holiday. After Iris' talk, I decided to try to stop swearing, so as to keep negative energy away from me. I also pared down my Christmas list to one or two gifts per person to reduce stressful spending. My guest list this year included only Matthew, Ava, Ian, Samantha, Noah, and Bryan. I decided on a free and easy food setup. I had ordered the meal from a local store and at noon, I started transferring the meal to serving dishes.

"Oh, diddle-toot!" I shouted as one of my good serving bowls slipped out of my hand, crashing into pieces on the kitchen floor.

"Did you just say 'diddle toot'?" Matthew asked, suppressing a laugh.

"I'm trying not to swear," I stammered. "It just came out. And yeah, I did. I said diddle toot! That's so stupid, right?" I said, suppressing a laugh.

"You've got to come up with a better replacement," he said, giggling.

I looked up from the mess and saw him standing there with a broom, smiling at me. We both started to laugh uncontrollably.

"I love you," he said, putting his free arm around my waist.

"I love you, too," I said, leaning my head against his chest.

After we cleaned up the mess and recovered from our laughing fit, we put all of the food on the table—ham, mashed potatoes, gravy, green beans, mac-n-cheese, and pies— there for the picking all day long. On my small buffet table, I had Ava and Ian put out cheese, crackers, and a vegetable tray. For plates and utensils, I used the fanciest plastic-ware that I could find, because the last thing I (or anyone else) wanted to do was wash a sink full of dishes.

It was an overcast day, so I turned off the lights in the house and lit candles for a warm golden glow. The boys sat around the TV playing the new Xbox, while Ava showed Samantha how to make polymer clay jewelry. Luxuriating in our domesticity, Matthew and I lounged on the couch with glasses of eggnog. The golden fireplace flickered, a silent accompaniment to the classical Christmas music playing in the background. The effect was transportive, just as this month's Goddess Tribe Meeting had been. There in the corner was our fresh-cut tree. On it hung my new golden monarch butterfly glinting in the firelight.

Chapter Seventeen

As I opened the door to enter this month's meeting, I was delighted to see that the holiday décor continued. This month, the room was decorated for a celebration of the New Year—all in silver. With this month's color, very appropriately, being silver, all of the ladies were rocking it in silks, satins, and metallics. With my raise in pay, I had taken myself shopping the week before and had happened upon a little boutique in town which was having a big clearance sale. Everything in the store was 70 percent off. And wouldn't you know it, I found the perfect silver dress right there hanging in the window—a pretty satin sheath dress that fell just above the knee. I paired it with gray pumps. On my finger, I wore Ma's silver spoon ring, one of my favorites.

"Happy New Year to my favorite Goddesses," Maymie boldly proclaimed from the podium. Maymie looked like a New Year's Goddess in a silver lamé toga and matching sandals. This time, she had silver leaves braided into her long mahogany hair. She wore a silver laurel leaf arm bracelet and matching earrings.

"If you have not tried the coconut cake yet, by all means get some. It is truly heavenly!" she said, sweeping her long curls off her shoulders. As she did so, I noticed that these last two meetings, Maymie seemed younger, freer, and even bolder, if that was possible.

"Now ladies, let us all join hands in prayer for the Power of Will in this glorious new year," Maymie continued.

I am the power of Will

Using my talents for the greater good,

Following my divine calling.

Through prayer, I discern the best path to follow

As I reach understanding in my mind, body, and spirit,

My power of will propels me toward my divine purpose

With good judgment, zeal, and imagination,

I boldly take steps to become the person I am meant to be

I powerfully claim all that is mine to do

And I follow my spiritual path in grace and steadfastness.

For inner knowing, I am grateful.

And so it is.

Amen.

"Today, the Power of Will is presented by the lovely and talented Patsy."

We all clapped as Patsy took the floor, holding her goddess poster high for all to see. "Happy New Year!" Patsy said smiling brightly, "Who wants to make this year the best year yet?" she asked.

All hands flew into the air to the sounds of "YES!" and "WOOT!"

"Still a wild bunch of church ladies," I thought, smiling.

"Our Power as you know is Will and our Goddess for this month is Ishtar," she said as she placed the Goddess poster onto the easel.

"Ishtar is goddess of love, beauty, sex, desire, fertility, and political power. I chose Ishtar to represent Will, because each of these is dependent upon Will in some way. What is Will? First it requires divine understanding in that you must understand your own inner divinity in order to hold to Will. Will is being steadfast in the pursuit of your calling," Patsy said. "How do you receive your calling?" she asked.

Again, all hands were in the air.

"Your calling comes from divine inspiration," said Sarah.

"And how can we receive divine inspiration?" Patsy asked.

"Divine inspiration comes through listening, through silence, through meditation," Sarah replied.

"That's absolutely right, Sarah." Patsy said smiling. "So how can we apply Will in our own lives? What is the practical application?" she asked, pointing to me.

"When you are called by divine inspiration to act on a great idea, you have to be steadfast and unwavering in pursuit of it. Because if you love the idea and it feels right to you, then it is your path. It is your purpose, or at least one of them," I said confidently, finally starting to understand this stuff.

"Yes!" said Patsy enthusiastically, "I like that you said that you have to love the idea and it must feel right to you. All divine inspiration comes from the Power of Love. If the idea is not based in love, it is not divine, and you should not act on it," Patsy continued.

"For example, if a voice in your head is telling you to burn your neighborhood down, by all means, stop what you're doing and seek therapy right away!" Patsy shouted from the podium as the ladies chuckled.

"The voice of the divine only asks you to do good. It never asks you to cause harm or suffering," she said. "And how are you going to do that in this wonderful New Year, Diana?" she asked.

"Well," I said, "the idea to start my own business has been nagging at me, but I have not pursued it yet. Right now, it's just an idea. But the more it pops into my head, the more I understand that I have to do it. I am called to do it," I replied.

"So, I am making lists and setting goals to start my business this year," I said timidly.

"I think that's great, Diana!" Patsy encouraged, sensing my lack of confidence.

"Let's all hear it for Diana, the business woman!" she cheered.

And of course, the ladies of the Goddess Tribe all cheered enthusiastically.

One evening, I was sitting at the kitchen table coming up with logo ideas when Matthew pulled up a chair.

"Hey, these look great, Diana, I didn't know you were an artist," he said with surprise.

"Well, I dabble," I said.

"I like this one, he said pointing to the one I had just finished. "Monarch Designs and Marketing. Very official sounding," he said. "Speaking of official, have you filed your papers with the state yet?"

"Um, I don't know how to do that," I said, suddenly realizing that there was a lot to starting a business that I hadn't considered.

"Here, it's easy. You can do it online," he said, turning the laptop toward him. "I have a side consulting business, but I don't do a lot with it. I just keep the records up to date for when I decide to jump in with both feet. You're much braver than I am," he said, touching my hand.

He pulled up the state website on the laptop and showed me the online form. I filled it out, paid the fee, and that was that. Next, I printed my certificate.

"Hey, I've got just the thing," Matthew said, retrieving an empty picture frame from the coffee table. I carefully placed the certificate in the old frame and stood it on the table in front of me. We both gazed at it proudly.

"The Articles of Organization for MONARCH DESIGNS & MARKETING, LLC," Matthew said. "I am so proud of you," and he kissed my forehead.

Suddenly I heard Patsy cheering, "Let's all hear it for Diana the business woman!" and I was filled with excitement.

The following weekend, I planned on going to look at possible office spaces for my new business. I tallied my budget and scanned real estate ads for something I could afford. I came up with three buildings to visit. Matthew offered to drive me, and I gladly accepted, figuring that his company would make the trip much more pleasant. I also decided to bring Samantha along so that she could see my process from the start, and maybe even apply it to her own life one day. As we entered the first building, I immediately noticed a chemical smell, similar to pesticide and ammonia . . . or cat pee. As I looked around, I saw orange stains on the ceiling tiles, mysterious burns and discolorations on the cheap linoleum floor. When the landlord took us to see the office itself, we entered through a crooked door with a broken door knob. The office appeared to be recently vacated, still having scraps of paper on the floor and the odd broken surge protector here and there.

"I don't think this is quite right for my . . . brand," I said apologetically. "But thank you for your time," I said, grabbing Samantha's hand and backing out of the office hurriedly.

The second place we drove to was a seedy office building/ motel with hookers standing out front. "No," I said flatly, my disappointment obvious to Matthew, "just keep driving."

By the time we reached the third and last location, my spirits were quite low. This looks like it's going to be a really nice building . . . when it's finished," Matthew said.

I looked out the window to see a lovely modern building about eight stories high. But as Matthew said, it was still under construction. We walked into the sales office and were greeted by an energetic young woman named Mandy.

"As you can see, the building is still under construction, but we have a demo office that we can show you. Right this way," she said, her stylish heels clicking on the polished gray hardwood floor.

As we entered the office, I sucked in a deep breath. The walls were exposed brick that had been painted white. The light fixtures were large oddly shaped industrial style exposed bulbs—one round, one oval, one elongated, and so on. The desks were long white tables and there was a large whiteboard on the wall. Everything was white—white computers, white coffee pot, white mugs. "This is just as I imagined it," I said in disbelief. "Matthew, I saw this place. I . . . this is the place," I said, not finding the words.

In hearing that, Mandy instantly perked up, "We're running a special this month for our first renters. If you sign today, you get half price rent for the first year. Are you forming a start-up, Diana?" she asked. "Yes, I am," I smiled. "Well, the special price will give you plenty of time to get the profits flowing in, right?" she said enthusiastically, her large white teeth bright against her shiny red lips.

"Is the furniture included?" Matthew asked.

"Well, not normally, Mandy wavered, "this is a demo," she paused, putting her hand to her forehead as if deep in thought, "But, I can include this furniture," she said placing a hand on one of the chairs, "if you sign the contract today. We are scheduled for completion in June, and then you will be able to move right in. First and last holds your space," she said confidently.

"Okay," I said, "how much will that be today?" I asked.

She told me the figure and I must have made an odd face because Matthew took my hand and said, "This is a good deal, Diana, I'll help you with the deposit."

"No, no, it's okay," I said. "I want to do this and you're right. It is a good deal," imagining my ultra-modern office, where I would invite potential clients and show off my fancy white desk, white laptops, and white coffee mugs. I pulled out my checkbook and filled out the check. Then into Mandy's expectant hand went all the money I had in the world.

Chapter Eighteen

February is my beloved birthday month and I look forward to it each year. I love that I was born on Valentine's Day and get the benefit of pink roses and red hearts; not to mention the chocolates. So I was more excited than usual to prepare for the Goddess Tribe meeting which had added an extra 'holiday' to my favorite month. I opened Ma's jewelry box to reveal my abundance of gemstones and selected a large round peridot ring. Today the color was chartreuse, and the ring was perfect. But I guessed that the bright yellow-green color would be a challenge for anyone to pull off, except for Maymie, of course. She always looked good, whatever the color.

However, having just spent my savings for the deposit on my new office, I didn't have the money to go shopping. Instead, I found the perfect chartreuse Goddess dress hanging in the window of a thrift shop as I drove home from work. The tag said $15, and honestly, I didn't even want to spend that much, but it was so pretty. I asked the attendant if I could try it on and she kindly removed it from the manikin for me.

As I continued to shop around the color-coded racks, some-thing pretty and pink caught my eye. I walked over to the pink section and reached for the garment. A pale-pink, satin trench coat, perfectly tailored, and my size. I immediately put a terri-torial hand on it as my heart started to pound. I pulled the tag closer, revealing a very expensive designer label. I was so excited that I was beginning to get confused. I eagerly grabbed the coat off the rack and claimed it as mine before even trying it on. When I found a mirror, I put the coat on, noticing again, that the original price tag was still affixed. My eyes almost popped out of my head as I read $825 on the tag, noting that the thrift store price was six dollars. I tried on the coat and, to my utter glee, it fit perfectly. I took the pretty dress and my newly claimed designer coat to the dressing room where I tried them on together. Chartreuse and pale pink—the effect was charming. The fabric of the dress was light cotton with eyelet lace in green chartreuse. It was sleeveless with a scoop neck and fitted waist. It tied at the waist with a sash of pink satin and it flowed exquisitely just below the knee. This, my absolute least favorite color, became my absolute favorite dress. The colors were bright and joyful, childlike and carefree.

I was on cloud nine at this simple shopping experience. I could not believe my luck. As it turned out, it was red tag day, so when I took my purchases to the cash register, the cashier jovially rang them up and said, "That'll be ten dollars and fifty cents." I looked at her in disbelief and quickly paid, almost laughing aloud at my good fortune.

On Saturday, when I entered the church, I could already smell the aroma of roses and I followed the scent into our magical tearoom. The colors seemed more vivid and the smells more vibrant. As I looked around the room, I saw the source. The ladies had generously decorated the room with dozens of fresh pink roses which were illuminated by pink mini-lights that were strung around the room. The pink glow intensified the visual of a dozen ladies all decked out in chartreuse. I removed my pink satin trench coat, hanging it on the coat rack before joining the group.

The dessert was chartreuse macarons. They were the cutest things I had seen in ages. The cookie was chartreuse with a pink strawberry filling. And on the top of each one, the creator had expertly sculpted three tiny pink roses, complete with little green leaves. I had seen roses like these before—Ma used to make them in bulk. She would line cookie sheets with parchment paper and carefully create each little rose with her pastry bag and frosting tips. She would often let me help her on rainy days if I was misbehaving due to boredom. Giving me something to focus on with the promise of getting to taste my work usually did the trick to settle me down.

"These are adorable," I chimed.

"Aren't those precious," said Zelda, her face all smiles. Zelda was as cute as the cookies in a satin chartreuse sheath dress. It was sleeveless with a dropped waist, pink sash, and ruffled skirt. "Virginia made them. She's really got a talent for baking and cake decorating. Her little catering business is doing real good," she chimed in her southern accent, taking a dainty bite of the cookie.

"She's doing well because she follows divine law," interrupted Maymie.

Maymie seemed to have permanently put aside her wardrobe staple, the turban, in favor of letting her spiraling locks flow freely. Today, she wore a chartreuse and gold headband with a vibrantly printed chartreuse, pink, and gold kaftan. Her earrings were pink and green lotus blossoms and she wore a large lotus blossom necklace to match. Her sandals were sparkling gold. From head to toe, she was as bright as the sun on the first day of spring.

"And speaking of divine law, that's what we are here to talk about. Let's get started, ladies," she said abandoning the dessert table and quickly making her way to the podium.

"Ladies, Angels, Goddesses," Maymie boldly declared. "Today our lesson is Law and our presenter is the lovely Sarah."

"But first, let us join hands in prayer and bless this wonderful meeting," Maymie said, closing her eyes.

I am Divine Law

Invoking the powers of Judgment and Understanding

In order to identify Divine Inspiration.

Through prayer and meditation, I receive my calling.

Through Divine Will, I remain steadfast, acting on Divine Inspiration.

According to Divine Law, I must do what I am called to do.

When I act in accordance with Divine Law, I live in Joy, Abundance, and Love.

If I act against Divine Law,

I struggle.

I suffer.

And I wage an uphill battle against myself.

With this Great Knowing, I forge ahead joyfully heeding my call,

And living life according to Divine Law.

For this, I am grateful.

And so it is.

Amen.

Maymie then gestured maternally to Sarah, who began to shyly make her way to the podium. She still reminded me of a China doll with her creamy skin and thick black hair. Today, she wore a chartreuse polished cotton dress. It had a scalloped neckline, full skirt, and cinched waist, tied with a blue-green satin sash. The dress was very young-spirited with little puffed sleeves and a crinoline underneath the skirt. She wore blue-green ballet slippers on her small feet. Her long black hair was tied with a blue-green ribbon, perfectly matching her large eyes.

"Also, let's be sure to thank Virginia for the dessert! She did such a wonderful job," Sarah said, trailing off as the applause and cheering overtook her speech. Sarah paused primly waiting for the group to quiet down and cleared her throat. Then she began to speak quietly but with an authority and self-assurance that surprised me.

"Today, as you know, our topic is Law. The Goddess I have chosen to represent our lesson is the Egyptian Goddess, Ma'at. She is Goddess of Truth, Morality, Law, and Order," Sarah said, pointing to the Goddess poster on the easel.

Ma'at was pictured as an Egyptian goddess with long straight hair. On her wrists, were cuffs which attached two long feathered wings to each of her outstretched arms. She wore a red dress, green necklace, and an ostrich feather in her black hair.

"When we speak of Law and Order in the Universe, we are in the realm of the Goddess Ma'at. She keeps the world from chaos, by enforcing order in all things. From the growing seasons, to religious practice, to laws of civilizations, Ma'at presides over order and balance in all things," Sarah continued.

"However, in keeping Law and Order in our own lives, although one can look to the Goddess Ma'at for help, the answer lies within each of us. Divine Law says that we each are unique spiritual beings and that we each have a purpose to fulfill. It states that no one else can fulfill your purpose, therefore it is paramount that you discover it and act on it."

"Please understand that divine purpose is based in the Power of Love and must serve the greater good. Your divine purpose will always help others in some way. But how can you find your divine purpose, or calling?" Sarah asked.

Hands flew into the air as if on cue.

"Zelda, how do you find your purpose?" she asked, nodding to Zelda.

"You've got to pray and meditate on it," Zelda replied in her southern drawl. "Your calling will come to you, but you probably already know it deep down in your heart. Your divine purpose is simply doing what you love and using it to serve the greater good. So, if you love teaching, then you should teach. If you love the arts, then you should do something to expand the arts in your neighborhood. If you love taking care of people, you should be a doctor or a nurse, or work in a hospice. If you love children, then you should work in a field that allows you to help and serve children," said Zelda.

"Yes, Zelda, you are exactly right," Sarah replied happily.

"We all know that if you break the law, you are punished. You may have to pay a fine, perform community service, or go to jail. However, if you break divine law, you are only punishing yourself. You are in fact creating hardship for yourself by not following your correct path. You are in effect, making a hell on Earth for yourself. Your eternal punishment comes in the form of failure, frustration, and struggle in life because you are living out of balance. You are out of order, so to speak, and you are breaking the law," she continued enthusiastically.

"However, the key to your prison cell is in your own hands. To free yourself, you must heed your calling and follow your divine inspiration. If you don't know what that is, you must ask through prayer and meditation. The answer will come to you. Most importantly, your divine calling is always something that you love. If you don't love it, then it is not your calling. Seek your calling and it will be presented to you," Sarah concluded.

"Now, do you ladies have any questions?" Sarah asked.

I timidly raised my hand.

"Yes, Diana, go ahead," she prompted.

"Sometimes it's impossible to act on our divine purpose because we've got bills to pay," I said, thinking of how I would love to quit my job now and work for myself full time. Then I could bring Samantha to the office and also mentor more girls. I could offer internships and workshops for young women in business.

"That's always the question, Diana. It's difficult to do, but you must act in Faith in order to achieve your goals. All of the Goddess Powers that we have discussed work together to get you where you need to go in this life. Faith, Strength, Imagination, and Love go hand in hand to propel you to achieve your divine purpose. If you know that you can do it. If you imagine yourself doing it. If you love it. If you have Faith that you can. Then the universe will move mountains to make it happen, because that is divine Law, my dear."

"Happy Valentine's Birthday Day," Matthew said, smiling.

I noted the excited tone of his voice and the accompanying wide smile.

"Thank you," I said suspiciously, as I took the card from his outstretched hand. "But it's not until tomorrow."

"Just open it!" he said, now almost hopping in place with expectation. He was still so impossibly cute.

"Okay, okay, I'm opening it," I said, as I tore through the red envelope.

As I opened the card, out fell two tickets for a dinner cruise in Costa Grande, Florida, a beach town about an hour south. It was a tourist destination with miles of white sand, luxury hotels, and plenty of tiki bars that served drinks with umbrellas.

"A dinner cruise, how romantic," I said, wrapping my arms around him.

"And," he said, pausing for effect, "We're staying all weekend at the Costa Grande Resort! I got us a suite!"

"Oh, Matthew, that sounds amazing! How did you know I needed a weekend away?" I asked.

"You've been working really hard lately with the long hours at work, plus starting the new business. You need some R&R and I want to take care of you," he said, kissing my forehead.

He was right of course. I had been putting in extra hours in the office at Jacob's insistence. Meanwhile, my nights were occupied with planning my new business—writing the business plan, mission statement, financial goals, and researching prospective clients. I had even managed to score my first client. I had been hired to create the website and logo for my favorite salon. Unfortunately, Matthew and I had not seen much of each other in the last few weeks. I could tell that it bothered him—my sudden, yet unintentional, neglect. I was just feeling so overwhelmed lately. In fact, I had planned on staying home this weekend to work on the logo. Suddenly, I felt a twinge of worry in the pit of my stomach.

"Everything okay, Diana?" Matthew asked, concerned.

"Of course," I chimed, "I'm very excited about this weekend. I can't wait!" I said, leaning in for a kiss.

That Friday at work, I tried to hurry through all of my work so that I could leave on time. I even worked through lunch. Matthew and I were going to drive to Costa Grande right after work. Our bags were waiting in his car so that we could maximize our time at the resort. I watched the clock like a hawk, and at five o'clock on the dot, I practically sprinted for the door.

"Diana," Jacob called. "Got a minute?" he asked.

My hopes for getting out on time were immediately dashed because I knew that a minute in Jacob's vocabulary could easily time-warp into an hour or three.

"Sure," I said, "but I'm leaving town for the weekend, so I really can't stay late tonight."

"Oh, this won't take long at all, I just want you to take a look at this marketing analysis for a client," he said, handing me what looked like a one-hundred-page document.

"Um, Jacob," I began, kneading my forehead, "I'll have to take this with me and review it over the weekend. We planned on leaving town right after work. Our suitcases are already in the car." I said, gesturing to Matthew, who was fidgeting uncomfortably beside my empty cubicle.

Jacob suddenly got that same look of nausea on his face that I had seen before. "Oh, okay, just . . . ," he stammered, "Just look at it over the weekend then. I would like a synopsis on Monday morning."

"Are you kidding me?" I thought. "Who does that? Who just works all weekend every weekend? Oh, that's right," I said to myself, "Jacob does." Although I greatly appreciated the raise in pay, the sooner I could get my own business underway, the better. Jacob was a nice guy, and he had put a lot of faith in me, but I was beginning to feel taken advantage of. I knew that he did little else besides work. But that wasn't my style. I liked my new life and I wanted to enjoy it.

We drove into the porte cochère of the five-star Costa Grande resort in Matthew's old Jeep Wagoneer. The enormous

hotel was flanked by a manmade lake and a perfectly manicured golf course. The ocean served as its backyard. The long
driveway was lined with majestic queen palms. As we rolled to
a stop, one valet opened my door while another jovially gathered our bags from the back and piled them onto a luggage
cart. We received our room keys and complimentary glasses of
champagne from the front desk and took the glass elevator to
our floor. As the elevator rose, we could see the stadium sized
conservatory, which housed an entire eco-system of Florida
plants, fish, and birds. Fully grown Palms, Sea Grape, and Royal
Poinciana trees with their bright red blooms forested the area
inside the hotel. Walkways adorned with tropical flowers and
quaint wooden bridges took guests on an adventure through a
jungle populated with tropical birds and over streams teaming
with aquatic life—fish, turtles, and frogs. Our suite was large
and open with an ocean view on one side and a balcony for
the conservatory view on the other. In the gardens, an impossibly large banyan tree twisted upward, spreading its expansive
canopy just above us.

"Fancy shmancy!" I said twirling to view the luxurious
room in its entirety. "I don't think I'll need to leave this room
all weekend," I said, flopping onto the king-sized bed.

"We could take a walk through the gardens tonight, and
then eat dinner on our balcony, if you like," Matthew said,
"but we can stay here for a little while too," he said smiling as
he flopped onto the bed beside me.

Later we walked hand in hand, strolling leisurely along
the wooden walkways through the neatly manicured indoor
jungle. The air was warm and misty, and occasional calls of
tropical birds encroached on the silence. I couldn't help but
feel a little bit like I was a specimen inside a giant terrarium.
Despite the ostentatious waste, I had to admit that the place
was breathtaking.

"So, how's the business plan going?" Matthew asked as we stopped on a bridge to watch the giant koi converging in a small indoor lagoon.

"Slowly, but surely," I said. "I've been so busy with my paying job, that I haven't had the time to work on my dream job very much lately." As I said the words, I remembered what Sarah had said to me at the Goddess Tribe meeting and felt a pain in the pit of my stomach.

"You've been spending a lot of time at work, that's for sure," Matthew said, shaking his head. "You and Jacob are practically work spouses," he said, laughing uneasily.

"It's not his fault," I said protectively. "Jacob has placed a lot of faith in me in giving me this new role. Quite frankly, I need the money and I'm lucky to have this chance. Jacob lives for work. It's all he has. I'm afraid he doesn't understand the rest of us. He thinks that I am as committed to Web Synergy as he is. Honestly, I feel bad about keeping my plans a secret from him, but I know that what I'm doing is grounds for firing," I said, pausing.

"You don't owe him anything, Diana, he works you like a dog," Matthew said, with a hint of annoyance in his voice, or was it jealousy?

"Matthew, what I mean is that I like Jacob as a person. He's a nice guy and a good boss. He doesn't work me like a dog. He respects me and as a result, he expects a lot from me. I am honored that he gave me this new project. I had very little experience and he is taking a chance on me," I said. I wasn't exactly sure why I was defending Jacob, because deep down, I did feel like he was working me like a dog. But I didn't want Matthew to see me as helpless. I wanted it to be my choice.

"But, yes, you're right. For me, working every weekend and staying late most nights, it really doesn't feel right. I want to make my own decisions and yes, spend less time at the office.

I want to try it on my own. It's like I'm called to do it and at the same time I'm frustrated that I don't have the time to do it—to really throw myself wholeheartedly into starting my business. It's like real life keeps getting in the way," I said shaking my head.

"Diana," Matthew said, taking my hand, "if you need to borrow money to get things off the ground, I'm here. I'll help you. You could quit at Web Synergy and just focus on Monarch. It could be your baby! I won't interfere. Why not?" he said expectantly.

I was surprised by the offer. It was certainly tempting to borrow money from Matthew, quit my job, and just focus on my own business. But, if I did that, how would this be any different than my relationship with Jonathan? "No, it's got to be mine. All mine. I've got to earn this myself," I thought.

"No, Matthew, but thank you," I said, touching his cheek. "I need to do this myself. It's important to me that I build this my way. I've never taken a leap like this before and it's—it's everything to me. And when I am successful, I want to know in my heart that I did it. That I was strong enough and smart enough to do it on my own."

Matthew was visibly disappointed that I turned down his offer. I also suspected by his speech and his manner that he was jealous of Jacob and I imagined that his offer to help me had more to do with getting me away from Jacob than with actually helping me with a small business loan. We strolled back to the room in silence and ordered our dinner on the balcony. Down below a group of butterflies fluttered upward, and came to rest on the branches of the banyan tree.

"Are you mad?" I asked Matthew.

"Mad? No, of course not. What would I be mad about?" Matthew asked.

"That I didn't accept your offer. You understand, right?" I asked.

"Diana, don't worry about it. I only want you to be happy," he said reassuringly. "I know you can do this on your own. I just want to be there for you if you need me."

"How did I get so lucky?" I asked.

"I'm the lucky one," he said smiling back at me.

On Saturday, I packed my sunscreen and Matthew and I headed to the resort's private beach. I felt a twinge of worry that I should be working on that report for Jacob, but after Matthew made the crack about how Jacob works me like a dog, I felt self-conscious bringing work with me to the beach. We exited the dimly lit and air-conditioned hotel, into a world of lightness and sunshine. There were no clouds to block the sun, so the day was so bright it hurt my eyes. The sand was glowing white, the sky was bright blue, and the water a beautiful azure. Everything was so illuminated that my eyes involuntarily squeezed shut as I dug in my bag for my sunglasses. Finding them added a rose tint to my perspective as seagulls glided motionless, hanging in mid-air. They rode to nowhere on the constant breeze that blew in from the crashing waves. The air smelled of tropical tanning oil and salt water.

"I'm going in," I called to Matthew as I dropped my bag and ran for the blue waves. I dove in, forgetting my sunglasses. I plunged into cold salty water. Waves crashed over me and tiny seashells bubbled up with sand and found their way into my swimsuit. When I came up for air I saw my sunglasses drifting helplessly just out of my reach. I watched them go, allowing my eyes to adjust to the unimaginable brightness of my world.

"Matthew, come in!" I shouted, waving at him.

He waved and ran to the water, diving into a wave as I had done. We swam out past the breaking waves and bobbed leisurely in the crystal blue water.

"Thank you for this weekend, Matthew. This has been a wonderful birthday," I said, swimming close to him.

"And you know what I love the most?" I asked coyly.

"I don't know, what?" he asked.

"Doing all of this with you," I said. "There's nowhere I'd rather be right now but right here with you."

We spent the remainder of the day at the beach, swimming, sunbathing, and drinking margaritas, before going back to the room to get ready for our dinner cruise.

That night I put on my little black dress and we took the hotel shuttle to the marina. The luxury yacht was all lit up with neon lights that cast a purple glow onto the white table linens. Waiters in white tuxedo jackets made the rounds with champagne and hors d'oeuvres while a jazz quartet played softly. Surprisingly, the dining area was only about half full, allowing for a quiet table all to ourselves and an unobstructed view of the ocean. The other passengers onboard were mostly tourists, happily sampling from the buffet and making frequent visits to the open bar. A German couple, clad in matching pink and orange hibiscus print chattered happily, as they sipped their umbrellaed Piña Coladas from coconut shells. The ocean breeze was pleasant and cool, and as the sun receded in all its pink and orange brilliance, I reached for my shawl to ward off the night chill that soon overtook the warm day.

The buffet was immense, offering pretty much anything that anyone might want to eat—ever. I happily chose lobster, a baked potato, and a caesar salad. When I got back to our table, my eyes grew wide when I saw Matthew's plate. It looked as if he had, in fact, loaded his plate with every dish from the buffet.

"Hungry?" I laughed.

"Starving," he said, smiling back at me slyly, a look that made me giggle.

After dinner we took a walk around the boat and stopped to enjoy a view of the moon over the ocean.

"Diana, I have a gift for you," Matthew said, taking my hand.

"You didn't need to get me anything else, silly. This weekend has been the best gift ever," I said.

At that he pulled a small box from his pocket and opened it for me. Inside, was a sparkling diamond engagement ring. Immediately, my legs felt numb. I became sweaty and my full belly began to ache.

"Diana, I know that this may seem sudden," he stammered, "and you can take as much time as you like, but I know how I feel and there is no question in my mind," he began nervously.

"Diana, will you marry me?" he asked, his blue eyes sparkling with a hint of a tear.

"Oh," I said.

"You can think about it if you want to. A long engagement is okay with me," he said hastily. "I know it's sudden, but I also know that I only want you for the rest of my life."

"Matthew," I paused, taking his hands in mine. "You're right. This is sudden. I mean, I just got divorced," I said, trying to sound diplomatic.

"Over a year ago," he said reassuringly.

"And I'm just not ready to talk about marriage right now. In fact, I have to be honest with you. I may never be ready to get married again. I like us the way we are," I said, which I knew was the wrong answer to give this amazing and wonderful man. But I owed it to him to be truthful.

The look of disappointment on his face was almost unbearable. He wore it all right there on the surface and it was heart-wrenching to watch. However, I couldn't help but wonder if this sudden proposal had something to do with Jacob and I being so called 'work spouses.'

"Matthew," I said, touching his face, "You know that I love you. You are the best thing to ever happen to me. Maybe in a few months we can talk about moving in together. Maybe we will get married someday. I'm just not ready to say yes today."

"It's okay," he said sadly, "I understand."

For the remainder of the yacht voyage, Matthew was sullen. I tried to cheer him up by cracking lame jokes, and he, in turn, pretended to laugh. But the evening ended silently, awkwardly, and I yearned for things to be the way they were only a few hours ago.

We spent Sunday on the beach. It was another hot and sunny day. Small waves gently tumbled onto shore, tossing seashells onto the beach. Matthew lounged beside me while I attempted to review the stupid marketing analysis that Jacob had thrust on me at the last minute.

"Hey, what happens if you just don't work today?" Matthew asked. "I mean, you're going to quit in June anyway," he said, grabbing at the report.

"Yes, I'm leaving in a few months, but it's important to me that I do quality work for Web Synergy until my last day at the company," I said.

"Anyway, I haven't touched work all weekend," I said smugly.

"You're a good egg, Diana," he said, "If it were me, I'd tell him to shove this report up his—"

"Okay, okay, I get it," I said, taking the report from his grasp. "At least I get to review it here on this beautiful beach with you, instead of at the office," I said, putting my hand on his.

"Come on, let's take a swim," Matthew said, pulling at my hand. I felt so guilty about the night before that I agreed, abandoning my homework for frivolous play in the ocean.

When Matthew drove me home that night, I got out of the Jeep and walked around to get my suitcase. Matthew, ever the gentleman, was already unloading it and then he proceeded up the porch steps beside me. When we got to the front door, I stopped.

"Matthew, I think I want to be alone tonight. I'm going to be up really late working on this report I didn't do," I added a little laugh at the end, trying to make light of the situation.

Matthew breathed in and out in a way that I can only describe as a huff. I had never heard him do that. I had never upset him before this weekend, though. Now I seemed to be on a roll.

"Okay, I'll see you tomorrow," he said, planting a half-hearted kiss on my forehead before turning to go.

Chapter Nineteen

During the following weeks, my relationship with Matthew seemed different somehow. He felt distant, and I felt guilty and confused. I wanted to spend time with him, but when we did, our time together seemed strained and the conversation, clumsy. The sudden marriage proposal and my awkward refusal colored everything we did together. All the while, work and my new business were keeping me busy and I began to use them as an excuse to avoid Matthew. While I felt like I wanted a break, I also yearned to push the reset button and return to the week before Valentine's Day. Then, as if in answer to my prayers, Ava called with a pleasant surprise.

"Mom, I know this is short notice, but I forgot to invite you to Parent's Weekend," she began nervously.

"Oh, that's okay, honey," I began, "when is it?"

"It's in a few weeks," she said apologetically. "I'll email you the invitation. Do you think you'll be able to make it?"

"Oh, of course I can!" I said. "I'm looking forward to seeing you in your element!" I said happily.

"How is everything going?" she asked. "How's Matthew?"

"Oh good." I said, trying to sound natural. "And I've got my second client. So my new business is starting to take off too!" I said, changing the subject.

"I'm happy for you, Mom. Your life has really opened up. That's just what you needed," she said.

"Yes, I'm excited about it," I said, trying to sound positive. "And what I'm really excited about is seeing you soon!" I said, redirecting the conversation once again.

"Okay, I've got to run," she said hastily, "but I'll email you the details right away. Love you!"

"Love you too!" I said, feeling a sudden loneliness. My voice trailed off as I heard the line click on her end.

The following weekend, I awoke feeling relieved that my Goddess Tribe meeting was today. I felt nauseous and just downright bad about what was going on with Matthew. I was afraid that we had lost our spark and I really needed some wisdom from my Goddesses. Our color was appropriately cheery and one of my favorites—orange. I silently hoped that this event would brighten my mood to match the color. I had a favorite orange wrap dress, long banished to the back of the closet, that now fit me pretty comfortably, thanks to yoga and running. Although the bust-line was a little tight. I yearned to share my news about Parent's Weekend, my business, and my new clients. Mostly, I needed a boost. I was feeling down and losing my enthusiasm for all of the good things that were happening in my life. All of it boiled down to Matthew. I hoped that my tribe could help me with their wise and understanding words.

My mood continued to spiral downward as I approached the church and the gray sky opened up, sending a deluge of heavy raindrops to follow me as I sprinted through the parking lot. Now drenched, I entered the church to a burst of freezing cold air. Shivering, I pulled on the door to our meeting room and was greeted by a warm orange glow. The fireplace, which had sat empty and anonymous against the south wall of the building, now crackled with a welcoming fire. Warm orange mini-lights hung from the ceiling in a canopy and the flowers adorning the tables were orange mums. The scene brightened my attitude instantly as I bypassed the dessert table in favor of the fireplace.

"You've picked the right spot today," said Lil, removing her plastic rain cap which perfectly preserved her bubble hairdo.

"I love a nice fire," I said quietly, as I warmed my hands.

"Something wrong, Diana? You look downright melancholy!" said Zelda, seemingly appearing from nowhere.

"Oh, I'm just feeling sad today, I guess. Things are not so good with Matthew and I don't know how to fix it. I just want to turn the clock back," I said, shaking my head.

"What happened, Sugar?" asked Maymie with concern.

I recounted the story of my birthday weekend to them. I told them how he had planned a perfect weekend, how he had offered to give me the money to launch my business, how he had proposed, and finally, how I had turned him down on every offer. I also told them that he had demanded that I not work over the weekend and that he seemed jealous of Jacob.

"Well, Diana," Maymie began, placing her hand on my shoulder, "I understand why you don't want to get married this soon, but why did you turn down his help? Why not take the money he offered you?"

I was surprised by the question. It seemed a no-brainer to me that a feminist should not accept financial help from her boyfriend, but then I considered it at a deeper level.

What had I felt when he offered to give me the money? My thoughts traveled back to the moment when Matthew had offered to alleviate most, if not all of my stress and concern by just giving me money to focus on Monarch full time. I tried to relive the feeling that I had felt. It had been in the pit of my stomach. And it had felt familiar. It brought me back to Jonathan and his parents and how they had pressured me to marry Jonathan in order to solve all of my problems. How I felt that I had no choice, no power, and that I owed them all for the rest of my life. It was fear. Fear of repeating the pattern. Fear of owing someone for my life. Fear of rendering myself powerless.

"I was afraid," I said.

"I was afraid that my relationship with Matthew would turn into the same old thing that I had with Jonathan. That I would cease to matter, and that Matthew would be holding the money card over my head for the rest of our lives."

Maymie shook her head knowingly, as if reliving a memory herself. "Believe me! I get it, honey," said Maymie. "I had a bad relationship once upon a time ago, real bad. That man was mean as a snake, but when I found the courage to run away, my soulmate picked me up and dusted me off. We bought a little house and some land. Together we worked hard to make that old house into a home. We worked as equals and that's how we lived. And I was happy for the first time in my life," she said staring dreamily into the distance. "But if I had not accepted help when I most needed it, I would not have made it, Diana. Sometimes, when help is offered, it's just an answer to our prayers, and that's that," she said frankly.

"But enough about me," she crooned. "How is your relationship with Matthew anything like your relationship with Jonathan?"

"Well," I paused, considering. "It's nothing like my relationship with Jonathan. First of all, I was only twenty years old when Jonathan and I got married. I was still in college, and I was pregnant!" I said, my wounded pride bubbling up inside me. "To be quite honest, I was in a desperate situation and I felt cornered by Jonathan and his parents," I said, remembering my fear and loneliness from years ago.

"You poor thing," said Maymie.

"I felt as if I had no choice in the matter. I had to marry him and raise our child because I didn't know what else to do, and then I got lost. I became a wife and a mother and everything I wanted fell by the wayside," I said.

"It sounds like you're protecting your freedom and your self-expression—your ability to be Diana," Maymie said knowingly.

I nodded silently.

"But do you think that Matthew is going to want you to lose yourself? Think about it, Diana. You say you want to work for yourself. You say you want to set an example for young women, like Samantha. You say you want more time to pursue your interests. You are putting all of this out there, into the universe. And when it answers back with a gift, you say, 'No, thank you. I would rather bust my butt, ignore my loved ones, and complain about not having time to pursue my dreams.' Diana, the universe is overflowing with blessings, but you have to be open to receiving them as they come, my dear," Maymie said, patting my shoulder.

"I never thought of it that way," I said. "I've been so busy trying to control the outcome, that I have forgotten how to be accepting. In fact, I don't know if I ever knew how."

"Give it some thought, Diana. If Matthew is as wonderful as he sounds, I'm sure things will smooth over. Remember to have gratitude for the love you share and be careful not to take him for granted. He sounds like a real catch, Sugar," she said, smiling.

"Now if you ladies will take your seats, it's time to get started," she said, making her way to the podium.

The Power of Divine Passion flows through me,

Igniting my creativity, self-expression, and courage.

I thirst to express myself in Zeal.

Joyfully, I follow my spiritual path with enthusiasm

Denying the power of

Abdication,

Self-doubt,

Mediocrity,

And Conformity.

With much gratitude, I steadfastly pursue my Divine Calling.

Thank you, Sweet Spirit.

And so it is.

Amen.

"Ladies of the Goddess Tribe, today our Goddess Power is Passion and it will be presented by none other than the very passionate goddess, Zelda!"

All of the ladies clapped and cheered as Zelda stepped up to the podium with her goddess poster in hand.

"Today we're going to talk about Passion and the Goddess of Fire, Pele," said Zelda as she placed the poster onto the easel stand.

"Now Pele was a real firecracker, so to speak. In fact, her father almost banished her because of her hot temper. What finally did her in, though, was having an affair with her sister's husband! Oh yes, she was something else!" Zelda said enthusiastically.

"So, in searching the world for a new home, Pele decided to create the Hawaiian Islands and just hang her hat there for a while. Little did she know that her angry sister, the Sea Goddess, was hot on her trail and hellbent on tanning her hide!" Zelda recounted.

"A great battle ensued between the two sisters and Pele was killed. But being a goddess and all, she came back and still lives on Kilauea, causing volcanic eruptions to this day. Pele creates as she destroys and embodies fiery passion. For this reason, I chose her to represent the Power of Passion, Enthusiasm, and Zeal," Zelda said.

"Now how does the Power of Passion come in to our daily lives? I'm about to tell you how," she said coyly.

"We have learned about all of these incredible Goddess Powers—Faith, Strength, Wisdom, Love, Power, Imagination, Understanding, Will, and Law. None of them gets off the ground without passion. You have to feel it in your soul in order to make it happen. Wanting to achieve your calling or your divine purpose—wanting it sets the Universe in motion. But you must be passionate in your pursuit of it in order to bring it to fruition," she continued.

"When you feel passion for something, do not fight the enthusiasm that fuels your dreams. Instead, love it! Harness its power and fevered pace for your divine purpose. Unfortunately for Pele, she did not temper her passion with wisdom and good judgment. She hurt a lot of feelings and wound up dead at the hands of her own sister. On the other hand, when you use judgment combined with passion you will achieve your goal as joyfully and effortlessly as a flowing river. Just think, if everyone harnessed their passion and judgment to live out their dreams, we would change the world," she said.

"Now let's open it up for comments. Ladies, what are you passionate about and how are you using judgment to help you live your dreams?" Zelda asked.

"Diana," she called, pointing at me.

"I am passionate about starting my own business, but I'm afraid that I haven't been in the flow of things. I want to use my new business to mentor girls in design and technology. I want my business to provide a comfortable living for me and a legacy for my kids. Instead of reaching for my goal, I've said no to help. I've had less time to mentor Samantha and less time for Matthew. I've been on edge, trying to do everything. As a result, I am accomplishing less, feeling overwhelmed, and damaging my relationships. So basically, my passion has not been tempered with good judgment. I've been full speed ahead in the wrong direction, afraid of accepting the help that is offered," I said.

"Hear, hear for Diana's epiphany!" Zelda called. The ladies clapped and cheered for me, but I didn't feel like taking a bow. I had just realized that I had been stubborn and controlling instead of open and accepting. I hoped that it was not too late to set things right with Matthew.

On my way out, Maymie pulled me aside. "Diana, as you have probably figured out, we each take a turn at presenting a Power.

"Oh," I said hesitantly, fearing what would come next.

"And guess whose turn it is next month?" she asked, seemingly reading my mind.

"Mine?" I asked sheepishly.

"Yes, but I've made it easy for you," she said, smiling reassuringly. "Here is the packet explaining your power," she said, placing the stapled papers in my hand. "You choose a goddess to represent your power. You make a poster. You give a quick presentation and then you open it up for discussion. Easy-peasy," she said, guiding me out the door in the same way that she had when she volunteered me for key lime pie.

I drove home in the rain imagining a nice evening with Matthew. In my mind, I was happy and open to possibilities. I imagined the two of us laughing and toasting to a happy future together. I had no deadlines this weekend and no need to be edgy or controlling. I would relax and just have fun. I also made a promise to myself to accept whatever anyone offered me.

"I am open to receive blessings in unexpected ways," I said to my car.

Just as I was pulling into the gravel drive, my phone began to vibrate.

"Hi Matthew, I was just thinking about you," I said happily.

"Oh, I hope it was a good thought," he said warily.

"Of course it was, silly. I was wondering if you would like to have dinner together tonight," I said.

"Funny you should ask, because that is exactly what I was calling you about. Mike and Mayra asked if we might want to meet them at Jake's. I said I would have to check with you because you've been so busy lately," he trailed off.

"Yes, it sounds great!" I said enthusiastically. "I could really use a night out with you," I said, "and Mike and Mayra, too," I added, laughing.

"I will pick you up at seven, pretty lady. Looking forward to seeing your beautiful face," he said.

"Me too," I said, "I mean, I'm looking forward to seeing your beautiful face, too," I said, immediately feeling like an idiot.

Our double date with Mike and Mayra turned out to be a lot of fun. We met at Jake's and the casual jeans and t-shirts atmosphere was easy and relaxing. We all ordered beers, except for Mayra, whose baby bump was now starting to show.

"I am really looking forward to joining you all for a beer in a few months," Mayra said longingly.

"I'll bring a six-pack to the hospital. How about that?" said Mike jokingly.

"Yes, do that." Mayra said. "You think I'm joking, but I'm totally serious," she laughed. "I'll probably need it by then. The doctor said this baby is going to be big—maybe nine pounds!" she said.

It was fun laughing and joking with Mike and Mayra. Matthew put his arm around me, resting it easily on the back of my chair. When Mike and Mayra told funny stories about their kids, Matthew and I exchanged smiles. I was smiling because the stories were familiar, from a time when Ava and Ian were little. It felt cozy and homie. I wondered if Matthew was smiling for another reason. The crinkles around his blue eyes, the idea of him being a dad. A little blued-eyed boy to love and to snuggle. I began to rethink the idea of marriage.

On the ride home, I was still in my reverie.

"Maybe, it's not too soon to think about it," I thought. "This feels so effortless, so joyful, so—easy."

"Penny for your thoughts," said Matthew.

"Oh, nothing. I was just thinking that tonight has been nice. I've missed you," I said, touching his hand. "Will you stay with me tonight?" I asked.

"You bet!" he said enthusiastically.

As we rolled to a stop under the big old live oak tree, we both felt it, the familiarity of home. The porchlight glowed a golden light mesmerizing brown beetles who flew hard, crashed, and knocked themselves to the ground. Unable to understand what had just happened, some landed on their backs and struggled to right themselves. Once on their feet again, most gathered all of their resolve and launched themselves at the golden orb once more, only to find the same fate. A very few sensed danger and flew away to the safety of the oak tree. But most remained. Again and again, they flew at the orb. In the morning light, hundreds of dead beetles lie on the front porch. Having beaten their heads against the light over and over, hoping for some great reward. Their colleagues in the oak tree would shake their heads and say, "Those poor bastards, they were their own worst enemy."

Monday morning, I awoke to the sound of the alarm and an overwhelming sense of dread at having to go to work. After a wonderful weekend with the Goddess Tribe and with Matthew, I did not want to go back to the office. I did not want to have extra work or be asked to forgo my yoga class in order to stay late and eat Chinese food with Jacob. I just was not feeling it. I kissed Matthew on the cheek and rolled out of bed to get dressed for my morning run.

As I ran my usual route, it occurred to me that the idea that you have to struggle against the current in order to make a living is just not true. It's a myth that I had bought into. I thought, "If I want to be successful, I have to sacrifice my time and my happiness in order to get there." I saw it in Jonathan and in my parents. I considered the Goddess Tribe talk on passion. It seemed clearer to me now that if I have passion for what I am doing, then everything will fall into place for me. Meanwhile, I was struggling upstream with a job that I no longer felt good about.

"I need to keep it together for a couple more months and then I'll be ready to officially launch my new company," I reasoned. "Just keep it together for a little while longer."

Chapter Twenty

The week before Parent's Weekend had been more hectic than usual. I had worked late every single night and had not seen much of Matthew. It seemed that all of the good advice and all of the insight from the Goddess Tribe were now just interesting ideas. There was no way I could quit now. We were too busy. Jacob would have a heart attack if I left now. By Thursday, I was exhausted, grouchy, and looking forward to the weekend. As I sat staring glazed-eyed at my computer, the vibration of my phone startled me. It was a text message from Matthew.

"Dinner at Café Marnier? I'm craving their steak."

"Absolutely! I'm leaving town tomorrow, so tonight is perfect!" I texted back.

A few hours later, Jacob called me into his office.

"Diana, I need you to stay late tonight. We've got an unexpected meeting with Sam from Florida Innovative Energy Resources. He's in town tonight only, so this is short notice, but unavoidable.

"Oh, I see," I said reluctantly.

"I wouldn't ask if this was not a crucial meeting, Diana. I really need you there," Jacob said, almost pleading.

"Sure, okay, I'll stay. Just let me cancel my plans." I said.

I sent Matthew a text message explaining the situation. I waited for a response, but none came. I understood why he was upset with me and I heard Maymie's voice in my head,

"Don't take him for granted, Sugar, he seems like a real catch."

After the office had cleared out for the evening, I pulled out my legal pad and began making a to-do list for my newest Monarch client. Suddenly, Jacob appeared in my cubicle. I hastily popped the legal pad into my top drawer, face-down.

"What's up, Jacob?" I asked smiling.

"Diana, I've got good news," he said cheerfully.

Hoping that the meeting was suddenly cancelled, I smiled brightly back at him.

"We're having a dinner meeting at Café Marnier with Sam and his wife! This will be a great opportunity to entrench ourselves with Florida Innovative Energy Resources. We'll get to know Sam and his wife. They will like us, of course. BAM! We're in for life! Can you believe our luck?" he said enthusiastically.

I smiled a forced smile, grabbed my purse and jacket and trudged toward the door with Jacob. I thought about texting Matthew the change of plans, but I thought it would only cause problems. It was better that he did not know that I had gone to dinner with Jacob at the very restaurant that he and I had planned on.

We arrived at Café Marnier and were immediately seated near the entrance at a pleasant outdoor table. Sam and his wife, Sue, were nice enough people, both exceptionally tanned with big white teeth and boisterous laughter. Jacob was a nice enough person too, but I felt sick at the thought of being there with them instead of Matthew. I attempted conversation and laughed on cue, but I was sad and miserable. Then, as our entrées were being placed before us, I noticed a tall man in a blue shirt, with shaggy brown hair sauntering toward us on the sidewalk.

"No, it can't be," I lamented silently.

Yes, it was. Who should walk up to the hostess stand to pick up his takeout; to pick up the steak that he had been craving, but my dear Matthew. He saw me immediately and the look on his face was one I had never seen. His jaw tightened, and his mouth clamped shut into a thin angry line. His blue eyes seemed to be drilling a hole into my forehead. As I sat staring feebly at him from my table, I felt the heat rising from my neck to my face and knew that I was as red as a beet.

"Diana, are you alright?" Jacob asked, looking concerned.

Sue began frantically fanning my face with a drink menu.

"I'm fine, I just" I began, "I need some water," I said taking a huge swig from my sparkling water. It burned as it went down, making me feel even more nauseous.

I watched, biting my lip, as Matthew waited at the hostess stand for his takeout order. What took perhaps five minutes, seemed to take hours. Finally, a server appeared and handed Matthew a stapled paper bag. Matthew looked at me once more with disdain, then turned and walked away without a word. Afterward, I felt even sicker than I had earlier. I picked at my entrée and pretended to laugh at Sam's jokes, but I was devastated inside. It had not even occurred to me that Matthew would show up there. Unable to focus, and feeling terrible pains in my stomach, I gave my apologies and left the restaurant before dessert.

When I arrived home, Matthew's Wagoneer was in the driveway.

"Oh boy," I thought, "I don't even know what to say this time."

I parked the car and walked over to the driver's side of Matthew's car. I tapped on the window. Rather than getting out, he simply rolled down his window. He raised his eyebrows and exhaled, but said nothing.

"Matthew, I'm so sorry about tonight. I feel terrible. I didn't know it was a dinner meeting and I certainly didn't know where we were going. I didn't want to be there with them. I wanted to be with you. I'm so sorry," I said feebly.

"Would you have told me anyway?" Matthew asked.

"What? Of course I would," I said defensively, even though it was not exactly true. "Why are you so mad? I have to work to pay my bills and Ava's tuition," I said, my voice growing louder.

"I offered to help you, Diana. You refused my help, not once, but twice. I offered to help you with the office and you said no. Instead, you spent your last penny so that you had to work your ass off. Then I offered to help you launch the business so that you could focus on it full time and you said no. Instead, you stay late with Jacob every single night. You ignore your responsibilities to Samantha, who you are supposed to be mentoring. You ignore me! You're distant. You're still trying to protect yourself. You don't want to get married. You don't want my help. You know what I think? I think you don't really want me either!" he shouted.

"Hey, calm down," I said, feeling the sting of his words.

"I gave up the job in Orlando for you, Diana. I gave it up so that we could be together. I should have just stayed there!" he continued. "You just have to prove to yourself that you can work yourself into the ground and wind up all alone. That's what I think," he shouted again.

"Look, I only have to do this for a couple more months, Matthew. Then things will settle down. You just don't understand," I said.

"Okay, give me a call in a couple of months," he snapped. At that, he turned the key in the ignition and drove away, speeding out of the gravel driveway as fast as the bumps would allow.

I drove to Savannah with plenty of time to reflect on what had happened with Matthew. He was right to be frustrated with me. He had given up the higher paying position in Orlando for me and things had been wonderful as a result. How did we get so far from there? I had talked about my problems with work versus my goals at the Goddess Tribe meeting, but I had not heeded their advice. I had not channeled my passion to achieve my dreams. I was lukewarm at best, clinging to my job out of fear when my safety net would have been a plush, soft place to land—my sweet Matthew. My heart ached at the thought of him. I had promised myself that I would be open to receive. But I was not. I was still stubbornly trying to make things happen by working myself to death. Why did I say no to Matthew's help again and again, while saying yes to Jacob's demands? Why couldn't I just say no to Jacob? What was wrong with me? The more I thought about it, the more I tired of my own thoughts. I was feeling so sorry and depressed that my stomach began to ache again, despite having nothing to eat.

"That's it, time for some music," I said to the car, as I cranked up the radio as loud as it would go. I drove for hours with the music blaring, hoping to silence my painful thoughts.

I arrived in Savannah, Georgia to a clear day with a gentle breeze and a cloudless sky. I was meeting Ava, Ian, and Jonathan for lunch at Mrs. Wilkes. I walked down Jones Street, near the center of the Historic District, taking in the scenery of beautifully preserved Greek Revival homes. Savannah in the springtime is transcendent. The flowers are in bloom and all-around the town are dogwoods, magnolias, azaleas, and camellias. The thick scent of Magnolia blossoms filled the air. Historic buildings and antebellum homes, trees draped in Spanish moss—the squares, the fountains, the statues. Stepping out of my car and onto the street was like stepping backward in time.

I met Ava, Ian, and Jonathan outside, as a line had formed at Mrs. Wilkes. I was nervous about spending time with Jonathan, and it seemed that he was too. He stood on the sidewalk between our two kids, looking thin and small. He had lost probably thirty pounds since I had seen him last, and he seemed older, frail. My first instinct was to walk right up to him and give him a long tight hug. He hugged me back in what felt like an apology accepted. As we hugged I wanted to communicate that I was sorry. I loved him for all the time we had together, for our kids, the home and the life that we had made. I hoped that he understood. It was comforting being with the kids again, but in my heart, someone was missing. I longed to have Matthew there beside me. When the doors opened, we filed in and took seats in the dining room, the four of us sitting together at a table of ten. The restaurant that Ava had chosen, Mrs. Wilkes, serves family style and guests sit at community tables and break bread together.

On the menu was fried chicken, corn bread, green beans, macaroni and cheese, butter beans, black-eyed peas, mashed potatoes, candied yams, pickled beets, collard greens, okra and tomatoes, potato salad, baked beans, and cole slaw. It was a Southern feast. We found that our lunch companions were also in town for Parents' Weekend and we had a nice chat with them, never revealing that Jonathan and I were divorced. For that short period of time, we pretended to be a happy, ultra-normal family indulging in a southern-fried carb-fest before taking in the sights of Savannah. As I looked around the table at the smiling faces, I thought about how breaking bread together is an act of peace-making that has been forgotten, but ought to be revived.

After lunch, Jonathan and Ian went to walk off the heavy lunch in Forsythe Park, leaving Ava and I to shop. We strolled down the herringbone sidewalk underneath mammoth live oaks, window-shopping, and enjoying the springtime air, which had not yet turned humid. Ava was chatty and animated, so happy that we had all visited together. We wandered into a vintage clothing and antique shop filled with a Victrola, old leather-bound books, antique jewelry, and the smell of dust, pipe tobacco, and moth balls. Alabaster, jade, and ebony jewelry boxes, a Windsor rocking chair, a China doll, and other reclaimed pieces of times gone by strewn here and there.

"Good afternoon, ladies. Can I help you find anything in particular?" chimed a velvety Southern drawl. I turned to see a tall, regal woman with bright white hair and golden-brown eyes gazing sweetly at myself and Ava from behind the counter. She wore her silky white hair in a sophisticated bob. Although I guessed her age to be about sixty-five, her mocha skin was flawless. She wore a strand of pearls around her regal neck and a red Chanel suit, which her lipstick matched perfectly.

"Oh, hello," I said, rather startled. "I didn't see you there."

"I was in the back, trying to organize a little. We get so many new things in each week, it's difficult to keep up," she said.

"Beautiful shop you have. So many interesting and unique things. I'm just trying to take it all in," I said.

"Well, feel free to shop around and let me know if you have any questions as to provenance of a particular item. I'm happy to help," she said sweetly, her white teeth illuminated by the contrast of her red lipstick.

Ava and I carefully picked through the racks of vintage dresses with styles ranging from the 1920s to the present. Beaded flapper dresses, pencil skirts, and butterfly dresses hung together in a fashion time capsule of the twentieth century. Next, we eyed the jewelry cases, crammed full of Art Deco Bakelite, mid-century rhinestone brooches, western-inspired turquoise, 1980s chainmaille and neon, and every gemstone imaginable. Amid the sea of jewels, a tiny butterfly pendant caught my attention.

"May I see this piece?" I asked the woman at the counter.

"That little butterfly," she chimed, "so dainty. Yes, that's one of my favorites," she remarked, carefully sliding the door and removing it from the case.

"It's fourteen-karat gold and the little jewels are diamond, citrine, and onyx," she said. "It was hand-crafted by a local jeweler here in Savannah during the 1920s. There were two, made exactly alike as gifts for his two daughters. Note the craftsmanship," she said, handing me the pendant and a magnifying glass. "Truly made with love."

As I held it in my hand, examining every tiny detail, I suddenly felt wealthy and luxurious.

"I have its sister, if you're inclined to give these to your two daughters, as well," she said, reaching under the cabinet for a small white box.

"I have one daughter and myself to give these to," I laughed.

The woman only smiled expectantly in response.

Although this was a big splurge for me, I inquired about the price for both. Something about the shop, the queenly woman working there, and the uniqueness of the pendants took me over and I had to have them. Feeling prosperous and pleased with my purchase, I exited the shop with Ava, and we along with our jeweled butterflies, continued our tour of the city together.

Later that evening, we met up with Jonathan and Ian for a casual dinner of Mexican food at a popular college hang-out. The place was predictably noisy, with many families having the same idea, and we had to shout over our plates of nachos in order to be heard. After dinner, Ava asked to take Ian back to her dorm to meet her friends. Tired from walking all day and longing to sit in a quiet, comfortable place and sip a glass of wine, I agreed. I smiled and said goodnight to the kids and turned to walk toward my hotel.

"Hey, I was thinking of getting a drink," Jonathan said shyly. "I don't know," he said, pausing sheepishly. "You want to join me?"

Although it was late, I was grateful for the offer of company, so I said, "Sure," and we walked to the hotel bar next door.

The atmosphere was exactly what I needed—cushioned chairs surrounding a serenely lit gas fireplace. I sunk into one of the chairs and immediately felt sleepy.

"I'll go to the bar and order," Jonathan said kindly, noting my exhaustion. He returned with a beer for himself and extended a glass toward me.

"Still Chardonnay?" he asked, smiling.

"Yep, that hasn't changed," I laughed, accepting the glass.

He sunk into the seat opposite me and we sipped in silence, watching the fire.

"The kids are doing well," he said, pausing to sip his beer, "I'm proud of them."

"Yes, despite it all, Jonathan, I think we did pretty good," I replied.

"Here's to doing pretty good," he said, extending his beer glass in a toast.

I clinked my glass against his, smiling and took a sip of my wine.

"Wait," he said, "let's get a picture of this historic moment. We're being civil. I think we've finally buried the hatchet," he said, extending his arm around me for a selfie.

We both smiled brightly for the camera flash and then resumed our overtired countenances.

"Jonathan, I never meant to hurt you. I hope you can understand that. We got married very young and just grew apart," I said, "and it was no one's fault."

"I know, Diana, you wanted more out of life and I didn't understand that. I thought that running our home and doing all the kid stuff was your thing. You were good at it. I didn't think you needed more than that. I get it now. My therapist and I have been over it and over it a million times," he said, shaking his head. "But things are good now. Better for both of us," he said, smiling at me.

I smiled back, feeling easy and comfortable, as if I was having a conversation with an old friend. I felt no self-consciousness, no judgment. This felt like family. I guessed that he would always be family to me in a way. As I sat dreamily gazing at the fire and sipping my wine, a heat began to rise from stomach to my face. I suddenly felt weak and dizzy.

"Diana, what's wrong? Jonathan asked, concerned.

"I, I think I'm going to be sick!" I said feebly. "Can you just help me to the bathroom?" I said, voice cracking.

He carefully put his arm around me and guided me to the ladies' room door. I plunged inside, ran into a stall, and reluctantly hung my face over the porcelain. There, my Mexican dinner went flying. When there was nothing left and I was weak and withered on the floor, Jonathan crept in, making sure the coast was clear, and helped me to my feet and out the door.

"I should get a cab to my hotel. I feel terrible," I said.

"You're not going anywhere, Diana, I've got a suite upstairs. You can sleep on the couch. You're too sick to take a cab anywhere," he said assertively.

I feebly agreed, and Jonathan helped me into the elevator and then onto the couch in his hotel suite. I was so very sleepy that I felt heavy. I felt as though I was a lead weight sinking into the very cushions of the sofa. Down, down, down, inside the sofa is where I slept. My dreams were of the Goddess Tribe and butterflies made of jewels. I saw clouds of mist, oak trees, and Spanish moss. I saw the clear blue water of the springs and I was part of it; swimming along with the gentle current. I floated under the clear blue water for hours and hours and there was Matthew, extending a hand to me, beckoning me to come with him. Then, I awoke suddenly, gasping for air as if in my dream, I had been holding my breath. Through the blinds, I could see that the sun was rising to greet the new day. I still felt nauseous, but better than the night before, so I got up to wash my face and call a cab for my hotel.

We met the kids for a big southern breakfast, of which I did not partake due to residual queasiness. Then we said our goodbyes and I headed back home, feeling a sense of satisfaction that the weekend had gone so well with Ava and Ian and a sense of closure and a new beginning with Jonathan. At a rest stop near Brunswick, I checked my phone, hoping for a text from Matthew. Instead, I smiled as I saw the photo that Jonathan had snapped at the hotel bar. He had tagged me as a friend on social media, and I was comforted by it. We were beginning our relationship anew as friends and family, rather than husband and wife, and it was going to be alright.

Monday morning I awoke queasy again and dreading work even more than usual. Instead of going on my morning run, I ate a few soda crackers and did some yoga stretches on the living room floor before going to work. I guessed that it was a combination of nerves and that I had caught a stomach bug in Savannah. In the parking lot, my stomach tightened when I saw Matthew's Wagoneer. But to both my relief and my disappointment, he had already gone inside the building. I reluctantly trudged toward the building. As I reached for the door handle, I felt a sadness that there was no big hand reaching to open it for me. Before I even reached my cubicle, Jacob stuck his head out of his office door and asked to see me.

"Good grief," I thought, "can't I even put down my purse before he starts piling on the work?"

"Have a seat, Diana," Jacob said curtly, gesturing to the extra chair.

"It has come to my attention that you have violated your non-compete agreement with Web Synergy," he paused, taking a deep breath, "and I regret to inform you that I have to let you go."

Suddenly, the room was spinning, and I grabbed the desk in front of me for balance.

"I'm sorry," I said, "What do you mean?" I stammered.

"I mean that you cannot have a competing business while working here, Diana, and you cannot have a competing business within city limits for the next ten years. So, I'm sorry, but you and Monarch Design Associates are finished. You can't do your own work from my office and you cannot have a startup inside the city limits. So, you're done here," he said, pointing demonstratively at his surroundings, "And we're done here," he said pointing to the door for effect.

"I'm sorry, what do you mean, 'it has come to your attention?' What are you referring to?" I asked, confused, suddenly feeling panic at having put down a deposit, all of my savings, for an office. An office that I now would not be able to use!

"Matthew told me," he said smugly.

"Wait, what? Matthew would never—," I stammered. Suddenly, the nausea was back. In disbelief, I tried to speak, but Jacob quickly interrupted me.

"I suspected something was up with you. Your work has suffered lately. I can tell that you're tired and stressed," he said intimately. I cringed as his manner was giving me the creeps.

He continued as if he thought he was Sherlock Holmes wrapping up a difficult case, "When I approached him, he told me about your startup business," he continued smugly. "He knew that you were quitting anyway, and he didn't want to lose his job. So, he told me everything I needed to know. He honestly did not think this would affect you at all, since you were planning on leaving soon. Don't blame him. It's your own fault for violating your employee contract. Now if you will excuse me. We've taken the liberty of boxing up your things and security will escort you out," he said.

Then, just as if on cu,e two building security guards stepped into the office.

"Good luck, Diana," he said flatly. He then watched as I exited, tears welling in my eyes, passing my friends and co-workers, in humiliation, holding my box, and flanked by guards.

For the next week, I barely left the house, preferring to live in my old gray robe. I did my best to work from home for the two clients that I had. It was more important than ever to keep the money coming in. I was undecided about how to move forward or if I should move forward with Monarch. Owing to the fact that I would be doing internet marketing, Monarch would be considered a 'competing business' and I would not be able to use the office I had rented come June. I considered the idea of looking for a new job, but I just was not ready to give up my dream. Fortunately, I had a few months to plan and save before Ava's fall tuition was due, but I still could not shake the thought of Matthew's betrayal.

"How could he turn me in like that, regardless of whether or not I was going to quit? He knew that I was relying on that money for the next few months," I thought.

Then, as I absent-mindedly scrolled through my social media account, I saw a clue. "Oh, of course!" I said, feeling an icky feeling rising in my stomach, "he must have seen the picture of Jonathan and me at the bar! He must have thought we were getting back together," I lamented to no one. "But still," I thought. "He didn't even give me the chance to explain. He just jumped to conclusions. He got me fired, ruined my hopes for having an office, and jeopardized Ava's college tuition payment. How could he go so far? Why?" I asked sadly. One short week ago, I thought that Matthew and I would work things out and get back together. We only had a few misunderstandings, nothing big. He must have thought it was pretty big in order to do what he did.

And Jacob. He had been so stoic, so smug, and so heartless. I had actually thought we were becoming friends. All of the nights I worked late for him, thinking that we were a team.

"Good luck finding someone to replace me," I complained loudly to an imaginary Jacob, "Everyone else will tell you where to stick it," I sneered, pointing an angry finger at the air.

I was angry at Jacob, alright. But mostly I was heartbroken. I was feeling desperate and fearful about money, but I had to keep going now more than ever, for Ava. Ava had gotten a scholarship and she also worked as a tutor at the University. She was doing her part, and I had to follow through on my half. I sat down on my bed and dreamily touched my little jeweled butterfly which now hung on a gold chain around my neck. I remembered how prosperous I had felt the day I bought them. I thought of the sophisticated shop attendant and the regal way in which she held herself. I was instantly reminded of Maymie.

"Maymie! Oh no!" I suddenly recalled her putting the packet in my hand at the last meeting. "I haven't done anything to prepare my presentation for the Goddess Tribe!" I rolled my eyes at the thought of having to do homework for the Goddess Tribe now of all times. I begrudgingly set up my laptop at the kitchen table and started to work. But as I began to research my topic, what started as drudgery, soon became an engrossing project. I searched the internet for a 'Goddess of Release', but my results came up empty. Next, I tried 'Goddess of Letting Go'. Again, I received no results for a goddess, but instead came the words elimination, renunciation, and confession. I then searched for 'Goddess of Elimination and Renunciation' and I finally got a full page of results. I clicked my first result, the Goddess Tlazolteotl, and when the webpage loaded, I stared in shock and surprise at the computer screen.

Chapter Twenty-One

Her enormous blue, red, and green feather headdress, decorated with a red and black tower-shaped center piece, the white crescent moon shapes. She was bare-chested, and her skirt was made of the same style of red and black tower-shaped pieces, etched with white crescent moon shapes. As she now adorned my computer screen, I could see her prominent gold nose ring—a thick bar that pierced her septum. From her lips to the center of her chest, was an oily path of dark brown. Suddenly, I felt that familiar jolt of electricity shoot through me, as I realized that this was my Temple Goddess, the dirt eater, Tlazolteotl, Goddess of Renunciation and Release.

As I began to read the story of the Goddess, I learned that the cycle of destruction, death, and decomposition, into rebirth and life was the domain of Tlazolteotl. I remembered the discarded pottery and shells that had become the building blocks of the burial mound complex. All loved, well-used, revered, destroyed, and discarded items had been honored in that place which was an appropriate tribute to the thousands of loved ones who were buried there. In order to have life, we must endure destruction, we must have decomposition, and we must endure the deaths of times, relationships, and loved ones in this never-ending cycle. "But how does the act of release factor in to this cycle?" I asked myself. "In the death of ideas, beliefs, and stories we tell ourselves about the past, and even relationships that no longer serve us on our journey in this life?"

I had felt a heavy weight of guilt about divorcing Jonathan and not being the mother I always thought I had to be—the perfect mother. I had not measured up to my own unrealistic standard of parenting. As a result, I had punished myself daily by denying myself the joy of an easy life, the joy of love unencumbered, the joy of being the mom that I am, rather than who I thought I should be.

"I have so much to release," I thought. "This is why Maymie gave me this Power to present. She saw my guilt, my heartbreak, and my self-condemnation. From the first day I met her, she saw this in me."

I felt guilty that I was not there for Ian every day, the way I thought a mother should be. I felt like a failure for ending my marriage instead of trying once again to make it work for the sake of my family. I thought about Jacob, and what a demanding and unreasonable boss he had been. Why hadn't I looked for another job that paid the same salary or better? I had pushed myself hard at work, not because I was desperate for money, or had no other options, but because I was punishing myself.

"And what about Matthew," I thought sadly, feeling the sting of his betrayal deep in my chest. "Am I to release him too? Release all memory of him? Release the love I still have for him?" I asked the goddess on my computer screen.

"I don't know if I can do that yet," I said, shaking my head sadly. "I'm not ready to have a funeral for this relationship. But I guess Matthew already has."

I sat moping at my computer, staring forlornly into the black eyes of Tlazolteotl—those empty, lifeless black eyes. "Kind of how I feel right now," I said. Then a sudden memory hit me like a flash and I realized that the artist had gotten it wrong. "Her eyes were green, like Maymie's, not black," I said with certainty. "And she was much more beautiful than this painting suggests." I said, pointing to her face. "Her cheekbones were high and very pronounced, and her lips were fuller," I corrected. Suddenly an urge that I had not felt in years overtook me. A passion that I could not contain. My brain assumed a feverish pace as all of the good ideas for this project came rushing in at once. "I must go to the art supply store now! I have to paint my goddess for Saturday's meeting!"

I hurriedly threw on a t-shirt and a pair of yoga pants, slid my feet into my old flip-flops, then drove like a bat out of hell to the local art supply store. Once inside the store, I felt able to relax and make a mental list of what I would need: a two-pack of 20 x 24 canvases (just in case I really messed up on the first try), inexpensive acrylic paints in as many colors as I could afford, a few new brushes, and a new pallet. I had given most of my art supplies to Ava and had only done sketches for the past couple of years. It felt wonderful to be in an art store shopping for myself again and it was motivating to finally have a painting project that I was excited about. When I happily rolled to the register with my purchases, the woman behind the counter smiled at me warmly. She looked to be in her late sixties. She had shiny black hair cut in a severe bob, with perfectly squared off bangs across her very tanned forehead. She wore black bejeweled cat glasses attached with a silver chain and a black turtle neck sweater. Her silver dangle earrings were geometric shapes, circles, squares, and triangles hooked together and she wore a silver necklace to match.

"What are you going to paint?" she asked, as she scanned each tube of paint and casually dropped it into a paper bag. "Tlazolteotl!" I said, smiling with excitement.

She nodded at me very slowly, furrowing her brow with a concerned look on her face. Noting that I sounded like a crazy person, I toned down the excitement and said, "She's a Goddess—the Goddess of Release, Elimination, the cycle of death and decomposition . . . ," I trailed off.

"Oh, that sounds fascinating," she said, now reassured that I was not crazy. "Are you a member of the artist co-op?" she asked with interest.

"Oh, no," I said, "I don't paint much anymore. Haven't had the time."

"Sounds like you've got some time now, huh?" she prompted, "to paint the Goddess Tezazzotule?"

"Tlazolteotl," I laughed. "Yes, I wasn't planning on having this extra time, but honestly, I am so excited to get back into it," I replied enthusiastically.

"Well in that case, do you know about the art competition?" she asked, pointing to the brightly colored poster that was prominently displayed on the wall. Somehow, engrossed in my upcoming project, I had missed it.

Noting my clueless expression, she launched in with an explanation. "It's an open call to artists to submit for our yearly art show. First prize is $10,000, so it's a pretty big deal around here. Submissions are due in a few weeks," she said, folding an entry form and dropping it into my bag.

"Thanks, but I'm not really at that level," I said timidly. "I just draw and paint as a hobby," I continued.

"What do you think all of the artists at the co-op do? They started painting as a hobby and then boom! Before you know it, tourists are snapping up their work like hotcakes! Tourists love to buy scenes from their vacation—the blue water, the Spanish moss, and of course, alligators! People just love alligators," she laughed.

"Well, thank you," I said, taking my bag. "I'll think about it."

When I returned home, I unpacked my supplies with excitement. I set up my easel in the kitchen and laid out my new paints and brushes on the table. I started with a light pencil sketch, remembering as many details as I could of the stately Goddess atop the Temple Mound. Next, I painted the winding river and the trees below, and the blue sky above as her backdrop. I carefully added color to her head-dress—bright green, blue, and red feathers and white crescent moons. I painted her golden-brown skin and her long silky black hair. She was strong, and her countenance was that of a warrior queen.

Two days later, with very little sleep, my painting was complete. Exhausted, I wiped my hands on my apron, dropped my brush into the mason jar full of murky water, and stepped back from the canvas to regard my work. I had depicted Tlazolteotl firmly holding a feather-adorned staff, her arm outstretched as if claiming the land as hers, and her green eyes were aimed defiantly at the viewer. Looking into her green eyes, I remembered the state that I had been in when I began work on my presentation. I had been angry, hopeless, and heart-broken. Now, seeing my work to completion, I felt proud and satisfied. I even felt strength and confidence in having the talent, ability, and training to be able to create something so special. The feelings I had earlier in the week were now memories, and I was able to process them and release them. All except for my feelings for Matthew, as I would explain to the ladies at the Goddess Tribe meeting.

I got to the church early, thinking that I would be one of the first women to arrive. However, as I entered our tea room, I saw that everyone was already there. The color for today was bronze and the ladies were scurrying about in bronze silk, satin, and velvet, getting the room ready for our meeting. Like a well-choreographed dance, they set about, putting the chairs into the proper formation, putting out the dessert dishes, and preparing the coffee. The dessert was chocolate brownies with vanilla ice cream, and the room still smelled as if the brownies had just been taken from the oven.

Comforted by the scene, I glanced down at my ring-finger. Ma's root beer ring with its brown topaz color, glinted in the light reassuring me. I walked over to Maymie with my painting.

"Diana, what do we have here?" she asked with delight.

"I've had a rough few weeks, and a series of unforeseen events have prompted me to get back into painting," I said, gesturing to the canvas.

"This is the Goddess Tlazolteotl, whom I know very well. In fact, we've met once before, but she's a bit shy and ran off before I could snap her picture. Anyway, I got her this time. I think this is a very fair representation of her. Way better than most I've seen. Those other pictures don't do her justice at all. She will be representing the Power of Release," I said, proudly displaying my creation.

"Diana, you have such talent," Maymie said, holding up the painting. "This is beautiful! I hope you'll make more. You know we have twelve goddesses in this group," she said, smiling.

"Now, what did you say about a rough few weeks? What exactly do you mean by that, Sugar?" she asked with concern.

With a great sigh of relief, I began to recount the details of the past month to Maymie. I told her about my conflicts with Matthew and work, about the Savannah trip, about Jonathan, and finally about coming back to work only to be double-crossed by Matthew and fired by Jacob.

"Oh my goodness! Are you alright?" she said, enveloping me in her embrace. "You poor child," she crooned.

"I've thought a lot about the job, and to be honest, I was overworked and underpaid—once again. And I should have negotiated a raise and set some boundaries months ago. I can call it a lesson learned. But Matthew, that's another story. I am stunned and heart-broken over this whole thing," I said. "I loved him. And he loved me. At least I thought he did. He didn't give me a chance to explain, he just . . . got me fired. I'm shocked that he could be so vindictive. It's just so hard to believe."

By this time, all of the ladies had formed a circle around us and were listening intently to my sad story.

"It is hard to believe," said Patsy.

"Yes, the way you've described Matthew, he seemed so nice and kind—So . . . good," said Francie.

"Isn't he the one who kicked his wife out of their house? And when she was at her lowest point?" asked Zelda. "I don't think he's changed a bit. He's still got a mean streak," she said with certainty.

"Now, now," said Maymie, looking disapprovingly at Zelda. "It is hard to believe that Matthew would go out of his way to get you fired. And then to go to the trouble to make sure that you can't use your brand new office because it's a violation of some company agreement. That's a low blow, even if he is a little bit ticked off at you. In fact, I think that's going too far and it doesn't fit with the Matthew you've told us about. It's hard to believe, Diana. So, why on Earth do you believe it?" she asked.

Confused by the question, I furrowed my brow and stared blankly at her.

"I, well," I began, "I assumed that he saw the picture of Jonathan and me on social media and thought the worst. Matthew and I had gotten into an argument and I didn't even get around to telling him that I was going to Savannah, much less that I was going to be hanging out at a bar with my ex-husband. I figured that was the last straw for him," I said, now realizing how lame my theory actually was. "And Jacob said," I continued, but Maymie raised her hand, cutting me off.

"Jacob said that Matthew got you fired," Maymie began, "And what reason, pray tell, does Jacob have for telling you the truth?"

"Well, I . . . ," I stammered, not having an answer for her. "Isn't he legally obligated to tell me the truth about why I was fired?" I asked.

Maymie shrugged her shoulders, "Legal-shmegal, Diana. Who is going to know what he told you? Was anyone else in the room when you were fired?"

"No," I said quietly, now feeling stupid at my naiveté.

"Then why on Earth would you believe his integrity over Matthew's?"

"I don't know, Maymie," I said shaking my head. "It all sounds ridiculous now that I am telling you the story, but if Matthew didn't get me fired, then why hasn't he called me?"

"I don't know, Sugar. Why don't you just put your pride on hold for a little while, give him a call, and ask him yourself?" she said kindly. Then, realizing the time, she stood and addressed the group.

"Now, my dearies, the Goddess Train is about to depart. Ladies, please quickly serve yourselves some of those wonderful brownies courtesy of Patsy, and take your seats."

The ladies quickly filled their tiny plates and took seats in a semi-circle in front of where I stood at the podium. I had already placed my painting on the easel and was ready to launch in to my presentation when Maymie called us to order.

"Now let's all center ourselves for a renewing and purifying prayer of release," she said, closing her eyes.

I am the Power of Release

I am Renunciation, Elimination, and Purification

I breathe out anger, resentment, sorrow, and fear

I breathe in joy, acceptance, contentment, and strength

I Release thoughts, beliefs, ideas, stories, and memories

That no longer serve my highest self.

In so doing, I cleanse and purify my body temple and my soul.

For this, I am grateful.

And so it is.

Amen.

She then slowly opened her eyes and gestured toward me,

"Today Diana is presenting the Power of Release and the Goddess Tlazolteotl. And by the way, Diana painted that pretty goddess picture herself!" Maymie pointed out as I shyly approached the podium.

The ladies all clapped and cheered as they were known to do at every meeting when encouragement was warranted.

I cleared my throat and smiled, nervously glancing at the expectant faces before me.

"The Goddess Tlazolteotl is known in Aztec Mythology as the Goddess of Purification. She also oversees the cycle of death, decomposition, and the bringing forth of new life from destruction. She is the goddess of refuse and elimination. Tlazolteotl represents the power of release in this way. When we release old behaviors, thoughts, beliefs, and patterns that no longer serve us, we are able to make room for new, more evolved ways of thinking, acting, and being. We release bad habits, grudges, and fears to make room for healing, forgiveness, strength, and boldness. I have recently been through a destruction in my life—the destruction of my job and my romantic relationship. I can see clearly now that the job was not the right path for me; that it had served its purpose in my life and the time had come to move on. But I have not come to terms with the ending of my relationship with Matthew yet. Who knows, maybe Tlazolteotl has rebirth in mind for us. Right now, I'm just trusting and hoping for a miracle; that Matthew just needs some time, or that... I don't know," I said choking back tears. I paused for a moment to compose myself.

"Through all of the changes I've been through in the past year, all of the joy, the disappointments, and the heartaches, I have rediscovered my love of life. I love my farm. I love my kids and the newest addition to my family, Samantha. Now, in the heartbreak of losing Matthew and my job, I have rediscovered my love of painting and I was inspired by Tlazolteotl to pick up a brush and start creating again after many years. I'm learning to trust myself, to enjoy the journey, and also to realize that life—a good and meaningful life—can rise from the destruction of the old."

When I returned home, I thought about calling Matthew, but I could not bring myself to do it. What if he was still angry? What if he really did get me fired? Or what if he yelled at me about Jonathan? I just was not in a state of mind to handle any sort of conflict.

Instead, I called Teen Harbor to see about picking up Samantha for the weekend. I had missed her the past few weeks and I was sure that she would love some time away. Samantha was a quiet girl and she really seemed to crave the solitude that the farm afforded her—a world apart from the noise and regulations of the children's home.

Of course, she was happy to spend the weekend on the farm, reading in the hammock or gathering eggs. That afternoon, as I walked onto the porch, I glanced over to see Samantha with her long blonde braids, lazily reading while perched on a thick branch of the big live oak. "What a perfect scene," I thought, regarding her rolled-up jeans, her bare feet, and her faded t-shirt. I turned to go inside and retrieve my sketch pad. As I picked it up from the kitchen table, out fell the flyer for the art contest. Immersed in my Goddess presentation, I had forgotten all about it. But now it seemed I had my subject—a little blonde farm-girl, engrossed in her book while perfectly balanced on a branch.

I suddenly awoke with the unmistakable panic and queasiness that means 'I'm going to be sick . . . Now!' Dizzy, I made my way to the bathroom, where I hung over the bowl and vomited nothing but clear fluid until I was dry heaving.

"This is the worst," I thought, "I'm going to die here on my cold bathroom floor. No one will find me until after the animals have picked my bones clean," I moaned in both the physical pain and in the ridiculous realization that Ian may very well have been right in predicting my lonely demise.

I had felt nauseous intermittently since Parents' Weekend, but had thought little of it. I figured that I had probably caught a mild stomach bug in Savannah, but now almost a month later, I was feeling worse rather than better. As I hung over the porcelain bowl one more time, with no result but the dry heaves, a sudden panic hit me.

"Wait? What day is it? How long since Valentine's Day?" I questioned, panic stricken. I then ran unsteadily to retrieve my phone to pull up the calendar. "But how? Could I be?" Quickly, I got dressed and drove, still very nauseous, to the local pharmacy. The drive home was a frenzy of questions running through my mind. "How could this happen? What else could it be?" But mostly I very seriously worried, "What am I going to do?"

When I was safely inside the house, I took my purchase into the bathroom, opened it, and proceeded to pee on the stick while reading the small pamphlet of instructions.

"As easy as 1, 2!" the package proclaimed with confidence. "One bar, not pregnant. Two bars, pregnant!"

"No, it's not as easy as 1, 2, you stupid package! Raising children is very, very hard! Especially as a single, unemployed, forty-something woman, whose baby-daddy has just dumped her!" I yelled at the pamphlet, before tossing it angrily into the waste bin.

The pamphlet instructions read, "Place stick in urine stream. Then place on counter and wait up to five minutes,"

However, there was no need for me to place it on the counter, as soon as I brought the stick into my field of vision, I could clearly see the result—two bars.

"Positive . . . how could this be?" I said, waiting for the news to sink in.

"I've been on birth control pills for years! Did I miss one? No, definitely not. Could something have interfered with their effectiveness?" I wondered in a panic. I began to imagine finding the culprit who was at fault here and filing a lawsuit.

Armed with the idea that suing for millions would help me to raise this child, I went to my laptop and searched for 'things that interfere with birth control pills.' I scrolled and scrolled, but could not find anything that applied to me. "Had I taken antibiotics? Do I have inflammatory bowel disease? Did I store my pills at varying temperatures? Did I take antidepressants, anti-viral drugs, or sleeping pills? The answer was no on all counts. Then as I continued to scroll, I saw it there under 'Herbal Remedies.' All I could muster in response was a long drawn out and very high pitched, "Whaaaaaaaaaaaaaat?"

"Women on birth control pills should not take St. John's Wart. It may interfere with the effectiveness of the pill," read the warning."

"I have been taking St. John's Wart since last summer, totally clueless about this!" I thought, wanting to kick myself. "How could I be so stupid? How could I not be informed about this?" I lamented.

I then searched for 'Pregnancy Calculator'. Typing in the dates as well as I could remember, then clicked 'get my due date!' The results then jauntily populated the screen in a cheerful pink font.

'Your conception date is February 14th'—*my birthday.*

'You are ten weeks pregnant'

'Due Date: November 2nd'

'CONGRATULATIONS!'

"Oh no, what am I going to do?" I said aloud as I crumpled on the bed, "I'm divorced, unemployed, and my boyfriend hates me. Not to mention the fact that I already have two teenagers whom I am still supporting—one in college, one who might start college soon. Oh no, how could this happen?" I buried my head in the pillows, and although I felt exhausted, I could not fall asleep.

Chapter Twenty-Two

I still had not mustered the courage to call Matthew, so instead of dealing reasonably with my situation, I worried constantly. To take my mind off worry, I dove head-first into painting. It was the only thing that I could do that would completely take me out of time; take me out of my life and into a truly meditative state. I painted Samantha in the tree, on the porch, and holding a chicken. I painted the farmhouse, and the old boat, now halfway finished with no end in sight without Matthew. I painted the live oak, the chicken coup, and the old dilapidated barn. I painted the scenery of my life—forgetting deadlines, nausea, and worries. The kitchen now served as my art studio where partially completed paintings leaned here and there, covering my table and obstructing my pathway into the rest of the house.

Before I knew it, it was time for another Goddess Tribe meeting—the first of May and also high time that I dealt with my reality by checking in with a doctor. I was eager to see my Goddesses again because I needed their advice and support now more than ever. The doctor on the other hand, I was not so eager to see. I cringed at the idea of explaining my situation.

"I'm 41, unemployed, and no, the father is not really in the picture," I would say, trying to sound matter-of-fact, as if I was totally cool with the whole thing.

"That's just sad," I thought, shaking my head.

I pulled a gauzy red floral dress from my closet—a loose-fitting sundress that felt perfect for today. It had spaghetti straps and the print was yellow hibiscus. I paired it with red flip-flop sandals and pulled my hair up in a clip. As I passed my reflection in the mirror, I noticed Ma's jewelry box and had the sudden urge to pick a ring. As I carefully opened it, I smiled to see a sparkling ruby near the back, enshrouded in shadow. I happily placed it on my finger, admiring it in the light. One more special thing I added that day was to apply my perfect shade of red lipstick. Then I drove the short distance to the church to see my tribe and tell them my big news.

"Good morning, good morning! Welcome, my dears. We are talking about the Power of Life today." chimed Maymie warmly, as I entered the tearoom. She was boldly dressed in a flowing red kaftan that was embroidered with multi-colored flowers, vines, and beads. She wore a red hibiscus flower behind her right ear and large gold hoop earrings. Her cheeks sparkled with rosiness and gold shimmer. If anyone embodied the Power of Life, it was Maymie. The room was decorated with red tablecloths and bright red and yellow flowers. It was such a lovely and cheerful site for my weary eyes to behold.

"Don't you look pretty in red, Diana," Maymie said, "why, you absolutely glow today!" she smiled.

I cringed a little bit at that cliché, but there was no way for Maymie to know that I was pregnant. So instead of assuming that she was just trying to be nice, I opened up to receive the compliment. That Maymie had unwittingly picked up on my pregnancy glow made me smile inside. And I was comforted for the first time in weeks. I began to think about how much fun it would be to see my Goddess ladies through my pregnancy as the baby grows.

I made my way to the dessert table, more to greet my friends than to get the dessert. I was now thinking about my growing bodies, the baby's and mine. And I wanted to make healthy choices this time around. I remembered my first pregnancy and how I had baked cakes all the time to satisfy my cravings. Cravings that turned into a fifty-pound weight gain and a teeny-tiny, five-pound baby, Ava. "This time, I'll gain less and the baby will gain more," I thought, eyeing the gorgeous red velvet cake, but declining a slice.

"No cake for you, Diana?" asked Zelda curiously. "You watching your figure, Sugar?" she asked, demonstratively sliding her hands up and down her sides. She was dressed in ruffles as she often liked to do—a red chiffon knee-length dress with gauzy cap sleeves and a lazily ruffled hemline.

"Just committing to making healthier choices," I said, smiling. I had planned on telling the ladies my secret, but I could not find the right time. "Perhaps after the presentation," I thought.

"Ladies of the Goddess Tribe, if you will please find a seat as we begin our meeting in prayer," Maymie's voice boomed over the chatter.

I Am the Power of Life,

Joyfully experiencing all of the good that the universe offers me.

I Am health, vitality, and wholeness.

I Am joy, exuberance, and glee.

I delight in all of the beautiful gifts of my world.

Ideas such as illness, pain, and lethargy have no power over me.

For I am filled with the Spirit of Divinity.

And I express Divine Life every day and in every joyful way.

I am forever in gratitude for my body, mind, and spirt.

Thank You. Thank You. Thank You.

And so it is.

Amen.

Then, coming out of her prayerful state, she said serenely, "Today, Francie is going to tell us all about the Power of Life and the Goddess Yemaya,"

Francie brought her poster of a lovely cocoa-skinned mermaid goddess with long flowing black braids and a blue-green tail. She carefully set the poster on the easel as she began describing her Mermaid Goddess.

"Yemaya's story originates in West Africa. She is the Goddess of the Sea, the Moon, and all Life on Earth. Yemaya wears a crown of cowrie shells, its cords and strands hanging down appearing to cover her eyes. Across her bare chest, she wears layers of pearl necklaces which symbolize wealth and abundant life," Francie said, pointing to the poster.

"Yemaya, representing all phases of life, is also a healer and regenerator to those who call on her in prayer. She is often associated with fertility and childbirth ceremonies as a patron of motherhood. As the goddess of life, pregnancy, mother-hood, and healing, she oversees the processes of life in vitality, health, healing, and regeneration," Francie continued.

"As we consider Life as a Power, of course, we think of motherhood, birth, vitality, health, and healing. The Power of Life, requires that we incorporate all of our twelve Powers in order to live purposefully, abundantly, and joyously. With the Power of Faith, as we learned from Isabel, we have the ability to hold thoughts in mind and to bring about their manifes-tation, bringing the truth to us, that we are creators here on

Earth. With the Power of Strength, as Margie told us months ago, it takes a strong commitment and we must use strength and perseverance when it feels like nothing we are doing is working," Francie continued.

As she spoke those familiar words, I was taken back to the meeting last year, when I timidly brought my key lime pie and listened to Margie's talk in a room full of ladies dressed in green.

"That was right before I met Matthew," I thought, smiling.

"I had recommitted to my job and to making my life better here," I thought, recalling my list of 'What I Want and Don't Want.' "And it worked for a while. But where did I go wrong? Where did I miss the mark?" I wondered.

Francie continued, "And we learned all about using the Power of Wisdom and Good Judgment from Nancy, when she reminded us that often, we go through the motions with our careers, our relationships, and even our love-lives, without much thought to using wisdom or even using good judgment. You see ladies, combining our powers is the recipe for success."

I remembered struggling with the ideas of Wisdom and Good Judgment—how I had not used this power in my career or my marriage in the past. I remembered vowing to be more vigilant in using good judgment, especially with Matthew. "When did I go on auto-pilot?" I asked myself.

"We learned from Virginia, about the Power of Love. We now know that Love is the creative force that brings all things into being. Although we may try to harness the power of Faith in order to create, we must infuse that power with Love in order to manifest our dreams—in order to truly become creative beings. When you give the Power of Love to an idea and use the Power of Faith to believe that it is possible, you really can move mountains, ladies," she continued.

I considered this recipe—Faith combined with Love. "Had I given Love to my new business idea?" I wondered. I think maybe I had at first, then after the new job responsibilities started to pile on, I gave my idea stress and anxiety. I was sure that I had stopped giving it Love. The same was true for my relationship with Matthew. I had taken him for granted. I had stopped feeding our relationship with love. Instead, I gave it my second-best or whatever was left after a long day. Not enough.

"As Maymie told us in her presentation on Power, we ladies," Francie said pointing to the group. "We have the power to change the world for the better if we but use our collective consciousness to focus on solutions rather than problems."

"Is that what I was doing?" I asked myself. "Was I focused on the problem?" Over the months, work had become stressful. I was overloaded with responsibilities that I did not want. "Yes," thought, "I had been focusing on my problem—a job that was all-consuming rather than on my new creative life, with Matthew, and Samantha, and the freedom to build my own business exactly how I wanted it to be. I was not being a creator, I was simply letting the current and the waves toss me to and fro. I was allowing Jacob to monopolize my time, energy, and focus. In turn, I was placing all of my time, energy, and focus into a life that left me feeling overwhelmed, stressed out, and resentful. Even though I knew that giving Love was important, I had not given it to Matthew, to my Teen Harbor commitments, or to my new business. Those parts of my life had been put on hold. What was I waiting for?" I asked myself.

"Lil taught us about the Power of Imagination," Francie continued. "When we make quieting our minds through meditation a daily practice, we gain the ability to control our thoughts, calling to ourselves only good. We practice imagining the life we want and the world we want. Through this practice, we begin to visualize. When we visualize the life we want in great detail, we send a powerful message into the Universe that will be reflected back to us. In this way, we collectively use the Power of Imagination to create our world. Of course, the world we want to create is one of peace, joy, abundance, and life for all. We don't want to sacrifice and take less for ourselves. Instead, we want more peace, more joy, more life, and more abundance for all," she said, sweeping her long black ringlets off her shoulder.

When I closed my eyes to imagine, I saw a little baby with Matthew's big blue eyes. "What kind of life can I give this little baby?" I asked myself. My mind drifted as Francie spoke and I saw Matthew holding the baby. I saw Samantha, Ava, and Ian. We were enjoying a sunny day on the ocean in the newly restored boat. I could hear the waves gently nudging the sides of the boat. I could feel the gentle rocking motion and I could smell the coconut tanning oil in the air. I could feel the heat of the sun and coolness of the breeze. As I slowly came back to the present, I began to feel hopeful again—hopeful for my new future.

Iris presented for us the Goddess Concordia and Under-standing," Francie continued, gesturing toward Iris.

"When we are in tune with the Power of Understanding, we see that we are, in fact, creators on Earth. That we are goddesses expressing ourselves in human form and we can ask ourselves if our actions so far have been worthy of our inner Goddess."

"Have my actions so far been worthy of my inner Goddess?" I asked myself. In some ways, yes. I am kind, caring, giving, hardworking, and creative. I love my children and would do anything for them. I care deeply for Samantha. I want the best for her, in fact, I have even considered adopting her. But now with a new baby coming, I don't think that's going to be possible. I am a good friend, although I have not spoken to my friends from work since I left in disgrace. I have not spoken to Mayra since our double date two months ago. Okay, maybe I'm not such a good friend.

"But what can I do that is worthy of the Goddess within? I'm not rich or powerful," I asked Francie.

Francie smiled warmly at me, ignoring the fact that I had interrupted her presentation.

"Bloom where you're planted, Diana. You have children, friends, and family who love you. You are a talented artist, an amazing mother, and a great mentor. These are your spiritual gifts that you can put to use right now—today and every day. If we, everyone, were to shine our light in the small ways that we can, we could change the world," she said.

I instinctively reached for my charm bracelet, so lovingly pieced together by Matthew. I remembered how the little cornucopia on the bracelet had matched Concordia's cornu-copia at the December meeting—a coincidence like so many that happened with the Goddess Tribe, a magical little gift that helped to make me a believer. A believer in the power of this group and of their message. And of the goddess living inside me somewhere.

"And we learned about the Power of Will, from Patsy," Francie continued. "When we identify our divine calling, we harness the power of Will to see it through and make our dreams into reality."

"That was a problem," I said to myself. Remembering how overworked I had been. Yes, I was using my Power of Will to bring about change, but I was pushing forward without Love, Good Judgment, or Wisdom. I was stubbornly pushing toward my goal of running my own business while working full-time, saying no to the help that was offered, and hurting Matthew and Samantha in the process.

We talked about understanding and following divine Law with the help of Sarah. She showed us how to find our divine purpose, and to follow divine Law by seeking and carrying out our divine purpose. Sarah reminded us that divine purpose is based in the Power of Love and must serve the greater good. As I said to Diana, you don't have to make radical change, unless you are called to do so. You can shine your light right here and right now. Bloom where you're planted, ladies.

Zelda taught us about the Power of Passion and how it can propel us to our dreams. If you are passionate about your work, you will never work a day in your life.

I thought about harnessing my passion, and honestly, I had not felt it strongly when I was sitting at a computer building webpages or in creating logos. Lately, I had seen my passion ignited in my paintings of the farm. For years, I had missed painting, and now I realized that this unplanned time off had given me the gift of being an artist again. The words of the woman at the art store crept into my head, " . . . start painting as a hobby and then boom! Before you know it, tourists are snapping up their work like hotcakes!" "Could that work for me too?" I wondered, a smile flashing across my lips.

"And Diana, our newest Goddess, did such a great job describing the Power of Release with her presentation, of course," said Francie,

"But what I remember most about it was the beautiful picture that she painted of the Goddess Tlazolteotl. Always remember to do a mental and spiritual inventory. If the belief, thought, or feeling no longer serves you, then release it and let it go. Make space in your body, mind, and soul for more love," she said, looking directly at me.

This was certainly true, noting to myself that I had a little baby bean developing inside my body. It had not occurred to me that negative thoughts could affect my baby, but thinking about it here, shed new light on the idea. I now saw that shining my light and sending out Love energy was important not just for me, but my baby as well. I had to release. I had to tell the Goddess Tribe, and my friends from Web Synergy, and Matthew about the baby. This was my life now, and I had to move forward not back. Release the old and make room for the new.

After Francie's presentation, several of the women gathered round to thank her. I hung back for a split second, then, shedding my hesitation, I approached the group.

"Diana, how are you doing?" asked Francie.

"Did you work things out with your fella?" asked Lil.

"Not exactly," I said, feeling my own disappointment in my voice. "I haven't had the nerve to call him and now, well. I've just had some pretty big news."

"He was married all along!" shouted Zelda feigning shock and surprise.

"No, it's nothing like that," I said shaking my head. "It's kind of good news, actually," I said hesitantly.

"What is it? Come on and tell us!" said Zelda impatiently.

"I'm not back together with Matthew, but I'm pregnant. So . . . ," I trailed off, my gaze ending up on my feet.

"You're what?" shouted Maymie. "That's so exciting! We're going to have us a baby!" she chimed, hugging me tightly. The other ladies closed in for a group hug, each trying to convey their congratulations over the chatter and excitement.

"When are you due?" asked Isabel.

"November 2nd," I said, instinctively placing a hand on my abdomen.

"That is Día de los Muertos in Mexico. A reverent holiday when we honor our ancestors. And look," she said, gently touching the butterfly pendant on my chest, "La Mariposa Monarca! The monarch butterfly comes each year in November, representing the spirits of those who have come before. Your child will honor her ancestors. What a blessing," she said smiling.

"Have you told Matthew?" asked Maymie.

"I haven't talked to him since the argument," I said, shrugging my shoulder helplessly. "And now I don't know how to," I paused, looking for the words, but instead began to sob.

I was instantly enveloped in the group embrace of eleven women.

"There, there, sugar. You're going to be just fine," said Maymie reassuringly. "You've got this. You've already done it! Twice!" she said, smiling.

"Now, you know you're going to have to tell him pretty soon," she continued.

"I know I do, but now this looks like a set-up. Like a trap," I said miserably. "I feel the same way I did twenty years ago when I was pregnant with Ava—helpless. And I hate feeling that way. I don't want Matthew to think that I'm trying to trap him now that we've broken up. Anyway, I'm not even sure if I want to get back together. I haven't talked to him about Jacob and getting me fired and all of that," I stammered through tears.

"Now Diana, you know that I don't believe he got you fired. You're going to have to talk to him. You're going to have to ask him those questions. And, honey, you're going to have to release the old baggage that doesn't serve you anymore— Maybe never did. You're a grown woman now with skills, talent, and lots of brains. You don't need Matthew. You want him. I know you do. I can see it written all over your face. Now, we'll all be a lot happier, baby included, if you will just talk to him.

"I know," I said. "I will."

Later that week, I remembered the flyer about the art contest. So, having absolutely nothing to lose, I took my twenty-dollar entry fee, my application, and my painting to the Art Store to enter.

"Hello again," said the woman behind the counter. "How did the painting of Tezazzotule or whoever go?" she asked, smiling.

"Tlazolteotl," I corrected, "It turned out beautifully and my presentation was a hit", I said proudly. "And now, upon your recommendation, I'm here to enter the art contest,"

"Well, Missy, you just made it under the wire. Today is the last day for submissions," she said. "Let's see what you've got."

I handed her the painting and she examined it carefully. "this is quite lovely," she said quietly. "Uh, sorry, what was your name again?"

"Diana," I said.

"Well, Diana, I'm Anise, and here is your invite to the opening," she said, extending her perfectly manicured hand, shiny red nails, and a great big onyx ring. She handed me a small gray envelope. "Free wine and cheese—you can't go wrong there, and the winners will be announced that night, so be sure to show up and invite your friends," she commanded. "here's a few extra invitations, and here, my dear, is a brochure for the artist co-op. You should join. You'll meet a lot of interesting folks, artists, gallery owners, even agents. It's a great resource for rising talent," she said, smiling.

"Thanks Anise, I'll check it out. And it was nice to meet you," I said, as I exited the store. "Rising Talent," I thought, smiling at the idea. "Anise had referred to me as Rising Talent."

Sitting in my driver seat, I pulled the flyer out of my purse and read the address. "It's worth taking a look since it's just down the street," I said to myself, as I started the car.

The artist co-op was a big old brick building. It was an old warehouse that had been abandoned and restored by the city. As I walked inside, I smelled fresh coffee, oil paints, and linseed oil. The walls were exposed brick and hanging lamps created warm lighting.

"Can I help you?" asked a voice from behind. Surprised, I turned to see a man of about seventy years or so. He had full, bright white hair and a bright smile to match. He wore a khaki jacket, green shirt, and matching khaki pants. He walked with a slight limp and used a shiny wooden cane for balance.

"Someone, a friend, told me I should come by and maybe join," I said.

"A friend huh? Which friend?" he asked, trying to sound suspicious, but I could tell that he was teasing me.

"Anise, from the art supply store," I replied.

"Oh, well if Anise sent you, then I guess you're okay," he said, winking at me. "I'm Don," he said, extending his hand.

"Hi Don. I'm Diana. It's nice to meet you," I said, shaking his hand.

"Are you interested in shared space? You come in, find a spot, first come, first served. It's thirty dollars a month and you also get to participate in our group art shows. If you have enough work, you can apply for a solo show after you've been with the co-op for a year." He recited as if on cue. "Sound good?" he asked.

"That sounds good. My kitchen was not really built to be an art studio. What are the hours?" I asked.

"You'll be issued a card key which will get you into the building any time—24/7. We have quite a few artists who prefer to work through the night. That's just fine. But security is not available on holidays," he said, shrugging.

"Wow, this place is really nice," I said, looking around at the large open space. There was plenty of room to set up my easel or even an over-sized canvas. "And you have onsite security too? All for that price?" I said with surprise.

"We are funded by grants and sponsorships. You know our president is a very talented fundraiser."

"Is that right?" I asked with interest.

"Well, she's your friend, right? You ought to know that about Anise," he said, winking at me again.

"Yes, of course," I said, smiling. "I totally knew that about her."

After the tour, Don took my application and my thirty-dollar fee, issued me my card key and co-op ID and sent me on my way.

"Now there's just more thing I need to figure out," I thought. "Since I've got a lovely studio space for thirty-dollars a month, I can continue to work from home for my web design clients. But I've got to get my money back on the office space. I'm going to need it in the coming months."

I drove over to my office space, and to my surprise, it looked to be in the same state of partial completion that it had been in months ago. I walked to the sales office where Mandy sat forlornly at her desk.

"Mandy?" I asked "I'm Diana Davis. I rented space here— to move in next month."

"Of course, Diana," she said smiling. "Actually, I was just about to call you. We've run into some permitting issues and unfortunately, we are not going to be ready for you next month."

"Oh?" I asked feeling relieved. "When will the office be ready?"

Mandy strained to smile and replied, "We have a new target completion date of October 1st. That's just a few month's delay and we are happy to give you an additional month's free rent for your inconvenience." She said, smiling as hard as she could.

"I'm sorry, Mandy," I said, shaking my head slowly, "but I cannot take you up on the offer. I came here today to ask for a refund."

"Certainly, I understand, but is there any way I can change your mind?" she pleaded.

Knowing that I was not legally able to open a web design/ marketing firm within the city limits, and that I needed that money back as soon as possible. In fact, I needed that money to live on now. I could not believe my luck and I was very grateful for the permitting issues. They had saved my bank account. I simply said "No, thank you. I am going to need that refund, please."

"Certainly," she said, producing cancellation paperwork and then cutting me a check for the full amount, on the spot. I then walked out of the office feeling lighter and freer than I had in months.

The following week, I finally scheduled a doctor's appointment. I had called the only OB/GYN in town, but she was booked up for weeks. Due to a last-minute cancellation, she was able to fit me in if I hurried right over. I reluctantly put on a loose-fitting dress, ran a brush through my hair, put on my lucky root beer ring, and went to the doctor. I hate doctor's offices. I hate doctor appointments. I do not like being prodded and judged in a cold gray room, wearing nothing but a backless paper dress. I do not like blood, or things that deal with blood. Or god forbid, having my blood taken—even a finger prick can cause me to lose consciousness.

"Maybe I'll just do a home birth down on the farm," I thought. I recalled a movie I had seen where a mother had given birth alone in some godforsaken wasteland and in her fierceness and bad-assery, had bitten the umbilical cord to sever it.

"Not me, I think I'll call a midwife," I chuckled to myself as I sat in the cold waiting room. I rifled through the magazines, seeing cover after cover of joyful, blond, twenty-something pregnant women. Bored, I just sat, staring at the exit sign, fantasizing about escape. Then suddenly, I was startled. I needed to hide. I needed to run out now for real, but she was blocking the door. Mayra, now very pregnant, had just waddled in and was now beaming at me with excitement.

"I didn't know you were pregnant!" she exclaimed, waddling very quickly and then taking the seat next to mine. "Matthew must be ecstatic!"

"SHHH," I said, putting my finger to my lips. "He doesn't know. I haven't told him yet."

"Oh, it's a surprise! How cute! How are you going to do it? Got something special planned?" she asked, her large eyes filled with excitement.

"No, no," I said shaking my head, "It's not like that. I haven't told him," I paused. "I haven't told him because we broke up," I said sadly.

"What the heck happened?" she asked, a stunned look on her face. Then her face suddenly changed, and her eyes grew wide in realization.

"The baby's his, right?" she whispered conspiratorially.

"Of course, the baby's his!" I whispered loudly.

The other pregnant women were now glancing at us sideways, wondering if there might be a juicy story here.

I breathed in deeply, then I told Mayra the whole story. When I finished, she just looked at me crossly, shaking her head.

"That Jacob!" she said angrily. "I would never have thought he would stoop so low," she continued.

"What are you talking about?" I asked. "What do you mean, stoop so low?"

"Diana," she said, as if talking to an idiot, "Come on! You don't believe him, do you?"

"What? I don't really know. Why wouldn't I believe him? Why would he lie?" I asked, confused.

"You mean you don't know?" she said with surprise. "At the barbeque, you said you knew all about Matthew and you were fine with it."

"Okay, well," I stammered. "I thought I did! What are you talking about?"

"Diana, you know that Matthew kicked his wife, Amy, out of their apartment and sent her to her brother's house, right?" she asked.

"Yes?" I said expectantly.

"Diana, who the heck did you think Amy's brother is?" she said.

My eyes grew wide with sudden realization.

"Jacob was Amy's brother," Mayra said.

Suddenly I had been furnished with the missing puzzle pieces and it made sense.

"Matthew said that her family never forgave him for what happened to Amy!" I replied, as if a light bulb had been turned on in my brain.

"Of course Jacob would lie about Matthew. I'll bet he has been seething ever since you and Matthew started dating," Mayra continued. "Matthew has been the happiest I have ever seen him over the last year. You've been his world. You've brought him back to himself! Jacob probably thinks that Matthew doesn't deserve happiness after what happened to Amy."

"Diana," she said taking my hand, "you've got to tell him. I promise you, whatever stupid argument you two had is not worth it. It's not worth throwing away all of the good that you have brought to each other, just because of your foolish pride. And I mean both of you," she said sternly.

"I don't want him to think that I am trying this as a tactic to get him back. I don't want him to feel trapped. It's not like that. This was as much a surprise to me as anyone. My plan was to start my own business, and now I've got no job and a new baby on the way. I don't know how I'm going to do this," I sighed, shaking my head sadly.

"With help, Diana. You'll do it with help. Tell Matthew," she said reassuringly.

The day of the art opening, I was filled with excitement. I had invited Mayra and Mike. I then called Monique, Shyla, and Paul, apologized for being distant, and invited them to the opening as well. I did not tell them that I was pregnant. I was looking forward to having a fun night out after being cooped up in the house for so long and I didn't want to be brought down with worries of how I'm going to support my baby.

The night before, after I made the calls, I pulled up Matthew's number on my phone. As my thumb hovered over the dial button, thoughts of our argument flew into my mind. He was so angry with me. He had said things that he believed—that I didn't want him, that I would rather stay at a job that I hate than spend time with him. None of those beliefs were true. I did love him very much. I just wanted to prove to myself that I could do it alone. But that is not what life is about. We all need help from time to time. We need each other to make our lives work—to make the world work. "No woman is an island," I laughed. "Especially now," I said, touching my abdomen. My thumb hovered over the call button, wavering on whether to give it a gentle tap, but instead, I shut my phone down for the night and went to sleep.

As I carefully chose my outfit for the art opening, I looked at every dress hanging in my closet, examining, and then passing to the next. I wanted to look artsy, but not pretentious. I settled for a sleeveless black sheath dress and turquoise jewelry. As I looked in the mirror, I remembered the turquoise necklace that Isabel had worn the first time I saw her. I remembered how I had wanted to be like her. Now, as I looked at my reflection in the mirror, I saw that even though life had not turned out the way I had planned, it was turning out just fine. I was growing. I was going to an art opening with friends, and most of all, I was healing from the past.

When I arrived at the art supply store, a little late due to the time it took me to choose a dress, Mike and Mayra were already there checking out my competition. They scanned each painting one after the other, offering their expert opinion, which amounted to "I like your work much better, Diana."

"Thanks guys, but I really am just happy to be here," I said, smiling.

"I haven't been out much since I lost my job. Samantha has been over a lot, and it's been fun. We take care of the farm, cook, read books . . . ," I trailed off. "But it's nice to have a grown-up night out." As I said those words, what I was really feeling was that I wanted to share this evening with Matthew. Once again, I took out my phone, only to put it away again. A little while later, Monique, Shyla, Paul, and Marco appeared. Of course, Marco had brought a bouquet of flowers for me.

"Congratulations on your artistic debut," he said, kissing me on the cheek.

"Thank you. These are beautiful, Marco," I said.

"Don't I get a kiss too? I made him bring them for you. That deserves some credit," said Paul jovially.

"Of course," I said, "and thank you for coming out."

"I can't turn down free wine and cheese. I'm heading for the bar. Diana, can I get you something? I know you love your Chardonnay," said Paul.

"Oh, I'm," I said, suddenly looking at Mayra in a panic, "I'm watching the calories. Just a water for me, please."

"Water it is!" he said as he turned and sauntered toward the bar.

"Mayra and I smiled at each other conspiratorially, and then suddenly Mayra's eyes were on the door. She looked surprised and a little confused as she took a deep breath in. I slowly turned to see what she was looking at. When I did, there stood Matthew, a pained expression in his blue eyes.

"I need to talk to you," he said, taking my hand and pulling me toward the exit.

Just then, Paul showed up with my water and tried to hand it to me, but I shook my head at him as if to say, "Not now," and he nodded and hung back with the group.

Matthew led me out the front door and onto the sidewalk.

"Look, Diana, I wanted to call you, but I didn't think you would want to hear from me. Especially after I saw the picture of you and Jonathan in Savannah. I didn't know what to think."

"Matthew, no," I said, "No, I'm not getting back together with Jonathan. We just . . . we had the kids there, and we— well, we've forgiven each other and we're on good terms now. But no, we're not anything more than friends."

"Jacob told me that you were the one who reported me and got me fired. That's why I didn't call you. I thought you hated me," I said.

"Diana, you should know that I would never do anything to hurt you. I would never do that. Even if you were with someone else, even if you didn't love me. I would never, could never, hurt you," he said, still holding my hand.

"Why did you come here tonight? How did you know I would be here?" I asked.

"Well, only everyone in the office was talking about it today, so I kind of invited myself. And—Mayra told me that I should come. She said I should talk to you instead of acting like an idiot," he said, looking at his feet.

"Well," I began, trying to find the words to tell him. "Matthew, um." I looked at my feet and he touched my chin so that I would look back up at him again.

"Whatever it is, you can tell me," he said. "I love you and I just want you in my life. I can't stand this anymore. I've been going crazy thinking about you."

"Okay, here goes," I said, "I want you to know that I love you too. That I have loved you since the moment we met."

"Okay? I love you too, and I want us to be together. What's going on? What's wrong?" he said with concern in his voice.

"Matthew, nothing is wrong. At least I don't think anything is wrong, but I guess it kind of depends on your reaction," I said.

"Okay, now you're scaring me. What is it. Just tell me."

"I'm," I paused, cringing, "pregnant," I said, sounding foolish, not at all like I had imagined this moment.

"Wait? What?" he said, laughing. He wrapped his arms around me and enveloped me in his embrace. "You're pregnant," he said, still giggling. His laughter was infectious, and I began to giggle too. There we stood on the sidewalk, just laughing our heads off.

"Diana, this is the best news I have ever gotten," he said smiling. "Hey, you think you might want to be my girlfriend again?"

"Yeah, I think I do," I said, taking his hand, "I think I like being your girlfriend."

Just then Monique was at the door gesturing wildly for us to come inside. "They're about to announce the winners!"

Matthew and I walked back inside hand in hand. I was feeling so happy that I didn't think the night could get any better regardless of who won the prize money.

Anise was standing in the center of the room, flanked by the show's sponsors, a tall man in an official looking gray suit and a small Asian woman in a red power suit with matching red stilettos.

"First of all, I want to thank everyone for coming out tonight. Doodle Canoodle Art Supply is happy to host events like these for the arts community and in turn, we really appreciate your support. And just so you know, the registers are open, so feel free to shop after the event," she said, smiling.

"Now please join me in thanking our sponsors, Spectrum Oil Paints," she said, gesturing toward the man in the gray suit, "and Aqueous Water Colors," gesturing to the woman in the red suit. They both smiled and waved uncomfortably.

"Ladies and Gentlemen, our Third Prize is an artist gift set from Spectrum Oil Paints valued at $1000," Anise said with excitement. "And our Third Prize is awarded to Annemarie Stout. Annemarie, are you here? Come on up here." Annemarie, a young woman who looked to be in her twenties, slowly made her way through the crowd. She had wavy, ash-blonde hair and wore a gray cardigan and blue jeans. As she reached Anise, she was greeted with handshakes from the sponsors and a hug from Anise.

"Congratulations, Dear," said Anise.

"Now our Second Prize, folks, is an art supply extravaganza from Aqueous Water Color Company valued at $2000. And Second Prize goes to Alan McDaniel. Alan, come on up here and claim your prize!" said Anise with excitement.

Alan timidly made his way through the crowd, a man who appeared to be about thirty years old, sporting a beard and red flannel shirt. He happily accepted a prize envelope and shook hands with the sponsors.

"And now for the moment you have all, I am sure, been waiting for. Oh wait, that was the moment we set out the wine!" said Anise teasingly.

"The First Prize is real actual money! A Prize of $10,000, courtesy of Doodle Canoodle, The Artist Co-Op, Spectrum Oils, and Aqueous Water Colors. We in the arts community work together to raise this prize money each year. We feel that it is important to reward the emerging artists in our community and give them a boost to keep at it! If art is your passion, then you must live it. Hopefully, this prize will make that dream a bit easier to attain. Am I right?" Anise said with authority.

The crowd answered with nods, claps, and subdued cheers.

"Without further ado, our First Prize Winner is—Diana Davis! Diana, come on up here, my dear," Anise said, gesturing toward me.

I was shocked that I had actually won. I could not believe that I had won $10,000 and that Matthew was there by my side.

"Such a perfect night," I thought as I stepped forward, but suddenly I felt heavy, as if my feet were made of lead weights. I felt as if I was sinking to the floor and I felt a big slow ache starting in abdomen and then taking over my body, until blackness.

I opened my eyes to a bright white light. It was so bright that it hurt my eyes, so I brought my hand up to shield them. It was then that I realized where I was. My hand was attached, via a needle and a tube, to an IV next to my bed. I could hear the beeping of the heart monitor. Suddenly, I felt a panic and a deep sadness. I struggled to sit up in bed. As I fumbled with my blanket and pillows, I heard a quiet voice.

"Hey, looks like somebody is awake." I turned to see that Matthew had been sitting in the chair next to me but was now drowsily making his way to my bedside.

"How are you feeling?" he asked, kissing my forehead.

"I don't know? What happened?" I asked.

"Well, we were all excited for you and clapping and waiting for you to go up and get your prize, but then I looked, and you were just gone. You were out cold, on the floor," he said with surprise. "Of course, I was worried about you. We all were. I wanted to drive you, but Anise insisted that we call an ambulance, so I rode with you here. And here we are," he said, taking my hand.

"Is the baby okay?" I asked hurriedly, barely listening to Matthew's words.

"The doctor should be here soon. She said she would come back after you woke up. So, I should probably call the nurse and let her know," he leaned over and pressed the call button.

A few minutes later, my doctor walked in.

"How are you feeling, Diana?" she asked.

"I'm fine. How is the baby," I asked concerned.

"Let's just do a little check up and see," she said. "I'll just check the baby's heartbeat. This may feel a bit cold," she said, applying the cold gel to my abdomen.

She placed the monitor on my abdomen and began to move it around. Silence. She moved it again, and then again. Still, we heard nothing.

"I'll just move it over here, I think your baby is hiding today," she said, smiling. But the look on her face was of concern. I looked over at Matthew. He seemed worried too.

"Okay, little one, where are you?" she said, moving the monitor again.

Then suddenly, I heard the familiar fast pumping of a little heart. Swish, swish, swish, it went.

"There you are," she said with relief. "Sounds nice and strong," she said, smiling.

Matthew took my hand and we listened, with tears in our eyes, smiling a secret smile together.

"Is this Dad?" she asked, referring to Matthew.

"Yep, I'm Dad," he said proudly.

"Diana," she said, looking at me, "you're dehydrated and run down. Did you drink any water at all today?" she asked.

I thought about it for a moment, "A little, maybe one glass. I was getting ready for the art opening and I lost track," I said.

"Well, I'm going to have to recommend that you stay here for a few days, unless you have someone at home to care for you.

"That's me," said Matthew abruptly. "I can work from home for a few days."

"And she's going to have to be on bed rest for those three days," she instructed, looking at Matthew.

"That means you only get up to use the bathroom. No cooking, no trips to the kitchen. Understand?" she said, now looking at me.

"Matthew, you will need to keep a full pitcher of water by the bed so she can stay hydrated. It's very important that she rest."

"Yes, no problem," he replied. "I'll take good care of her," he said sincerely.

"Okay, if you're all set, then I'll discharge you in the morning. But Diana, make an appointment at my office first thing next week. I'll be sure and fit you in." she said, closing her folder and quietly leaving the room.

After she was gone, Matthew leaned over and kissed my forehead. "I love you and I promise to take good care of you and our baby," he said.

"I know you will," I said.

Chapter Twenty-Three

June—1 year of Goddesses

After everything that happened in May—winning the art contest, getting back together with Matthew, and forcing myself to rest after being hospitalized for dehydration, I was excited to go to the Goddess Tribe meeting and fill them in on all of my news. As I started to get dressed, I realized that I didn't have the meeting packet. I had gotten this one last June—a year ago. And we had completed the twelve month study of our Goddess Powers. Not knowing if we would have a special color or theme, I picked a blue-green floral print sundress and pulled my hair back in a clip, because it was starting to get hot. I made sure now to bring a water bottle with me everywhere I went, so I couldn't forget to drink. Drink water, drink water. It seems that's the answer to everything when you're pregnant.

When I arrived at the church, the parking lot was empty as usual, but as I reached the front door, I found that it was locked. I tried it again, and it would not budge. Confused, I began to knock—quietly at first, and then louder. I carried on knocking for a few minutes and then decided to walk around the back of the building. I had always assumed that there was another parking lot. To my surprise, when I reached the back of the church, there was nothing but a field of overgrown weeds. Confused, I walked around to the front door. Once again, I began pounding on the door.

"Can I help you, Ma'am?" said a voice behind me. I turned to see an elderly man. I imagined that he was a landscaper or groundskeeper. He was very tan with skin like a leather saddlebag. He wore dirty overalls, and stood regarding me with concern as he wiped the sweat from his brow with a faded red bandana.

"Hi there, I was just looking for the women's group. We meet here on the first Saturday."

"I don't know nothing about a women's group," he said, looking puzzled. "We rent the facility out to AA on Wednesdays. You looking for AA, honey?"

"No, it's not AA," I said, trying to explain. "It's a lady's church group. We have been meeting here for over a year, as far as I know. Do you have a key? We meet just off of the Narthex, in that little tea room," I said, growing impatient.

"Well, okay, I'll open the door, but there ain't no ladies group in there," he said, sticking the key into the lock and turning the knob.

As I entered, the air was thick and warm, moldy. I walked toward the tearoom door and slowly turned the knob. I pushed the door about halfway, but it was obstructed on the other side by something. I squeezed in the opening and could not believe my eyes. Our adorable ladies' tearoom had been reduced to a moldy gray storage room. Gone was the welcoming smell of coffee and dessert. Now, dusty tables and chairs were stacked against the moisture-stained walls. The once cheerful yellow and white wallpaper sprinkled with little rosettes was now discolored and peeling. The once shiny wooden floor was dusty and worn, and the boards were splintering in places. I stood in the middle of the room. I looked around for anything familiar but could find nothing. I began to question my sanity. Had I been here?

"I know that I was here—at this church last month and the month before that—for a year. I know that I was here in this room with Maymie and Zelda and Lil and Patsy, and Sarah! With Francie, Virginia, Margie, Nancy, Isabel, and Iris—my Goddess Tribe met here in this very room. I know it!" I said aloud.

"Ma'am, are you alright in there? Do I need to call someone for you?" asked the groundskeeper with even more concern this time.

"No, no," I said, regaining my composure. "I'm fine. I'll just go now," I said with sadness and disappointment. "Does this church offer services on Sunday?" I asked.

"No ma'am, the congregation dwindled down to nothing a few years ago. I come out every once in a while, to cut the grass and fix leaks. Seems folks don't like to go to church these days. It's a shame," he said, shaking his head. "Nice old building like this."

When I arrived back at the farmhouse, I was so confused and upset that I could scarcely think. "If I imagined all of it, then that means I am psychotic—out of touch with reality," I thought in a panic. "I am pregnant and quite possibly completely nuts! With a child to raise and a foster child to care for," my stream of consciousness continued. "But then, why would Teen Harbor let me near Samantha if I am nuts?" I questioned. "I passed the psychological evaluation and it was exhaustive. So, either their test is severely flawed, and they are letting nutcases in left and right, or I am not crazy," I concluded.

"There has to be an explanation for this," I thought as I clumsily entered my bedroom and began removing my jewelry in haste and frustration. As I pulled the aquamarine ring from my finger, I yanked too hard and the force of my hand came back and knocked Ma's jewelry box and all of its contents onto the floor. I knelt on the floor to retrieve my beloved rings and then I noticed something—a piece of yellowed paper was sticking out of the lining of the jewelry box. I carefully tugged at the paper and the lining opened up to reveal a hidden compartment. Inside were several small paper cards, yellowed by the passing of time. Now intrigued, I sat down on the floor and took the stack of cards out of the box. The first one read,

"The Goddess Tribe Dessert Recipe #1 Faith & Blueberry Cobbler"

"What? What is this? Did Ma have a Goddess Tribe too? How is that possible?" I asked as I fanned the recipe cards out in front of me. There were twelve recipe cards, each one listing the dessert and the Goddess Power for the Goddess Tribe Meeting—for my Goddess Tribe meetings. Suddenly, it hit me like a flash of light. "The rings!" I said, "there are twelve rings, one for each month of the Goddess Tribe," I frantically took out each ring and placed it upon its corresponding month's recipe card. "Of course!" I said in amazement. "Ma wore these rings to her Goddess Tribe meetings too!"

I sat there on the floor for several minutes, marveling at Ma's recipe cards and the fact that she had a Goddess Tribe too. Suddenly I remembered,

"The box!" I said, frantically running toward the hall closet.

"What are you doing, in there?" asked Matthew with concern.

"I'm just—just looking for stuff," I said as I rummaged through the closet. "Ah-hah!" I said triumphantly, pulling the box into the hallway. I frantically tore at the tape to open it, desperate to know what lay inside. Matthew's hand appeared with a swiss army knife and quickly cut through the tape. "Thank you," I said, looking up at him briefly before I returned to my frantic search.

Inside the box was a set of old china carefully wrapped in newspaper. I pulled the dishes out and continued to search the box. Next was a set of pretty glass Christmas ornaments. I put that aside as well. On the bottom of the box was an old black photo album that I had never seen. I carefully lifted it from the box and placed it on my lap. Nervously, I opened the album. There on the front page, I recognized my grandmother, Ma, standing over a sheet cake and smiling brightly. She looked to be in her early thirties. She wore a tailored wool suit with a pencil skirt and her hair was cut short in a trendy style of the era. On the next page, there she was smiling brightly surrounded by friends. But when I looked more closely at their faces, I could not believe my eyes. I recognized these women! Standing beside my grandmother were three women who looked like Patsy, Virginia, and Lil, but older! My eyes went to the inscription below. It read "Sisters, Edna, Patsy, Virginia, and Lil, June, 1956."

"But this doesn't make sense," I whispered as I turned the page frantically. On the next page were even older pictures. As I scanned the faces, I saw Zelda, with her familiar smile, holding a baby. The inscription read, "Mother and Daughter, Zelda & baby Edna, 1924."

"Zelda? My great-grandmother?" I asked questioningly as I turned to the next page. I saw old photos of Iris, with her daughter Zelda. I saw family reunion pictures of Francie as an old woman, with her daughter, Margie, and her grand-daughter, Nancy. Next, I saw a picture of Sarah. In it, she was holding a baby and standing next to a man in a poncho. The inscription read Aunt Sarah, Uncle Miguel Ángel, Baby Isabel, Mexico 1900. I turned the page once more, my hands shaking at the thought of what I might find. As I beheld the photograph, my head started to spin. There was a picture, as plain as day, of Maymie. She stood proudly in front of my farmhouse, looking rather like a pioneer with her hair in a long braid that fell across her left shoulder. Beside her was a tall man with a kind face. Standing in front of them, were three little girls. I followed my fingers along the inscription to keep my place as the tears began to flow,

"Great Grandmother Maymie 1840-1910, born a slave. Pictured on her farm with her husband, William Klaur and three daughters, Sarah, Frances, and Gramma Iris; Heritage Springs, 1875."

Chapter Twenty-Four

One Year Later

Matthew and the boys have finished restoring the old boat and we take it out as often as we can. Noah, now in college in Gainesville and doing very well, is enjoying dorm life. Bryan, having joined the Army, will be leaving for boot camp next week. Ian has remained in high school and has improved ten-fold since joining the Jr. ROTC program. He is now hoping to win a scholarship to college and continue ROTC there. Ava is still happily living in Savannah and loving her studies. This summer, she is interning as an illustrator for a wilderness and outdoors magazine in Colorado. And what about Matthew and me? We are now Samantha's foster parents and have applied to legally adopt her.

After winning the art contest and being on doctor's orders to remain as stress-free as possible, I turned my career focus to my artwork. Drawing and painting filled a space in my soul that had been missing for years and I can only describe it as my divine calling. Through my art, I use all of my twelve goddess powers every day—Faith, Strength, and Judgment; Love, Power, and Imagination; Understanding, Will, and

Law; Passion, Release, and Life. I use them all in creating my artwork and in making a living from it. Although I was heart-broken and angry when my idea for Monarch Designs fell through, I now realize that I was still thinking very much inside the box. I had not set my imagination free to dream big. As a professional artist, I love my work so much that I live in a state of joy every single day.

I am still in touch with my friends from Web Synergy. And I heard it through the grapevine that no one told Jacob about my side business. Instead, he found my legal pad by snooping in my top drawer. Afterwards, he easily found my articles of incorporation—which are public record—online. I am not angry with him. Though his actions were motivated by bad intentions, he freed me from that office. He gave me the shove I needed to realize my true calling. Matthew, my wonderful partner in life, was inspired by my sudden success in the art world, and feeling his own divine passion, cut ties with Jacob and with Web Synergy. He needed to do that for his own growth—to free himself from guilt and condemnation. To use the Power of Release to forgive himself and let go of Amy's memory. He now works with a consulting firm which gives him greater freedom and higher earning potential.

Despite our busy lives, this weekend we are blessed to be all together as a family. We took the boat out and have anchored it near a shallow reef. The sun is bright. The sky is azure blue. The water is clear blue-green. I see our big family snorkeling around the shallow reef together. Ava, Ian, Noah, Bryan, and Samantha swim in a group as brightly colored fish swim by unconcerned. We are not allowed to touch them. It's illegal here in the national park. I sit on the boat holding my seven-month-old daughter, Mari. She is chubby and happy, with auburn hair, rosy cheeks and fair skin, which I am careful to keep out of the sun. Matthew and I both wear gold bands on our ring fingers, although we are not married. We call them partnership rings. Our daughter, Mari, has corkscrew curls and green-gold eyes, like Maymie. On the side of the boat, I painted twelve butterflies in flight in honor of my ancestors— my Goddess Tribe.

Sometimes, in fleeting moments in the middle of the night, I wonder if I made a mistake in turning my kids' lives upside-down with the divorce. But then I am quickly brought back to my bliss when I hear my daughter stir in her crib, or I feel Matthew's hand next to mine. Although initially change can be painful, it is the only way to grow. So often, I remember the wise words of my Goddess Tribe.

"We, as creators, have the ability to shape our own lives"

~ Isabel

"Strength to advocate for those who are powerless is the gift that mothers all share"

~ Margie

"When we sit in meditation, we are able to tap into the Goddess within"

~ Nancy

"Love is a creative power and as women we are the keepers of it"

~ Virginia

"We have within us the ability to solve all of our problems by giving our divine energy to what we Love, not what we hate"

~ Maymie

"When we visualize what we want in great detail, we send a powerful message into the Universe that will be reflected back at us."

~ Lil

"As a divine being, your speech should always be positive and uplifting, because your words have great power"

~ Iris

"When you are called by divine inspiration to act on a great idea, you have to be steadfast and unwavering in pursuit of it."

~ Patsy

"If you love it and if you have Faith that you can, then the universe will move mountains to make it happen, because that is divine law, my dear."

~ Sarah

"When you use Judgment combined with Passion you will achieve your goal as joyfully and effortlessly as a flowing river"

~ Zelda

I'm learning to trust myself, to enjoy the journey, and also to realize that life—a good and meaningful life - can rise from the destruction of the old."

~ Diana

"When we are in tune with the Power of Understanding, we see that we are, in fact, creators on Earth. That we are goddesses expressing ourselves in human form and we can ask ourselves if our actions so far have been worthy of our inner Goddess."

~ Francie

As I reflect on these words, I am eager to pass their wisdom on to my own children. Although I always have been free, now I feel free to make my own mistakes and to live as I choose. I embrace not only Faith and Understanding, but all of my Goddess Powers. I am a creator of my own life. As a creator I am empowered to live passionately. I paint the pictures of my life. And I stand in my power. No one else has the power to fix me or to heal me; or to hurt me for that matter. I am spirit. I am light. And so, after so many ups and downs, so much blaming, and unnecessary heartache, I now know that in my little way, in my little corner of the world, I can work to create heaven on Earth.

And so can you.

Acknowledgments

I am deeply grateful to my many friends, colleagues, and mentors whose wisdom has pointed me in the right direction and ultimately lead me to my spiritual path. Through a series of happy accidents and minor tragedies, I found myself on the front steps of Unity North Atlanta and then Unity of Pompano where I have met many living goddesses.

Through this journey, I have been inspired by the words of Charles and Myrtle Fillmore, Linda Martella-Whitsett, Paul Hasselbeck, and Cher Holton. I would like to thank Carmela Garone, Bev Spivey, Sandi Warner, Dina Shimeck, my fellow Prayer Chaplains and the Women of Uni-Tea at Unity of Pompano for your support and encouragement on this journey.

When I encountered stumbling blocks, I had many cheer-leaders including Mary Davis who truly shared my vision and encouraged me to think big. Kimberly Peticolas has been constant source of knowledge and inspiration. I thank Kelly Henning and Jordy Marin, who have both continued to nudge me forward; Nidhi and Nikia, who are smart, strong, and compassionate women of power. My husband, Nik, for being my rock and my spiritual partner, and Claire and Sky, without whom, I would have a very boring story, and Dad and Marie, who continue to encourage me to shoot for the stars.

Finally, I am forever grateful to the women in my family who provided inspiration for the ladies of The Goddess Tribe: Ma, Mom, Sandra, Lilly Mae, Patsy, Grandma, Nancy, Margaret, Martha, Sarah, Ruth, Anise, Sandra, Janice, Rhonda, Laura, and Emily.

94352508R00183

Made in the USA
Lexington, KY
28 July 2018